Caught Up With A Real One

Taniece

Join my mailing list
Stay up to date with releases and receive exclusive sneak peeks!
https://mailchi.mp/f706027718f3/taniece

Disclaimer: This is a re-release of Trap Kings Fall In Love Too.

Contents

Taniece

Synopsis

Miles Karrington, known as "Reapa", was the most feared man in all of New York. Because he ran with the same people he made it with, Reapa thinks that his foundation is solid and airtight. After his relationship with his ex, Ava, goes to hell, his trust is messed up, and he completely throws away the idea of ever being in love. By the time he realizes what he's gotten himself into with Unity, it might be too late for him to do anything about it.

Unity Galore grew up being the joke amongst her peers for her dark skin and her country accent. As she got older and matured, she pushed the jokes to the side and focused on her one true love- kickboxing. All that changes when she receives a business proposition that changes her entire life. But will putting up with the extras be too much to bear after she finds out the real reason they call Miles, "Reapa"?

Phoenix "Nix" Quartz is anything but a good girl, constantly spending her time in and out of jail behind her boyfriend, Axel. But after one time too many of looking stupid, Phoenix puts Axel behind her and makes a decision one night that changes the course of events forever.

Blake "Kase" Watts once loved his baby mama, Harper, more than anything else in the world, but that was then, and this is now. After realizing she's no longer the person he fell in love with and he doesn't see a future with her anymore, he's forced to pursue other options. He never expected to run into the beautiful Phoenix, and he never expects to fall for her the way he does. But Harper refuses to allow herself to be put in the background and what she has planned for Kase could ruin his whole life.

Miles "Reapa" Karrington

"Wassup Ava?" A nigga said as he grazed her forearm with his thumb while walking by. When my eyes landed on her, hers bucked. She already knew the thoughts that were running through my mind. That nigga had really just tried me, walking up on my bitch in the club; it wasn't enough that he spoke to her, but he had the fucking audacity to touch her as well. Shit wasn't about to go down like that.

"Aye, my nigga, how the fuck you know my girl?" I asked, staring him directly into the eyes. I wanted him to say something wrong to give me a reason to put a hole between his eyes. My trigger finger always itched; that's how I got the name Reapa in the first place. I was lowkey as fuck, but when niggas saw me, they knew somebody's head was about to get to rolling like a bowling ball.

"Babe, just let it go," Ava cried, gripping my arm as I went behind him. I snatched away from her and kept walking. She was acting like he was going to tell me something she didn't want me to know. Better yet, something that I probably needed to hear.

"Ava and I go way back," he answered with a smirk. Apparently, I was missing something. I knew of every nigga she ever fucked with. The lifestyle I lived, any bitch that I even thought about communicating with, went through a thorough background check. I didn't need any shit popping up on me out the blue or stressing about someone trying to set me up. He sure as hell wasn't on the list of niggas she used to fuck off with, so someone better get to explaining something.

"It's nothing like that I swear," Ava pleaded behind me.

"Who are you to be questioning me and shit?" he asked, licking his lips, gawking at Ava. I chuckled slowly, nodding at his stupid ass. Obviously, this nigga didn't know who he was talking to, but I was going to remind his ass.

"Please, Miles, not here," she begged, but I just tuned her out. That nigga had disrespected me one too many times, and I was not about to keep putting up with his shit. I rolled my sleeves up on my Armani button-down shirt slowly strolling toward him, popping my neck at the same time.

"I'll deal with you later, Ava," I told her, pulling my Glock from my waistline. "I'm going to ask you one more time. How the fuck do you know my bitch?" The terror in his facial expression told it all; he was fucking my bitch. I would've thought that with all the good dick I had been giving her, that she would've been satisfied but I guess I was wrong. On the days I been taking my business trips, he probably been sneaking around and dicking her dizzy ass down. The dumb bitch probably had the nigga riding in the brand-new whip I just bought her and all. I was about to dead that shit real quick. Not on my watch.

"It was only one time, Miles, I promise you," Ava wept. She must have figured out that I had put two and two together in my head if she was snitching on herself. Turning around, I shot Ava right in the knee.

"Ahh!" she screamed out in pain as she dropped to the floor. I had given that bitch two years of my fucking life. I kept her laced in designer shit, ice around her neck and wrist, had her pushing the baddest whips and that was how she fucking repaid me by fucking another nigga behind my back. Not even one that was on my level at that. A fucking bum! The least she could've done was upgraded as if the shit was even possible. There was no one in the state of New York that was even close to touching my level. I was my own breed, cut from a different cloth. These niggas were just napkins with their clone asses. There would always be one authentic Miles "Reapa" Karrington.

"Did you really just shoot me?" she asked as I stood over her with my smoking gun. Everyone stared on, but they knew better than to say shit to me. I had the whole state on lock. The police were even under my belt as well as a few of the best judges. You might as well say that I was the fucking king of NY. Once they saw that it was me that pulled the trigger, they went back on about their business like the shit was normal.

"You really thought you could play me and get away with the shit?" Placing my gun back in my waistline, I kneeled down and picked Ava up off the floor. I may have been one dirty ass muthafucka, but I wasn't about to just leave her down there bleeding all over the fucking floor like that. There was some sort of love left in my cold heart for her ass deep down somewhere. Like really deep down. The least I could do was take her to a hospital.

"You didn't have to shoot me." Tears streamed down her beautiful bright red cheeks. Once I got outside, the valet pulled my cocaine-white Lamborghini up to the door. I dropped her inside and hopped in myself.

I couldn't even be mad that the ho tried to play me. What really surprised me was the fact that we had been together for this long. Usually, I would've been got rid of a chick. I was far from the relationship type of nigga and now we see why. I couldn't trust anyone as far as I could throw them. It was insane that Ava even got me to trust her this much, but I'd never do that shit again. She fucked it up for every bitch after her.

"It hurt Miles," she whimpered as I whipped in and out of traffic. The way I was feeling about her ass at the moment, I should've driven at a snail's pace so that she could feel every bit of that got damn pain. Better yet, I should have shot her ass in the head. Ava was lucky as fuck I didn't really fall in love with her ass because if she would've done something like that while I was in love with her, things could've been so much worse for her right now.

"Stop crying like a bitch. Should've kept your fucking legs closed. Spreading them bitches like they a got damn twenty-four-hour fast food joint." She kept on with all that damn crying, I had the right mind to push her out the door into oncoming traffic and keep going. If niggas could get back all the time and money they wasted on shitty ass relationships, things would be so much better after a breakup. Me, I wasn't even stressing it. I had more than enough money for one lifetime, but I hated when a muthafucka wasted my time.

Pulling up to the emergency entrance, I threw the car in park and got out. Ava was still crying when I pulled her out the car and sat her down on the bench that sat right in front of the double doors. "You not even going to take me in?" she had the fucking nerves to ask.

"Nope, better walk on that good leg or get to crawling. Better yet, call that nigga you were fucking and ask him if he'll take you in there. You lucky I even brought your ho ass up here in the first fucking place." She had me fucked up. I slammed my door and went around to the driver's side, and hopped in, peeling out of there.

Phoenix "Nix" Quartz

*M*y leg nervously bounced up and down as I sat there waiting to hear my fate. I swear I was tired of Axel's cheating ass and everything he stood for. Ever since I had been dealing with him, I've found myself in all sorts of bullshit. For me, this was the last fucking straw.

"Ms. Quartz, if I see you in here one more time, you're doing some time. I promise you that," Judge Martin said. Just as soon as she said that I released the breath I had been holding in. That time, I really thought I was about to go down that road. The other day when I had gone by Axel's house to see him, he had another bitch in there, so I set his shit on fire with him in the muthafucka. Sure the fuck did. Lucky for me, he and her made it out just in time. Every part of me was low-key hoping they both would've died in that damn fire. I don't give a fuck what nobody says, the shit really hurt when you go hard for someone and put your all in them and end up getting shitted on. That's exactly what the fuck Axel had been doing to me— shitting the fuck all over me. Niggas be having a good girl by their side but still be out there searching and shit. Like what you looking for sway? A nigga?

"You won't see me again. I'm going to get my act together," I promised her with a smile.

"Oh, you better because I'm not playing with you." Her gavel slammed, and I rushed out of there. Spending the weekend in jail wasn't fun, but I had grown accustomed to it by now. My best friend, Unity would've come and gotten me out without hesitation, but I was too embarrassed to even bother her with that phone call again. It was evident that she was tired of bailing me out of jail. Knowing her, she would never tell me that. Unity was always my savior. Looking down at my phone, it was almost nine, and I was going to be late for work if I didn't get a move on it. Standing on the curb, I stopped a taxi and hopped inside.

"*RK Fitness* on 42nd Street."

When I got inside the gym, I ran full speed toward the locker room so I could grab my scrubs, take a quick shower, and get dressed. I always kept an extra uniform in my locker just for days like this. There was no way I was going to be able to go all the way home to Manhattan, shower, then make it to work on time.

"You're late," Jessica, one of the other masseuses said when I stepped into the locker room.

"Tell me something I don't know." I rolled my eyes and grabbed my things then headed straight for the showers.

With my mother, Olivia being a five-star chef and owning one of the most expensive five-star restaurants, I didn't really have to work, but I chose to. It was something I loved even though I was starting out small. One day, I planned to be in the big leagues making way more money than I was now. Everyone had to start somewhere, right?

Pulling my curly ink-black wet hair up on top of my head, I headed out onto the floor to see how many people I had for the day. I prayed for a slow day so I could fuck off with Unity. She worked at the same gym as I but was a personal trainer and kickboxed on the side. I scrunched up my face when I looked down at the whole list of names I had to do for the day.

"Mr. Brady," I called out the first name that was at the top. A heavyset guy stood up and walked toward me. I almost vomited in my mouth just thinking about having to touch him. "Follow me."

∞ ∞ ∞

"Ouch, you're hitting too hard," I cried as Unity punched the mitts on my hands. If my shit was bruised up by the time we were done, I was kicking her ass or at least trying.

"Somebody needs to beat yo' ass. Where the hell you been at all weekend, huh? I been blowing yo' phone up like crazy and even came by the house but Ma said she hadn't seen you." She threw another intense punch that I felt through the mitt.

"I was in jail," I said, trying to shake the dreadful pain from my hand before sticking it back up in the air.

"Again, Nix?" I ran my tongue across my teeth. That was the last time I was losing my cool over a guy. They were going to make me adopt a fuck all niggas mentality. I was tired of giving them my all and ending up with nothing in return. Love was never what it's all cracked up to be. The shit that you see on the TVs in the movies or heard on songs were nothing like what happened in real life. Someone needed to kick them bitch's asses for lying to us all these years or mine for being so dumb to believe it.

"Man, that was the last time. I'm over Axel fareal this time." I wasn't sure who I was trying to convince more; me or her.

"I tried to tell you that nigga wasn't any good when you got with him but nah, you just didn't wanna fucking listen. That fake love be feeling real too, Nix. Yeah, he promised you the world and sold you all types of dreams. Where the hell did you think the rest of us were gonna live?"

I hated whenever Unity wanted to dig in my ass, but it was all just love. With her not really having much of a family, she and I had been joined at the hip ever since she moved up here from the south seven years ago. That was my best friend, and I wouldn't trade that chick for anything in the fucking world. She kept things raw and uncut. What more could a girl ask for? Feeling my phone vibrating in my pocket I pulled it out and saw Axel's name flashing across the screen.

"Bih, you answer that phone, and I know something. Put him on do not disturb and move on with yo' life," she encouraged. I nibbled on my lower lip trying to debate if I wanted to answer it or not. Axel and I had been together off and on ever since I was sixteen and now I was twenty-three. As much as I kept saying I was done with his cheating ass and moving on, my heart still was in the mix.

"It's hard though, you know how I feel about that fuck nigga," I stressed.

"Ho, you better shed you a tear or two, cry you a muthafuckin' river, whatever the fuck you gotta do but MOVE THE FUCK ON. The shit is life, sometimes shit happens. You never know there just might be someone else better that's waiting on the sidelines, but you'll never know 'cause you're so wrapped up in a nigga that doesn't deserve your time." She pulled the gloves off her hands then wiped the sweat from her forehead with the towel that she had wrapped around her neck. Sometimes I envied Unity for being so strong. Maybe the things she had been through was the reason she was the way that she was. She definitely didn't look like the things she had been through.

The phone rang again. Unity glared at me, I was well aware of her feelings from the displeased look she gave me. "Just let me see what he wants. It might be really important since he was calling back to back."

By the time I placed the phone up to my ear, it was rudely snatched away from me. She threw it to the floor and stomped it repeatedly until the screen had gone completely black. "Bitch get yo' life," she said, walking away leaving me standing there with a dumbfounded expression on my face.

Unity Galore

"You're pretty for a dark-skinned girl." Was that really supposed to have been a compliment? I hated whenever niggas did that shit. He certainly killed any chance he ever thought he had when he opened his mouth, and that bullshit flew out of it. Apparently, his mother didn't raise him right because all black women were beautiful no matter their skin tone.

"So, what are you trying to say? Dark skinned girls can't be beautiful too?" I asked with a raised brow. Stupid niggas just like him were the reason I constantly had to remind myself to fix my crown; embrace my melanin. Who gave them the bright idea that light skin was better? That they were always winning? We win too.

In all reality, I wasn't that dark, but I was far from light. Not to toot my own horn, but I was a bad ass bitch. Standing at five foot six, I was a deep brown beauty slim thick shorty. I may not have had all the ass in the world, but I had enough. Little booty chicks matter too.

Growing up, I was always joked on for my rich skin and big ass head. People said that my head was way bigger than the rest of my body. Thank God I finally grew into that head of mine. There were stupid ass jokes like, I know your neck tired of holding up that head or how your black ass get freckles aren't those supposed to be for light skinned chicks? Things like such were what caused me to form a tough exterior. Instead of beating bitches on a daily, I wandered my way into a gym one day and I been there ever since. Now I was a walking killing machine. If I get into it with a bitch, I try to calm myself down, so I don't end up killing her ass with my feet and fists.

"No, that's not what I was saying."

"Yeah, I bet." I left before he embarrassed himself even more than he already had.

Climbing the flight of stairs to my grandmother, Justine's apartment, I used my key and let myself inside. Even though I no longer stayed with her, I made it my mission to come and check on her at least twice a week to make sure she didn't need anything. When I was fourteen, my mother, Shona died from a heroin overdose, so I ended up being shipped to New York to stay with my grandmother to avoid being put in the system. I never knew my father and honestly, don't think my mother even knew who he was her damn self. Transitioning into staying in a foreign place was hard especially with that thick ass southern accent I had. How long I had been staying in New York, you would think I would've lost my accent by now, but it was still evident in my voice.

"Hey, Ma." I kissed my grandmother on the cheek then sat down on the couch beside her.

"Hey baby, I didn't know you were coming by today," she said, softly squeezing my thigh.

"I had to bring your medicine." I set her diabetic medicine down on the coffee table. My grandmother looked so worn out. She was the reason I went hard the way I did. Since she had taken me in and really didn't have to, I felt like I owed her my life. That woman would never be pressed for shit as long as I'm around.

"Baby, I keep telling you that I'm good. You need to stop coming by here so much and focus that time on finding you a man somewhere. I do want me some great grandkids while I'm still around and can enjoy them." Children were the last thing on my mind. I did want children one day, but at the moment, she could miss me with that shit. So far, there was no man out there worthy of me giving them my time. The most expensive thing I could give a nigga was my time, and I'll be damned if I was going to allow them to waste it.

"I'm good on that, Ma," I told her, reaching into my pants pocket pulling out my vibrating phone. "Yes, ma'am," I answered.

"That's right respect your elders," Nix joked. I screwed my face up at the phone and then placed it back up to my ear.

"What do you want, Nix? And how come you're calling from your mama's phone?"

"Uh, have you forgotten that a certain someone stomped my phone out the other day or no?" I giggled at her silly ass because I actually did forget I did that.

"Yeah, I did but it was only to save you," I made known. Someone had to hold her back. She claimed that she didn't want to deal with his ass anymore, so I was just trying to stop her from relapsing.

"Ma said that she has a big ass party to cater tonight and she needs all hands-on deck for servers. In other words, have your ass at the house in a couple of hours." A lot of times whenever Nix's mother, Olivia did those massive parties, she would pay us to help her out if it was overwhelming for her. I never mind lending her a helping hand, I could always use the extra money no matter how much it was.

"So y'all weren't going to ask, you just were going to tell me?" I joked.

"What did that heffa say?" I heard Olivia ask in the background.

"She said that she isn't coming Ma," Nix lied then giggled.

"Have your little ass here at seven, dressed and ready to get to work. It's not like you have anything else to do anyway. Don't make me have to come and hunt you down Unity because you know I will." Olivia was just like another mother to me, and she treated me as such. Sometimes, I hated my mother wasn't around any longer. I envied the relationship Phoenix had with her mother knowing that it was something I would never have.

"Yes, ma'am; I'll be there."

∞ ∞ ∞

"Whose party is this?" I asked Nix taking a look around the big ass kitchen we stood in. The shit looked like it was bigger than my one-bedroom apartment. Couldn't even imagine what the rest of the house looked like. Olivia needed to hurry up and tell us what she wanted us to do so I could do some wandering around. I took a peek out of the kitchen door at all the people that were mingling around the house in their expensive clothes. "Like seriously, whose house is this?" I queried, shutting the kitchen door.

"I don't know, Ma didn't say, and you know me, I don't be asking questions unless necessary." Nix poured champagne in some glasses that sat on the granite top island before placing them on a tray.

Olivia came in the back door with the most gorgeous cream and gold colored stacked tier cake I ever seen. It was so beautiful that I felt like they shouldn't cut it. No cake that looked that good should be for eating. I was sure it cost them a pretty penny too because that woman was not cheap. "You two heffas supposed to be working not in here running your mouths," she fussed, placing the cake down on the counter.

Nix playfully rolled her eyes, "What you think I'm doing. I can multitask. Now that ho over there, I don't know what she calls herself doing. She hasn't been working since she got here. She too worried about who house this is."

"You two are here to work not flirt with those boys. With all that money that they got, they probably no good anyway." Olivia picked up one of the trays that were filled with champagne flutes and shoved it into Nix's hands. When she said that, it just intrigued me more to know who house it was.

"You don't pay me enough to be dealing with this stank attitude of yours," Nix said, trekking toward the kitchen door. Olivia stuck her tongue out at her as she disappeared behind it. I grabbed another tray and went to work behind her. As I moved through the crowd, my eyes wandered around to see who all was there. Someone softly gripping my wrist, caught my attention. My eyes landed on the sexiest specimen I ever seen before in my life. He was tall standing at about six foot four. The black waves that covered his head were so deep that I could drown in them. From what I could see from the unbuttoned top buttons of his white shirt, he was covered in tattoos from the chest down. He glared back at me with a pussy dripping scowl on his creamy caramel face that my pussy twitched.

"Damn ho, stop staring at my nigga like that. We just wanted two glasses, then you can take your ass on back about your business," the girl standing next to him spat, reaching over taking two from the tray. I was so lost in his hooded deep-brown eyes that I didn't even notice her standing there. Like most niggas I encountered, he obviously saw something he liked as well because his hand was still wrapped firmly around my wrist.

"I suggest you put your chick on a leash 'cause I promise you she got the wrong one," I warned after finally shaking myself from the daze he had me in and letting the corner of my lower lip go.

"The wrong one? Bitch, you aren't nothing but the hired help. Fuck out of here," she laughed, but was the only one that thought what she said was funny.

"It's always the dry scalp bitches that wanna talk greasy. They got some shit called head and shoulders, invest in it 'cause them flakes on your shoulder ain't cute, bitch." From the glare in her eyes and the redness of her face, I knew she was embarrassed and pissed all one in the same.

"Forget you," she scoffed, gripping the guy around his arm holding on to him for dear life like she was scared he was going to go somewhere.

"Ho, I'm unforgettable, ask yo' man in a couple days." I chuckled then snatched my wrist away from him and bounced away.

Blake "Kase" Watts

"Harper, your ass supposed to be at home with Baylee. Who the hell watching her anyway? It better not be your mama with her coke head ass." I roughly snatched her by the wrist pulling her into my bedroom closing the door behind us so that no one could hear us arguing. I was tired of this back and forth shit with her ass all the time. There was one point in life where I loved this girl more than life itself but lately, I could feel things between us slowly withering away and she was the one to blame.

"No, I left her with Brittany. Did you really think I wasn't going to show my face at this party? No thirsty bitch about to get her hands on you on my watch." That was always the reason that we were getting into it. Harper swore up and down I was cheating on her ass when that's not the case. She was so insecure when it came to me which I never understood why because she was a bad bitch. That woman had more curves than a coke bottle. Bitches stayed hating on her. I never could grasp how a woman that was as gorgeous as her could be so fucking insecure at the same time.

"If you don't take your ass home to my seed where you're supposed to be. We not even together right now anyway. Have you forgotten that you broke up with me two weeks ago?" I scrubbed my hand down my face. Her crazy ass popped up out the blue and broke up with me for no apparent reason. She came to me with some bullshit talking about Brittany told her I been fucking some bitch she knew and just like the bird she was, she believed her over her nigga. That ho never liked me ever since I shot her down, not wanting to give her dusty ass the dick. Harper slowly strutted toward me, placing her small manicured hand on my chest.

"I want to get back together now." This was exactly the shit I was talking about. Why she always had to be with the shits, bruh?

"No, it don't work like that. Go home," I said, gripping her wrist slightly shoving her away from me. She knew I wasn't a crash dummy while she was always trying to play games with me. That shit was on her if she wanted to lose a good nigga for listening to her dumb ass friend that couldn't even keep a man to save her fucking life so how was she giving her relationship advice?

Harper sucked her teeth.

"Why do you have to be so mean to me? You see I'm trying to work things out with you." I opened the bedroom door and held it opened so she could find herself on the other side of it. It was my parents' anniversary and it was supposed to be a celebration, but she was fucking up my mood. I'd just have to deal with her ass on another day, but now wasn't the time.

"Fine." She stormed out of there and I pushed the door closed behind her. Between Harper and the streets, I was stressing more than I was supposed to be. I took a seat on the edge of my California King bed placing my head in my hands just thinking about life. If it really wasn't for Baylee, I think I would have left her a long time ago. She played more games than a fucking jobless nigga played on an Xbox.

When my bedroom door opened, I thought that it was Harper coming back for round two. My mouth was already fixed to curse her ass out some more but was sadly mistaken when another girl was standing in the doorway. She was so beautiful almost the most gorgeous woman I ever seen in my life aside from my mother, Karen. Don't get me wrong, Harper was fine as fuck, but the babe that was standing before me was on a whole other level. Baby girl was slim, nowhere near as thick as the women that I was used to going for.

Even though she was dressed in some simple black slacks and a white short-sleeved button-up shirt, it didn't take away from her sex appeal. Her naturally jet-black curly hair was balled up on top of her head. She diverted her attention away from me when her slanted cocoa-brown eyes met my intense gaze. Apparently, she was nervous, her flawless golden honey brown face had turned scarlet red.

"What the hell you doing up here?" I finally asked breaking the ice.

"I'm sorry, I was just trying to get away from all the noise so I could make a phone call," she admitted finally bringing her eyes back up to mine.

"Why you didn't go outside for that? Nobody supposed to be up here." She rolled her eyes to the ceiling. I was taking my anger for Harper out on her and that wasn't fair on her part.

"Excuse me then Mr. Rudeness," she said, stepping back into the hallway trying to close the door. For some reason, I found myself jumping up from the bed and rushing over to where she was. My first instinct was, that I wasn't ready for her to leave just yet. I quickly grabbed the door stopping her from closing it. I wasn't sure if it was because I felt lonely and empty inside and just wanted the comfort of a woman, or if I wanted the comfort of this particular woman. Either way, I wasn't about to just let her leave.

"My fault. You can make your call in here. I wasn't trying to take my shit out on you, Ma," I confessed, gesturing for her to come on into the room. She hesitated at first, but then pushed past me on inside. I looked out in the hallway before closing the door behind her just in case Harper's crazy ass didn't really go home like I told her. The last thing I needed was her popping up on my ass with another woman in the room. I'd never hear the end of that shit.

While she stood there trying to make her phone call, I went back over to the bed. Her eyebrows furrowed as she paced impatiently waiting for whoever she was calling to answer. Whatever nigga that was playing games with her was a damn fool. Obviously, he didn't know what to do with her and was going to fuck around and lose her to a real nigga. Once you go Boss, you never go back and that's a known fact. She just might be the one that could make me leave Harper's ass alone for good if she played her cards right.

"Did you hear me?" she asked, bringing me back from my thoughts.

"My bad, I was zoned out. What did you say?" I brushed my hand across my waves.

"You look like you got a lot on your mind. You good?" She stopped, standing directly in front of me, giving me the perfect view of that fat ass pussy that stared back at me. How come the slim girls always had the fattest pussies? I really didn't know but I had to bring my eyes back up to hers before my dick grew on the side of my thigh. Those juicy lips begged for a nigga to kiss 'em. To stop myself from doing something I knew I didn't need to, I reached into my pocket and pulled out the pre-rolled blunt I had in there.

"I do; you just don't know." I placed the blunt between my lips and lit it. Before I could even take a puff from it, she snatched it, putting it between hers. Shorty had a lot of nerve. That was something I wasn't used to. She plopped down on the bed beside me, taking a couple pulls from the blunt.

"You don't know how much you just saved my life," she said, blowing the smoke out. I snatched the blunt away from her.

"I'm not paying your little ass to smoke and take personal calls." She screwed her face up at me.

"Actually, you're not paying me for shit... period. My mama paying me, not you so I can do what the hell I want." She didn't waste any time taking the blunt back from me and relaxing back on my bed like she belonged there. It was already bad enough she was invading my personal space, but now she was taking it a bit further by making herself at home. "Tell me what's on your mind."

I didn't usually pour my heart out to strangers, but I was getting this strong vibe from her and she hadn't even been in the room that long. I felt like I could trust her, so I told her my problems leaving out a few major details of course. We sat there cooped up in my bedroom for what felt like hours just rapping with each other, straight vibing.

That was the first time in forever I ever felt like I could just be myself around someone and didn't have to worry about them judging me, because she didn't know who I was, and I didn't know who she was. We were just two strangers sitting there smoking and talking. I wished it was that easy when it came to Harper, but we couldn't even talk long before things went left. She was so used to getting her way all the time and I was the only one to blame.

"I been looking all over for you, Nix," a girl said when she barged into my bedroom. Nix and I both looked at her at the same time. She handed me the blunt back and pulled herself up from my bed putting her shoes back on. I knew she was about to leave me, but I wasn't ready for our time to end.

"Sorry, I have to go. I've already been gone for too long as is," she announced, rushing toward the door.

"Wait!" I got up from the bed and went behind her gripping her softly by her hand. "Will I see you again?" I asked her, staring directly into her eyes.

"I doubt it, but good luck with your girl." Her hand slipped away as her friend pulled her down the hallway.

Reapa

"Wassup Reapa," Markell said, walking into my backyard with Kase right on his heels. I nodded my head and continued smoking my blunt like everything was kosher. Markell was called over to my house for a reason and I was going to get to that in a moment when I felt like addressing the situation, but right now I was just going to play things as cool as can be.

Markell almost jumped out of his skin when he looked down beside me. I let out a chuckle because that was almost always everyone's reaction when they saw Cocaine especially his. No matter how many times he seen her, he always gave the same response. "Do you have to sit there with that thing like that?" he asked, taking a step back but Kase pushed him forward. Cocaine was my all-white tiger that I kept for a pet. Most niggas had pit bulls or some shit, but I wasn't most niggas.

"What your problem is? You scared of a harmless tiger? She don't bite," I chortled. Truth was, she was just as ice-cold as I was.

"Bruh you lying. I'll just stay over here as far away from you and her as possible." I loosened the heavy chain a little bit that was tied around her neck, giving her a little more leeway. Cocaine paced back and forth in between me and the pool.

"Scary ass. You know why I called you here though, right?" I asked, taking another toke from the blunt then blowing the smoke out in his direction. Markell, Kase, and I had been together since before the sandbox days. Our bond was tighter than a virgin's pussy. We all jumped off the porch around the same time and got it out the mud together. Taking in my backyard, I realized that we had come a long way from the dope house.

A nigga was living like a true king and I'll be damned if I let anyone take the shit away from me that I worked my ass off to get. Even though I was now sitting in a big ass mansion up on a hill somewhere; I was a straight hood nigga at heart. What nigga you know that made it all the way to the top and was still a hood nigga? There was a certain code that we lived by and I still expected them to go by it. What fucked me up was the fact that Markell was no longer living it. There was too much he say-she say shit going on, so I had to address it and put an end to all the madness.

"No," he replied, keeping his eyes on Cocaine.

"Go take a look over into the pool," I told him, and he did just that. He eased over to the edge and saw Dez lying face down in a pool of his own blood.

"Type of shit you got going on?" he queried, locking eyes with me. Terror overtook his face, by then I was sure he knew he was caught red handed. Dez had come to me earlier saying he saw Markell talking to a detective the other day. What I couldn't wrap my mind around was the fact that he hadn't come to me when he was *supposed* to had seen the nigga. I sat there listening to everything he had to say but once he was done, I put a bullet in his ass. I was always taught to shoot the messenger too because somebody playing both sides of the fence are more dangerous than your enemy. Facts.

"See, Dez told me a funny story today. You want to hear it?" I leaned over putting out the blunt. Cocaine's chain loosened a little bit more. Recognition dawned on his face. Markell knew he was fucked and there was no way around it.

"Whatever he told you, that nigga was lying." Of course, he would say that when Dez wasn't here to defend himself. Markell knew me better than that; I was far from stupid. A nigga had street smarts and common sense so he can try that shit with someone else.

"Your stupid ass already snitching on yourself. That just confirmed what he said was true 'cause I hadn't even said that it was anything about you." I fully let go of Cocaine's chain and she charged toward him. Kase and I watched as she mauled him like he was a juicy deer.

"Damn, you had to do your cousin like that?" Kase asked, pointing in Markell's direction with his thumb before coming over and sitting in the chair next to me.

"I'on give no fuck, one fuck's too much." I placed the blunt back into my mouth relighting the tip. "It's better to get a nigga before he can get you."

Nix

"Help me, I think I'm about to do something stupid," I cried into the phone to Unity. I finally got a new phone after she broke the old one I had. She really did me a favor because I finally got that Galaxy 8, I been wanting for the longest but was trying to be cheap and not buy it. If she hadn't broken my phone, I probably would've squeezed out at least another year with my old one.

"Please tell me you're not talking about Axel." She sighed.

Unity was tired of me complaining about Axel and she let it be known. She never liked him in the first place but there wasn't really anyone that she too much liked.

"Yeeesssss, I'm so close to running back to the dick," I whined. It had been a while since I had some dick and I was fiending for Axel's shit. He may have been disrespectful as hell, but that nigga had the best pipe game I ever had. So far, I hadn't met anyone that was able to touch his ass. That was the only reason I put up with all his bullshit for so long. There was no other bitch out there more dickmitazed than I was. Good dick would have you dickstracted, dickcombobulated, even dickoriented and I think that I was all the above.

"Bitch, you need to get yo' fucking life. That nigga ain't thinking about yo' ass and here you are tryna go running back to the muthafucka like always. If he needs convincing or extra pressure to be with you then he ain't the nigga for you," she lectured.

"But Unnnniiiiitttttyyyy, I need some of that death stroke. My shit getting super-duper wet just thinking about that pipe game. Stop denying me my dickquil."

She burst out laughing, "Ho, what the fuck is a dickquil?" she seriously asked, furrowing her brows.

"You know that deep stroking, hair pulling, ass smacking, deep gut banging, waist gripping, neck choking 'til your eyes bulge, leg seizure shaking, shit talking type of fucking." My lower lip poked out because I had just made myself want the dick even more.

"Bitch, get off my phone." Unity hung up in my face. She was a fool if she thought I was going to stay here and torture my damn self. Getting up off my canopy bed, I slipped my feet into my all-white Huaraches and quickly grabbed my keys off of my dresser heading straight out my bedroom toward the front door.

"Phoenix Lynn Quartz where the hell you think you're going!" My body froze in place before I could even make it to the door. I spun around on my heels with a big Kool-Aid smile on my face.

"When did you get here?" I asked, hanging my head; I was guilty as fuck.

"I was on my way when you first called. Something told me you were going to try and relapse on my ass, so I came straight over." Unity got up from the barstool that sat in front of the island in the kitchen. She gripped me by the forearm and took me over to the lime green sectional. "You need AA sis. That dick ain't that good. Why don't you call someone else to dick you down?"

"My phone is dickless. I basically pay almost two hundred dollars a month for a calculator, calendar, and to talk to your ass."

I shrugged.

"Bitch you need some new dick in yo' life," she laughed. I let out a harsh breath.

"And you're one to talk... when's the last time you got some dick, tongue, your ass ate like groceries... anything?" She wanted to laugh at me and shit for wanting some dick, but I hadn't seen her with a nigga in what felt like ages. I was starting to think that my bitch turned gay on me or something. "I mean sis, if you gay it's safe for you to come out the closet. It's twenty-seventeen, nobody going to judge you." Unity mushed me in the head and smacked her teeth.

"I'm not gay. Not everyone wants to be a thottie like you. I'll just leave that shit up to you. What about that guy I saw you with a week ago at that party that we helped Ma with? You were locked away with him for the longest. Thought that something good could've come from that," she brought up. I had completely forgotten all about him. With everything that was going on between Axel and me, there wasn't any room to bring someone else into my life at the moment. It wouldn't be fair on their part when I wasn't fully over him just yet.

"That nigga had a girlfriend anyway. I don't have time for that shit. You already know me, no girlfriends or baby mamas allowed and that nigga girl is both. The only way I'm fucking with that nigga is if his baby mama is dead. I'm sorry." I brushed off the shit she was talking. I didn't have time for no baby mama drama and shit. Unity already knew how I was, and I would fuck a bitch up with no hesitations. And if I couldn't whoop a bitch my damn self, she would be brought into the equation. Drama wasn't for me, but I definitely knew how to address it if it came my way.

"Ho, you gotta start thinking. Your soulmate might be in a relationship. It's your job to ruin the shit and live happily ever after with yo' nigga. The fuck you mean?" That was the exact reason why I fucked with her ass; she was always with the shenanigans. She and I slapped hands laughing.

"It really doesn't even matter now though 'cause I probably would never see him again anyway." He didn't look like the type of nigga that you would run into on the streets somewhere. It'll be a miracle if he was to grace my presence again.

"You never know," she said twisting up her face.

Unity

"Aaahhh," I hissed as I grazed my index finger across the cut that was on my lower lip. That bitch really did a number on me the night before when we were in the ring. Trust me when I say that one punch she got in was the only one that she got. Not long after, I hit her so intensely in the chest that it knocked the wind right out her ass. After she was down, I tried my best to kill her ass, they had to pull me off of her. That'll show her to aim for my face again. She really tried it. I just hated I had to come to work with my lip looking like that. It wasn't like I worked a regular nine to five so putting on makeup to cover it up was totally pointless. By the time I started sweating it was just going to come off anyway.

"Unity, your client is out there waiting for you," Amber the receptionist made known, walking into the locker room. I closed my locker and headed out onto the floor. Standing by the front desk, there was a tall handsome chocolatey guy. I bit down on my lip wincing in pain. For a slight second, I had forgotten the cut was even there.

I quickly grabbed Amber's arm, "That's my client?" I asked, getting all eager. He had muscles for days, so I didn't understand what he needed a personal trainer for. Unless he was stalking me. He probably saw me here once before then booked me thinking he was going to get some play. The way I was feeling, I wouldn't mind giving his sexy ass a little of my time.

"Yeah, he's sent from the Gods isn't he." She smirked when we approached him. "Omarion, this is Unity," Amber introduced us with a bright smile on her face. He lustfully gazed over at me and I mugged him with a smug look on my face.

Walking away from him, I thought he was smart enough to come on behind me but when I didn't feel his presence, I turned around. "What are you waiting for? You coming or are you just going to stand there looking stupid?"

"You have to be so rude?" he asked me, jogging over to catch up with my speed walking. Once we got in a good stretch, the first machine we went to was the lat pull-down. He eyed me suspiciously before taking his seat. "You call this a real work out with them little ass weights on there?" Since he thought he was doing something, I went behind the machine and placed a hundred pounds on the already forty that was on there. Let's see how he feels after I force his ass to give me a hundred reps.

"A hundred reps," I told him flashing a fake ass smile. He had only been with me fifteen minutes and I was already prepared for him to get the hell out of my face.

"That's nothing." He smirked and reached up grabbing the bar. By the time that he left there, he was never going to want to come back to deal with me again. Just the way I wanted it. He was on his fortieth rep when Nix appeared beside me.

"What you want Nix? Ain't you supposed to be working?" I queried, keeping my eyes on Omarion so he wouldn't try to cheat me on the reps. Something in my peripheral caught my attention, so I turned my attention to her. Nix was standing there scratching the hell out of her skin like a crack head that was fiending. If she was to go any harder, she would probably break the skin. "What the hell is wrong with you?"

She leaned over by my ear, "I need some dick before I go fucking crazy," she whispered. I screwed my face up at her; she was really pathetic. No matter what she said, I thought she needed to go to AA for her dick addiction to Axel. There isn't any dick in the world that could have you that captivated.

"Nix, I swear if you don't get out my face with that shit, I know something. I'm busy; I don't have time for this." I shooed her away, taking a deep sigh. My friend really needed some help and if she kept on, I was going to give her ass an intervention.

"Done," Omarion called out, bringing me from my thoughts.

"Come on." I headed over to the weight bench and stacked a hundred pounds on both ends of the bar. He looked like he could lift it, so I didn't think much of it. He laid down on his back steadily gripping the bar. I stood directly behind his head so I could spot him in case it was just too much for him.

"How many reps do you want?"

"Just go 'til I tell you to stop." He lifted the weights up and brought them down. His gaze met mine, but I quickly turned my head away from him. Something about him felt a little off to me and I wasn't trying to get mixed up in his shit.

"You're sexy as fuck. When I saw you the other day, I just knew I had to get a session with your sexy ass." When he said that, my assumptions about him turned out to be correct. He didn't need any help; he was just like all the other niggas thinking he was about to get some ass, but I was far from easy. You would have to go to hell, battle with the devil, and come back to get this pussy. Nigga was wasting his time and money.

"Thanks," I dryly said, trying not to be rude about it.

"You want to hear a joke?" he asked, bringing the bar down to his chest and lifting it back up.

"Not really, but I'm sure you're going to tell me anyway." Just as soon as I said that the joke was already escaping his lips.

"What's the difference between ohhhh and ahhhh?" From the blank expression on my face, he could tell I wasn't about to answer his stupid ass question. I didn't even have the answer to it anyway. "Three inches... you get it?" He laughed.

"I see you like jokes. Do you like movies too? 'Cause I got a good one for you starring my fist in yo' dick hole." I pushed the bar all the way down to where it dropped on his neck and stepped away. He struggled to push it back up. Out of nowhere someone came over and pulled the weights off of him.

"What the hell are you doing!" his deep-voiced boomed. My eyes were still fixated on the rude ass nigga that thought making sexual jokes were funny. I was going to show these niggas I was nothing to play with.

"THAT NIGGA JUST DISRESPECTED ME!" I yelled at the guy that had helped him. When my eyes finally landed on him, my mouth almost dropped to the floor. It was the same guy I saw at the party Olivia catered a week ago. He was dressed down in some blue sweatpants that showed the top of his Burberry boxers with no shirt on and sweat dripping from his sculpted body. How the hell did I miss that sight?

His jaw immediately tightened. "What did you say to her?" he questioned an angry Omarion that rubbed his neck where the weights once were.

"All I did was tell her a joke. That bitch needs to be fired. I'm going to your manager," he scoffed, rising to his feet.

"You told me a sexual joke you fucking pervert!" I shouted, feeling heat coursing through my veins. I was pretty sure that everyone was now looking, based on how loud I was, but I didn't give a damn; he pissed me the fuck off.

"You just disrespected her again. I'on give a fuck what she did, that's a Queen and in my presence, you going to treat her as such," he warned, hands balling into fists.

"Nigga, who the fuck you think you are?" Omarion asked, getting all up in the guy's face. I saw no fear in his eyes so I was sure he could probably handle his own. My messy ass just stood back, waiting to see if something was going to pop off. It intrigued me that a total stranger was taking up for me. That was something that had never happened before. Usually, I had to fight my own battles and some of Nix's as well. He seemed like a breath of fresh air for me.

"I look like the nigga that own this muthafucka that's who the fuck I look like." Out of all the time I been working here, I never knew who had owned the place. When I got hired, I went through the manager, Charles. Just wait until I tell Nix ass about this. Omarion backed down and walked away.

"Thank you," I softly said. I went to leave, but he stopped me.

"Didn't we meet before? Your hair didn't look like that, but I'm sure that I met you."

A smirk crept up onto my face. "I told yo' bitch I was unforgettable."

Kase

"What the fuck you mean you can't find my seed!" my voice roared through the phone. More and more each day, Harper proved to me she was incapable of being a mother. She's more obsessed with the dick than she was with taking care of my fucking child. At the rate she was going, I was going to end up taking Baylee away from her ass. I quickly got up off my couch in my man cave and headed for the front door.

"I'm sorry, Blake! One minute she was there and then the next she gone. You know I wouldn't lose her on purpose. I'm scared just hurry up and get here. I'm about to call the police," she frantically cried.

"How the hell I'ma hurry up and come somewhere when you didn't even tell me where the fuck you at?" Was the bitch stupid or was she fucking stupid? Did she think I had magical powers and could read her mind to know where she was at? If she did, then she knew something about me I didn't even know my damn self.

"At Fort Tryon Park, please hurry Blake." I disconnected the call and rushed out the door. Hitting the unlock button on my metallic green Bugatti, I hopped inside and pulled off. If something happened to Baylee, Harper's ass better be out of sight because I was going to wring her fucking neck. Today was going to be the day I didn't care about going to jail for murder. The police probably were going to have to pry my hands from around her fucking neck.

Baylee was my world and she knew it. I'd travel the universe behind that little girl. There weren't many things on this earth that could scare me but when she came into the world months early premature and having everyone thinking that she wouldn't make it, I was scared as shit. Now it was four years later, and she was healthy and strong.

Before I knew it, I was pulling up to Fort Tryon. I quickly threw my car in park and hopped out. Rushing through the park, I yelled out Baylee and Harper's name. By the time I found Harper, she was standing there talking to two cops. My massive hands balled up into fists when my eyes landed on her. Part of me hopped she was joking around when she said she couldn't find Baylee but standing there glaring at her talking to the cops, that was when I knew this shit was real. I stormed up to her, wrapping one of my hands securely around her throat. She clawed at my hands, trying to get me to let her go.

"How the fuck could you lose the only thing in this world that I loved?" I was a big strong muthafucka. Standing at six two, I was a good two-sixty, pure muscle so I was sure that my hand being around her neck was crushing her windpipes. There was murder in my deep-brown eyes and Harper was my victim.

"Sir, please let her go," one of the cops pleaded from behind me. I softly sat Harper back down on her feet. She gasped for air.

"I swear to God if something happens to Baylee, you dead," I warned, walking off meaning every word. I wandered around that park for twenty minutes looking for her until I found her in a woman's arms at an ice cream cart. She was licking on a strawberry ice cream cone. "Baylee!" I called out rushing over to her.

"Hi daddy, Nix got me some ice cream. You want some?" she asked with a smile on her face, shoving the cone into mine. The woman turned all the way around. As she was turning her curly hair swung in what seemed like slow motion. There before my eyes was the woman that I had met a month ago. After she had left me that night, I thought I was never going to see her again. Never did I think I would find her so soon or better yet she found Baylee.

"Hey, it's you... the guy from that party. This little one yours?" she questioned with a huge smile on her face. Was it possible she looked even more gorgeous now than she did the night I met her? The tights she wore showed off her small curvy hips and that onion booty. She had more ass than I thought she did. I licked my lips after my eyes roamed up and down her frame.

"Yeah, and it's you, the woman that ran off from me." I took Baylee from her arms and kissed her cheek. "Baby, you can't be wandering off from your mama like that. You had me worried thinking something happened to you." Baylee poked her lower lip out at me. This was the first time she wandered off on her own like that. It made me wonder what really happened.

"It's okay; she was in good hands. I found her and spent like thirty minutes searching for her parents but couldn't find them. She saw the ice cream cart and begged for an ice cream cone, so I bought her one," Nix calmly explained.

"Baylee!" Harper shrieked. For a moment, I forgot she was in the park as well. She hurried over to us and took Baylee from my arms. I didn't feel safe with her having her, so I grabbed her right back. The police were hot on her tail, so I went over to talk to them. Not long after we were done talking, I heard screaming and shouting. When I turned around, Nix and Harper were arguing. Taking a deep breath, I stepped between them to try and prevent something from popping off. I should have known Harper was going to cut the fuck up. She couldn't stand whenever another bitch was anywhere near me.

"See, this is exactly why I don't do niggas with baby mamas. Check for me when you lose this dead weight," Nix announced and walked off before stopping short. "And bitch you welcome for finding your kid." She gave Harper the bird finger then left.

Nix

"Yaaassss, bitch, you wearing the hell out of that dress babe," I boosted up Unity's ego. I loved hyping up my girl. What were best friends for? She was wearing a cream-colored dress that was sheer in only the front and had a gold and diamond design on the front of it. Underneath it, she wore a white bra and matching white thong set. My bitch looked good, and we were about to apply some pressure at club 718. "I see you whipped out Stormy for the night," I teased her.

"You know how I do." She stuck out her tongue and swayed her gray blunt bob cut wig side to side. I had never seen a dark-skinned baddie that could pull off any color hair like Unity could. I gave her, her props though because I loved to just wear my natural hair. Fuck a weave, why wear weave when you had a head full of hair? Don't get me wrong, Unity was far from bald-headed, she just loved her wigs. "Talking about me, you look good too, chica," she complimented with a smile.

"I do, don't I?" I placed my hands on my thighs and twerked my ass. I was rocking a denim tube jumper with the matching over the knee denim boots.

"Save all that shit for the club, let's go; you were already late." Unity pushed me out the door closing and locking it behind us. When we made it outside, she stopped a taxi, and we both climbed inside. "Club 718."

∞ ∞ ∞

"*Tone that shit down. You ain't never ball like this. Tone that shit down. Tell me who can ball like this,*" I sang along to Gucci Mane's *"Tone it down"* as we made our way through the packed club. Just like I knew, Unity headed straight for the bar. She had to get drinks in her system in order for her to fully turn up. I was right with her about to toss back shots like they were water.

"Let me get ten shots of Patron," she yelled to the bartender over the music. The bartender placed ten glasses down in front of us then poured the shots.

"Here's to both of us getting some dick tonight," I said, picking up my first glass and tossing it back.

"Is that all you be worried about?" Unity laughed then threw her shot back as well.

"You can't tell me that this shit isn't fate," a familiar voice said from behind me. I spit out the shot I just put up to my lips all over the front of Unity's dress. Obviously, this nigga was stalking me. This shit wasn't a coincidence that I bumped into him the other day and now tonight.

"I'm so sorry Unity." I grabbed a napkin off the bar and tried to help her wipe herself down.

"It's cool. I got it," she said leaving. I wanted to beg her to stay because I didn't feel safe being left alone with this man.

"Where your bitch at?" I asked, rolling my eyes. That ho was going to make me fuck her ass up. When he walked away that day at the park, she ran all off at the mouth. If he hadn't intervened when he did, she probably would've been on the ground gasping for air with my hands wrapped around her fucking throat. That ho's mouth was too fucking slick for me and probably couldn't back up any of the shit she was saying.

"She around here somewhere," he truthfully admitted. I looked around for the ho. I didn't need her trying to run up on me and shit catching me off guard. Sneaky bitches did shit like that because that was the only way they could win.

"Why the fuck you in my face then?" I brushed past him, but he quickly gripped me by my forearm pulling my body into his. From the feel of that third leg resting on his thigh, I knew he was excited to see me. I swallowed hard as I took in the sweet scent of his cologne. The feeling I was getting with my body pressed up against his was unexplainable.

"I want to be more than in your face," he teased, and I swiftly traced my tongue across my lips.

"What all you want to do?" I had to ask. I promise you that nigga didn't know who he was fucking with.

"I want to be all up between them legs in that slippery pussy of yours. I want to blow your back out so good that you can't walk straight for days. I want to devour that pussy like it's my last meal," he whispered in my ear and my pussy throbbed. A light moan escaped my lips. I quickly pulled myself away from him feeling my juices streaming down my inner thighs.

"Boy please don't play with me. I can suck a bullet out a Glock on safety. You not ready for me. I'll have your head all fucked up, not knowing if you coming or going."

"Show me." He gripped me by the hand and led me toward the exit. Normally, I wouldn't too much fuck with a nigga that I knew had a bitch, but I was going to take Unity's advice and get me some new dick. That shit was very much past due like a late power bill, and he was the only one that could handle that shit before it got disconnected. Before we could reach the door, his crazy baby mama jumped right in our path.

"Where the hell do you think you're going with this ho, Kase!" she yelled, tossing her hands in the air. The way shorty eyed me, I knew she was pressed. I didn't give one fuck; she couldn't whoop my ass.

"I'm about to go; what the fuck does it look like I'm doing?"

She tilted her head to the side.

"Are you fucking serious right now! You came here with me and now you about to leave with another bitch?" Her bright face turned beet red from embarrassment. If she knew exactly how she was looking at the moment, she would've dismissed herself.

"You damn right he is, now get the fuck out of this bitch's way before she move your ass," I warned. Hos always wanted to assassinate my fucking character. If she didn't find something to do with herself, I was going to show her just how much of a bitch I could be.

"Harper gone on somewhere. We aren't even exclusive. You already know wassup," he smoothly said, shutting her down really quick.

"What the hell do you want with this ugly ass skeleton in the first place. She don't have nowhere near as many curves as I do." She sounded stupid as fuck. I had to gone and check that bitch like a Nike.

"First of all, little bitch, just 'cause you got a phat ass don't make you a bad bitch. You just blessed by the waist and stressed by the face. Secondly, I'm tired of y'all thinking that you thick bitches are winning all the got damn time. Kase gone take this little ass booty and he going to love this shit. Get the fuck out the way." I shoved her ass, and she fell to the floor. "I'm about to go pop my pussy all over your nigga's dick. You can have him back in the morning." I pulled Kase out of the club while texting Unity at the same time.

Reapa

*L*istening to Post Malone's *"Rockstar"* had me reminiscing about my life. Once upon a time, I was on the same bullshit he was talking about in that song. Now, I didn't have to be wild and flashy for people to know my name. A nigga calmed down so much since then, but Reapa instilled fear in everyone's hearts just the way I liked it.

I pressed the ignore button on my phone again. Ava had been straight blowing a nigga's phone up ever since I shot her ass. I don't know why she thought that everything was going to be all good once I found out she was fucking another nigga behind my back. I would have just got a new number but that was my personal line and I didn't feel like giving out my number to everyone all over again. It wasn't like my trap, I tossed that muthafucka out every other day. There was no time for slacking.

Getting up from my seat, I went over to the railing and looked down at the crowded club. My eyes immediately landed on a woman. It was just something about her that seemed so familiar to me. I stood there observing her. Her sex appeal was off the fucking charts, straight bursting through the roof. The way that crème colored dress hugged her small curves had my dick trying to brick up. I didn't usually go for women that wore odd color hair; the shit was tacky as fuck to me, but somehow, she was making the shit look sexy.

"You seen Kase?" Harper walked up to me and asked. She knew I didn't fuck with her while she was all in my personal space and shit. The only reason I dealt with her was on the strength of my niece. If it wasn't for her, I would've put a hot one in her ass a long time ago. I didn't even give a damn she was Kase's girl and he loved her, if she didn't have Baylee, she would be dead. The ho was shiesty as fuck. Gripping her by her shoulders, I pushed her back a few inches.

"Respect my space," I told her, and she rolled her eyes. "But no, I haven't seen him, and even if I did, I wouldn't tell your ass."

"What have I ever done to you that you don't like me?" she seriously asked with a quivering lower lip. This muthafucka was really about to cry.

"I don't owe you no fucking explanation." I leaned forward on the railing, ignoring her ass like she wasn't still standing there with a scowl on her face. I knew exactly where Kase was, but like I said, I wouldn't tell her. My eyes trained back on the beautiful dark-skinned beauty as she bounced away. Keeping them locked on her, I made my way to the direction she was heading in. When she went into the bathroom, I posted up on the wall, waiting for her to exit.

The way she had me feeling, I was on some stalker type shit. This was the first time I desired someone other than Ava so I might as well embraced it. If I wanted you, there had to have been something captivating about you because there weren't a lot of women I craved. They didn't really have much to offer, but a nice shape and maybe some good sex if I was lucky. Their hands always wanted to be deep off in my pockets that's why I didn't give most of these hos the time of day. Normally, I'd just take 'em to a hotel, fuck 'em and be gone before the crack of dawn. But this one... she felt different.

"Shoot," she blurted, bringing me from my thoughts. I looked up and saw her standing there staring down at her phone.

"Something's wrong?" I questioned her. When she turned to me, I finally realized who she was; the girl from the gym the other day. It was as if she was a different person every time I laid eyes on her. One thing I knew for sure, she was damn right when she said she was unforgettable because indeed she damn sure was. I could never forget that beautiful face and those plump pouty lips. Those freckles even enhanced her beauty.

"Not that it's any of your concern, but my homegirl just left with my keys and money in her clutch so now I'm basically stranded," she fussed with a frown.

"You're never stranded baby girl when you got me," I confidently made known.

"Boy, I don't know you nor do I know anything about you," she quickly snapped. A smirk formed on my face. All those other bitches would jump for joy if I told them some shit like that. That alone told me she was different from the rest.

"This our third time bumping into each other, I would hardly call us strangers now." I was just calling it how I saw it. Shit, I had bitches that dropped their panties within seconds of meeting me. In my opinion, we were damn near associates by now.

"To me, you're still a stranger." If it was up to me, before the night was over with, we wouldn't be.

"For now." I gave her my infamous panty wetting smirk. From the way she bit down on the corner of her lower lip, I could tell it was working. "Tell me how come every time I see you, your hair is different?" I queried, running my hand through her hair.

"I love to switch it up; keep my man on his toes whenever I have one. Babe, dating me is like dating a different bitch every day of the week. You never know who you gon' get," she explained. I could second that.

I pushed myself up off the wall, "You still need that ride 'cause I'm about to bounce?" I asked her before heading toward the exit not even waiting for her to respond. If she wanted a way home, then she would bring her ass on. When I got outside, my driver pulled my cocaine-white Rolls Royce Ghost up to the door and got out so he could opened the back door for me.

"That's you?" she quizzed, walking up beside me. Something told me she was going to come along for the ride, that's why I really wasn't sweating it.

"Yeah," I replied. Usually, when women saw me riding around in the Royce, they got dollar signs and twinkles in their eyes. But her, she just shrugged it off and climbed over into the car. I hadn't been around her for long, and she was steady proving to me she wasn't caught up in my lifestyle. "What's your address?" I quizzed, climbing in behind her and shutting the door.

"Just drop me off in the Bronx on Matthews Avenue," she told Tyler, and he nodded, pulling off. She relaxed back in the comfy seats, drifting off in her own thoughts while gazing out of the window watching the city pass us by. My trap phone buzzed off the charts, so I pulled it out to see who was blowing me up.

"This better be important that you're calling me up this time of night." From my peripheral, I could see her staring at me sideways trying to figure out who I was on the phone with.

"We found that missing package. Do you want us to pick it up or what?" Jug asked. I was becoming eager as fuck because I had been waiting on that package to get delivered to me for far too long. I'd rather go pick it up myself.

"No, text Tyler the address and I'll be there. I want to handle it myself," I told him, ending the call with a smirk.

"You got somewhere you need to be? If you do, I can just catch the subway or the bus, even a taxi and get home." There was no way I was about to let her roam around this time of night all alone for something to happen to her. That was out of the question.

"We just making a slight detour then I will get you home safely. I told you I was taking you home and that's exactly what I intend on doing." Not long after we pulled up in front of a tall glass building. I shot Jug a quick text letting him know I was outside and for them to kill the cameras. "Wait right here; I'll be right back. Shouldn't take too long." She nodded, and I got out of the car heading inside.

Knocking on the door, I stood there patiently waiting for someone to answer it. A woman finally came to it. Terror crossed her face just the way I liked it. I invited myself inside, taking a glance around the spacious apartment. Jug and the other boys stood out in the hallway just in case I needed them. "Where's your husband?"

"H-H-Henry!" she nervously yelled out. I stood there with my hands crossed in front of my dick firmly holding on to my Glock.

"Just the man I wanted to see," I announced when Henry rounded the corner into the living room.

"What are you doing in my shit?" he questioned quickly grabbing his wife, pulling her to his side. I thought the little gesture was cute.

"You been looking for me, right?" I was never one to hide from no man. I faced my demons head-on every single time.

"Where you heard that from?"

"From a little birdie but that doesn't really matter. I'm here now so what the fuck do you want?" I took a seat on his couch making myself at home while eyeing his wife. She was all right looking for her to be a white bitch. The only thing that turned me off from her was that she was shaped like a fucking toothpick. I'd fuck around and snap her ass in two. From the dissatisfied expression on his face, I could tell he saw the way I was looking at her, so he pulled her behind him out of my view.

"You act as if the whole city is scared of you or something. I'm not afraid of you," he grimaced.

"Is that so?" I rushed toward him, pushing him out of the way and gripped his wife roughly by her hair, forcing her down to her knees. Placing my gun at her temple, I diverted my attention back to him. "You still not scared Henry?" Tears flowed freely down her cheeks. She begged for my mercy, but mercy was for the faint-hearted. Niggas like me didn't really have a heart.

"Please, just let her go," he pleaded, bringing his hands up to his nose and mouth. If he knew like I knew, he would've been praying because couldn't shit save his ass now.

"I had to murder my own cousin because of you, and now you want to beg for my sympathy." Tears shone in his eyes as he mugged me. I took the gun down from the side of her head, and he let out a sigh of relief. "Open your mouth," I ordered, clenching my teeth.

"Pleeeeaaasssseee," she pleaded with watery eyes.

I kept my eyes trained on Henry to make sure he didn't make any sudden moves. "Open your fucking mouth!" I barked, and she did just that. I shoved the tip of my strap into her mouth. "Suck that shit." Her cries muffled by my piece filling up her mouth like a dick. She slid her mouth up and down on the chrome as if she was sucking one. "Yeah just like that." *Pow!* Her body slumped down to the floor. "Oops, guess my finger slipped." I smirked.

"You son of a bitch!" Henry bellowed, charging toward me, but I aimed my bloody gun at him, stopping him right in his tracks.

"Now what were you saying? That you weren't scared of me?" I knelt down next to his dead wife's body and used the end of her dress to clean her DNA off of my gun. "Are you going to tell me what the fuck you were doing talking to Markell?"

"I'm not telling you shit. When I'm done putting my case together, I'm going to make sure you get the death penalty." I never liked threats; they always did something to me. They turned me colder than I already was as if that was fucking possible.

Storming over to Henry, I gripped him by his shirt, backing him up into the floor to ceiling glass door that led out on the balcony. A thought instantly came to mind. "We're up on the what?... Twentieth floor?" I grinned sliding the door opened with my free hand and pushed him out onto the balcony. His body stopped at the railing with his head leaning back. "Hope you can fly muthafucka," I said and pushed his ass on over the edge.

Tucking my strap into my waist, I stepped back into the apartment. Jug was already in there cleaning down everything, trying to get rid of all evidence that I was even there. "Make sure you find the files on everything he has here on me. And if you can't get 'em, then make a call to Carrie down at the station where he worked."

Unity

I wasn't sure what made me go against my better judgment and get inside that car with him. I didn't know this man, yet here I was riding around the city in this beautiful ass car like I was royalty or something. Things just seemed too good to be true. This was definitely nothing I was used to and just like Olivia had said, there probably were so many problems coming along with this handsome ass man.

He definitely was a sight for sore eyes, and I was trying my best just to keep mine off of him the entire time he had been inside the car with me. Being so close to him, his delicious smelling cologne was attacking my nostrils, and it was becoming hard for me to control myself around him. Hopefully, he would hurry up and drop me off before I found myself doing something I would regret in the morning. Lucky for me, I hadn't drunk all of those shots I ordered or else I would've been assaulting his sexy, juicy lips.

Since I didn't know anything about him and had left my keys in Nix's clutch, I was going to get dropped off on my street and walk the few blocks over to my grandma's house and stay the night there. I was brought from my thoughts when I heard a loud thud hit the ground outside and something red splattered on the window. I anxiously opened the car door and climbed out looking over the top of the car to see what it was.

With me being so short, I couldn't really see but knew that it had to have been something serious. People were standing around screaming and pointing, so I crept around the back of the car. When I saw what was lying on the ground, my entire body went rigid. My heart pounded rapidly in my chest as I screamed at the top of my lungs, looking at the dead body on the ground. A few moments later, he walked out the door, stepping over the man's body as if he was just some trash on the street. When he came toward me, I immediately backed away from him.

"D-d-d-did you do that?" I stammered because I was now scared for my life.

"Do what? Him?" Swallowing the lump that formed in my throat, I slowly nodded. "No... guess he jumped." He shrugged without a care in the world.

Something told me he was lying. I had a feeling he was the one that did that shit but since I couldn't really prove it, I just stopped backing away and allowed him to console me. That was the first time I actually seen a dead body that close, and quite frankly it scared the shit out of me. My eyes glistened with tears. He softly gripped me by the waist, pulling me into him, stroking my back as if he actually cared about my feelings. "You good?" he asked. How could he be so nonchalant about the shit when there was someone dead lying on the ground behind him?

"I don't know," I honestly replied. My body melted into him and it felt as if I belonged there. I needed to get home. There was no way that after all these years, I was going to let my guard down to a stranger. "Can you just take me home?" Breaking away from him, I took one last look at the body, then climbed back into the car.

The whole way to the Bronx the car ride was silent. I sat there lost in my thoughts not knowing what to say or do about the situation. Up until that moment, I kind of liked him, but he was now having me feel complexed. I'm not trying to get mixed up in no bullshit behind no man. Everything in me was telling me he was trouble, but it didn't stop my eyes from wandering over at him every chance I got.

He sat there, not uttering a word with a mug resting on his face. Not one muscle in his face moved an inch and truthfully it was kind of sexy to me. My pussy began speaking another language. She itched an itch that he was the only one that could scratch it. Pressing my thighs together, I attempted to stop my pussy from dripping.

"You aight over there?" he finally spoke, turning to face me. His hooded eyes meet my lingering gaze making me feel a certain type of way. Pushing myself up from the seat, my body fell into his. I pressed my lips against his soft plump ones. They felt just as I thought they would. My juices dripped even more as he smacked me hard on the ass. I wasn't sure exactly what had taken control of my body to have me acting that way. All I wanted was to feel his hard dick sliding between my legs. We kissed so long that our lips had become sore to the touch. Feeling the car come to a halt, I finally came to my senses and pulled back.

"What am I doing?" I more so asked myself, falling back into the seat. I didn't even know his name, and here I was getting ready to fuck him in the back seat of his car. That was totally out of my character. Looking around, I noticed I was down the street from my grandma's apartment. "I'm sorry, but I have to go."

When I reached for the door, he stopped me by softly gripping my wrist. "What's wrong?" He licked his lips and my pussy twitched. I had to stop myself from giggling because my lipstick was smudged all over his mouth. If I was to fuck him, all he was going to do was disappear on me, and I'll never see him again or better yet just look at me as a ho, and I was far from that. No matter how much I wanted to have sex with him, I wasn't trying to be just a one-night stand. I wanted more, and judging by his lifestyle, I knew he couldn't give me that.

"I just can't do this," I answered honestly, then pulled my hand away from him and climbed out of the car.

Nix

*J*ust as soon as we made it to his door, I just couldn't keep my hands off of him. Suddenly, between pulling his shirt over his head and our tongues colliding, I stopped. "Wait," I panted, attempting to catch my breath.

"What's wrong?" he stared at me confusedly.

"I'm about to fuck you and don't even know your name," I admitted. It should've been something I asked a long time ago but now was when I thought to. Don't get me wrong, I love myself some dick, but I wasn't just about to lay down in the bed with a man and didn't know his name. The way things were already going, I wasn't too sure if we were even going to make it to the bedroom.

"Kase," he replied.

"Oh, yeah, I remember your baby mama calling you that." Snatching his shirt over his head, I tossed it to the side and continued to assault his plump, firm lips. As he pulled back, he brought my breath with him, gazing me lustfully in the eyes. His large hand went up gently stroking the side of my face.

"I've been wanting to do this for a long-" I hushed him with my lips. It felt like he was trying to make things seem more intimate than they really were. The truth was, this session was to feed my dick hunger, nothing more, nothing less. After tonight was over with, I had no intentions of ever seeing Kase again. It sounded harsher than what I was trying to make it seem, but that just was my reality.

Reaching down, I unbuttoned and unzipped his pants revealing his dick and dropped down to my knees. The sight before me was mouthwatering. His thick, long, curved dick was one of the biggest muthafuckas I ever laid eyes on. I licked my lips, getting them nice and slippery then engulfed the tip, swirling my tongue around. His body shuddered underneath my fingertips. All my mind focused on was making him drop his load off down my throat. Little did he know, I was about to milk his ass dry of every bit of cum he had inside his ball sack. By the time I was done with him, he was going to be looking for me in the daytime with a flashlight. I was confident of that.

Squeezing my jaw muscles and relaxing my throat, I took him all the way in. "Fuck, you about to make me cum," he growled, letting me know I had him exactly where I wanted him. The way I sucked his dick, I was sure his toes were curling in his sneakers. A few moments later, he emptied all his seeds down my throat and roared like a beast in the night.

Kase intertwined his fingers in my hair and grasped a handful of it, tightly pulling me up from my knees. He pressed his lips against mine, backing me up until the back of my legs hit the couch. I broke the kiss long enough to take my boots off and push my romper down. His eyes zeroed in on my body. From the way he licked his lips, I could tell he loved what he saw.

"Don't just stare at it, show me all that shit you were talking back at the club," I teased him, falling back on the couch, giving him the perfect view of my dripping wet, pink pussy. Glancing down, I saw his dick standing at attention with pre-cum oozing from the tip of it. Getting down on his knees, he came eye level to my pussy. His eyes fixated on her like she was a brand-new Rolex that he been wanting forever. He didn't even allow me to brace myself before he yanked me by the thighs and brought my clit straight to his mouth latching onto it.

A moan escaped my lips just as soon as he touched it. That nigga was putting in overtime trying to make that pussy squirt for him. Even though it was the worst time to be doing so, I couldn't help but compare his and Axel's sex. So far, he had him beat with the head game, and I was anxious to see what that dick was talking about.

"Aw fuck!" I whimpered. I was so close to climaxing, and that was the first time I had ever cum that fast from the head alone. I squirted my juices into his mouth. Kase licked me clean and brought his eyes up to meet my gaze. Biting down on my lower lip, I gripped him by the sides of his face, bringing his lips to mine, hungrily sucking my pussy juices off of them. He pushed his pants down just far enough where he could enter me with ease. Placing his dick at my entrance, he plunged straight into me without warning causing me to yelp out in pleasure and pain. I tilted my head back and dug my nails into his shoulders.

The way he was fucking me, I knew he was going to mess my head up afterward. I thought I was going crazy over Axel, but that dick wasn't shit compared to Kase's. With every thrust he gave, I matched it on beat. Every time he eased his dick out, my pussy sucked him right on back in.

Kase fucked the shit out of me for what seemed like hours. After I had cum numerous of times and he came twice, he finally collapsed on the floor with me in his arms and a fur throw blanket thrown across our sweaty naked bodies. As he laid there snoring in my embrace, my mind drifted off. He had just given me the best sex of my life. I mean, that mind-blowing, stalking, curse your bald headed mammi out over the dick, get you hooked kind of sex. There was no way I was going to be able to see this man again. The people that give you the greatest sex are never the ones that you're supposed to be with.

Once I collected my thoughts, I eased from underneath him, allowing his head to drop onto the throw pillow I was lying on and got up to grab my clothes. That was the fastest I ever seen myself get dressed. I snuck out of his place like a thief in the night.

Harper Davenport

K ase and his little scum bucket had me all the way fucked up if he thought he was going to treat me like my feelings didn't fucking matter. I was about to pop up on that ass and blow all the fun he thought he was about to have with that bitch. That was my dick, and I was staking claims on the muthafucka. I had been with him for far too long building far too much to just let another chick come in and take what I helped build. He thought I just be tripping on him over nothing when that's not the case. I loved that man more than life itself. I just wished he would understand that for once.

"Blake!" I yelled, beating his front door down. I knew he was inside because the Bugatti he drove to the club earlier was parked in the driveway. I prayed to God he didn't have that bitch inside the house with him. If he did, I was going to fuck both of their asses up on sight. The ho had an ass whooping with her name on it from that cheap shot she gave me at the club prior in the first place.

The door finally swung open, and I forced myself inside, taking a look around. Kase stood before me, wiping the sleep from his eyes in nothing but his Burberry boxers. Apparently, the bitch had been there from the clothes that laid on the floor. "Where is she?" I asked with tears shimmering in my eyes. I couldn't believe he actually done me like that with everything we been through together. My heart crushed into a million pieces, and with all the rugged edges, I don't think it will be able to be put back together again.

"Don't come up in here starting this shit with me. A nigga tired and shit," he complained, treading away from the door.

"Do you not know what all I had to go through just to get here since someone left me at the fucking club?" I queried, wiping the tears from my eyes.

"Nope, not that I care, but I'm sure you're going to tell me anyway," he nonchalantly replied. As if it was even possible, he smashed my heart even more.

"I had to take the subway, then two buses and walk the rest of the way to get up to this stupid ass house of yours."

"Why you didn't just call an Uber?" he asked, cocking his head to the side.

"THAT'S NOT THE FUCKING POINT! The point is that I was there with you and you just left me like I was some random bitch on the street. I'm no random bitch, I'm your baby mama, and I thought I was your girl, but you proved me wrong tonight when you disrespected me the way you did," I ranted. Kase had me on ten, and I was not leaving there until he knew exactly how I felt and where I was coming from.

"I was wrong for just leaving you the way I did, and I apologize for that. You feel better now?" The apology seemed somewhat sincere and knowing Kase, that was the best I was going to get so I better take it and just deal with it. Walking over, I stopped right in front of his face as he chilled back on the sofa.

"No, I don't feel better. You fucking hurt me, Blake. I thought you loved me. I would've never thought you would do me the way you had." The floodgates finally opened, and I couldn't stop myself from crying even if I wanted to.

"Yeah, I do love you Harper, but we not working out. I get tired of the back and forth shit with you all the fucking time. Shit gets old, you get tired of trying to work things out. You get tired of giving people chances, sometimes you just gotta let people go and you're one of those people. Let's just keep things cordial for the sake of Baylee," he implied. That was something I never thought I would hear leave his lips before. That bitch had her claws in him deeper than I thought that she did.

"CORDIAL!" I screamed, reaching my hand out to slap fire from him but he caught my hand in mid-swing.

"Don't fucking play with me Harper. I've never put my hands on you, so you better not put yours on me 'cause if you do, I swear to God I'm going to knock you the fuck out. Your ass going to wake up not knowing your fucking name, try me," he warned, letting my wrist go.

"Fuck you, Blake! That's why that bitch just fucked your stupid ass and left 'cause she sure as hell not here now. How the hell does it feels to be treated like a bitch!" I shouted and stormed out of there.

∞ ∞ ∞

"He just treated me like I wasn't shit. Kicked me to the side for some gold-digging bitch," I cried, dropping my head in my hands. The way Kase treated me still seemed surreal. The love we had for each other, I thought was that forever love.

"Fuck that nigga sis, you can do way better than his ass in the first place. I told you that when you first started fucking around with the fuck nigga," my brother, Axel said with a scowl on his face. Axel had never liked Kase nor Reapa, and I just couldn't understand why. Maybe it was because they were pulling in way more money than he was. Sometimes I could see the resentment in his eyes and knew that nothing good would ever come from it.

"But I love him, Axel," I wept. Axel probably thought I was stupid as fuck for crying over Kase, but that nigga had my heart. It was something he would never understand because he never kept a bitch no longer than a week except for that one that he would never let me meet; he was scared I would run her ass off or something. If only she knew the shit her so-called man was doing whenever she wasn't around including fucking the brains out of my best friend.

"Like Axe said, fuck that nigga," Ava said, coming from the back of the house with nothing but a towel wrapped around her dripping wet body. To me, the bitch was stupid as fuck to fuck up what she had with Reapa over my brother. I loved my brother to death, but that nigga wasn't shit and hardly bringing in as much paper as Reapa.

"It's not that easy. I can't just switch my emotions off like that. He's Baylee's father. I'll always love that man with all my heart; well what's left of it anyway," I responded.

Axel got up from the couch with a mug on his face. "Well, I'm going to make that nigga hurt just the same way he made you." He leaned down, picking up his Nine off the coffee table, cocked it, and placed it in the small of his back.

"Axel noooooo!" I cried out as he left out the door, slamming it behind him.

Axel Davenport

he other night when I left and went looking for Kase, I couldn't find his ass anywhere. Harper would never tell me where he laid his head at, so the shit was really up to me to find him. Not a lot of people knew where those niggas stayed since they didn't really trust anyone but their inner circle. But I swear to God when I found Kase, I was fucking his ass up on sight. He should've never fucked with my little sister's feelings. I never really could figure out what she saw in him in the first place—it had to be the nigga's money.

I called Nix for the millionth time while sitting outside of her building. It had been a while since I heard from her. Normally, she would be blowing a nigga's phone up, and now that I had some free time and wanted to put up with her ass, she was ignoring the shit out of me. I needed to see what the hell she was up to because it just wasn't like her to not pick up. When she didn't answer yet again, I got out the car and went inside. There was no doubt in my mind that she was acting up since she wasn't getting the dick. All it'll take is one good dick down, and she'll be right back on track. That's exactly what I planned on doing with her ass.

Her mother answered the door wearing a grimace. It wasn't any mystery that Olivia couldn't stand me and quite frankly, her hatred for me was mutual. I kept telling Nix she was too damn grown to be still staying at home with her fucking mother but could never convince her to move out. "What are you doing here?"

"Hi, Ms. O, is Phoenix here?" I asked her, flaunting a fake smile. The way I was feeling, I just wanted to reach out and strangle her ass.

She rolled her eyes to the ceiling then yelled out Nix's name before walking away from the door. "Phoenix!"

Not long after, Nix came from the back. I licked my lips. My baby was looking good as always. She was wearing a PINK sports bra with some white jeans. Her curly hair had two balls on top of her head while the rest of it just hung down her back. Once her eyes landed on me, her juicy lips turned into a scowl. She had the right to be mad how I had been doing her, and since I felt like she was slowly slipping away from me, I was going to try to do better by her for the time being. That didn't mean I wasn't going to stop slipping between Ava's legs every chance I got. That pussy was too muthafucking good for me to give up like that.

"What's up babe?" She gave me the same eye roll her ugly ass mother gave not too long ago.

"What you doing here?" she quizzed, folding her arms underneath her breasts. The way they poked out, it had my dick trying to brick up.

"I wanted to holler at you for a second." I reached out pulling on one of her curls. Nix briefly looked back at her mother before grabbing me by the hand, pulling me into the apartment, and shutting the door behind me.

"We'll be in my room," she told Olivia and dragged me toward her bedroom. I knew she was missing the dick while she was trying to play all hard and shit. I couldn't wait to plunge headfirst into that pussy. Just as soon as she shoved me into the bedroom and shut the door, I began stripping. "What the fuck are you doing?" I stopped mid strip because I was confused as hell.

"Thought you wanted the dick. Isn't that why you brought me in here?" My brow rose.

"No. Keep your fucking clothes on. I just brought you in here so that my mama couldn't hear what I had to say." I pulled my shirt back down over my head.

"What you mean?" I plopped down on her canopy bed already knowing she was about to be on some good old bullshit.

"I'm tired of this bullshit with you, Axe. Ever since I got with you, I've become a totally different person. I had never been to jail before but ever since I started fucking with you, I've been in and out of jail. This shit isn't me and just like my mama said, you're no good for me, Axe. I have to leave you the fuck alone."

The whole time she talked, she stared down at the floor. Something was telling me this wasn't really what she wanted, and I was about to feed off that bullshit just to get my fucking way. I really wanted to know where she was getting all this from. Like some other nigga had been putting a bug in her ear or something. Getting up from the bed, I sauntered over to where she stood, cupping her face, and gazed down into her eyes.

"You don't really mean that babe. You love me, and I love you." Her eyes moved side to side as if she was trying to read me. They were glossed over, and I knew I had her exactly where I wanted her.

"How do you love me? How, Axel? When you continually cheat on me like I ain't shit? Fuck your love if your loyalty isn't coming with it!" she spat and slapped my hand down from her face. Her new-found balls were quite intriguing. At that moment, I knew there was another nigga that had been in her head, and when I found out who the fuck nigga was, I was going to kill his ass dead. "Get the fuck out!" she yelled and snatched her bedroom door opened. When the door opened,

Olivia stood there with a mug on her face. She gripped me by the ear and drug me to the front door.

"And don't bring your black ass back!" she shouted, slamming the door in my face.

Kase

Shorty just up and left me the other night like it was nothing. That was the first time in history some shit like that ever happened to me and I couldn't lie, a nigga's ego was a little bruised. How could she just fuck a nigga like that and dip off on him? No matter how much I tried, I just couldn't keep her off my fucking mind. I just wished she would have left a number or something before she took off where I could reach her.

Now I was sitting here lost in a daze, trying to figure out if I had done something wrong or not. Even though it seemed impossible, I had it bad for her. This was the first time I couldn't function right because she just wouldn't stay off of my mind. When she said she would fuck my head up, she wasn't lying.

"Aye yo, you good fam?" Reapa asked, pulling me from my thoughts. I had almost forgotten I was sitting at this nigga's house watching the game with him.

"My mind fucked up," I admitted, running my hand across my waves.

"Your mind still on old girl?" He chuckled, but I didn't see anything funny. He was almost in the same situation I was. Reapa told me all about the girl he met at the club and how she threw herself at him but dipped off before anything could go down. Shit wasn't adding up to me.

"Yeah, what the hell is going on with us?" I confusedly queried. Usually, women stayed throwing the pussy at us, and we caught it with no hesitation, but now we had two women on our hands that wasn't shit like we were used to, and we had no idea of what to do with 'em.

"Nothing. Maybe we just found a couple of challenges. I still don't know what makes you want to chase her ass down when she gave you the pussy on the first night like that." He shrugged it off.

"It really wasn't the first night, that was my third-time meeting shorty. I just hate she disappeared on me like that without a trace. I would try and track her down, but all I know is her nickname and nothing else."

"That's where you're wrong. Didn't you say her mama did Ma and Pop's party? Why don't start there?" he asked me getting up from the couch, treading into the kitchen.

"Got damn, you not slow after all, Miles." I smirked, calling him by his government and got up. I never seen someone that hated their name as much as that nigga right there. Hopefully, her mother could tell me where to find her that's if she wasn't one of those strict, uptight mothers and shit.

"Where the hell you going?" he quizzed as I headed for the front door. I looked back, and he stood there with a scowl on his face and a bottle of D'USSÉ in his hand.

"Going to get my girl," I announced, backtracking to the door.

"Nigga, I didn't fucking mean now, the fuck." He frowned. I shrugged and left.

∞ ∞ ∞

As I strolled into restaurant O, I scanned the place, trying to lay eyes on Nix or her mother. Even though she had been working for her mother that night at the party, she told me she didn't actually work for her, just was helping out since she needed the help. Gripping the first woman by the wrist, I stopped her to ask if Olivia was there. To my surprise, it was just the woman I been searching for. Nix eyes poured into mine, and her face crept down into a frown.

"What are you doing here?" she questioned, pulling her wrist away from me. From the attire she wore, I knew she was probably helping her mother out tonight as well or lying about not working for her one.

"Was looking for you. I didn't like how you dipped off on me like that the other night," I confessed. Blowing air from her lips, she looked around then grabbed me by the hand, pulling me out of the restaurant. When we were far enough away from the door, she spoke.

"Look, Kase, I just got out of a relationship, and I'm not looking to get in another one. That night was supposed to have been nothing but a one-night stand, nothing more. I was only trying to quench my dick thirst," she truthfully disclosed.

"Why you lying to me? You feel the same shit I do. Why else would you run away while I was asleep?" She could sit there telling herself them lies all she wanted to but I knew the truth. The connection we had was undeniable, and she could feel it as well. That twinkle in her eye told it all.

"I'm not lying; I can't do this shit with you. My ex took my heart and I haven't seen that muthafucka since."

"Well, let's go get that bitch then." I grabbed her by the hand, but she pulled away.

"Why do you want me? I fucked you on the first night. I'm nothing compared to what you're used to. I'm a broken chick that needs to work on finding myself, and I can't do that with another man that might shatter me even more." My eyes bored into hers searching for her soul. Her looks were what caught my attention, but her personality was the reason I wanted to fuck with her so bad. Her being different from my norm was what I needed.

"Yeah, you right. You are different but a good different. Let me tell you something that you might not know. When a nigga first laid his eyes on you, his mind is made up from the jump about what he want to be to you. Having sex with me so soon was not going to change that. I could see myself being with you and nothing or no one going to stop me from being with you including you so cut the shit."

I snatched her phone from her front pants pocket and punched my name and number in it before handing it back to her. "Use that shit and don't make a nigga have to come and hunt your ass down. You gave a nigga that wet-wet and fucked up his head and shit. That shit mine now so whatever nigga you been fucking with, you need to let his ass know he dropped." Her mouth fell ajar, and no words formed. I had just checked her ass and was feeling good as fuck about my decision. "Hit my line when you get off."

Reapa

S ince Kase ran off and left a nigga, I ended up watching the rest of the game by myself. It wasn't the first time he left me hanging for some pussy. There were plenty of times he had done it when he was with Harper. The relationship they had was confusing as shit. One day, they would be together then the next they wouldn't be. If you asked me, both of them needed to get their fucking acts together and quick for the sake of Baylee. That new girl he was chasing, I didn't really know anything about her but could tell he was feeling her deep. Obviously, he was all for it, so I was with my nigga. Whatever made him happy, that was all mattered.

The knock on my front door brought me out of my thoughts. I got up from my couch and went to see who was at the door. I wasn't expecting anyone, so I didn't know who it could've been. "The fuck you doing here?" I asked Ava, a scowl plastered across my face. She stood on my porch with a bright smile on hers. When she saw I wasn't too pleased with her surprise visit, the tears glistened in her eyes.

"I tried to give you some time, Miles. I stayed away from you as long as I could so that you could calm down, but I miss you. Can't you just forgive me and move on from this. Swear one day we just going to look back on this and laugh." She brushed past me into the house and I shut the door behind her. This bitch must be crazy if she thought I was just going to forget about her fucking another nigga behind my back and take her back like the shit was nothing. If I would've done her the same way, she wouldn't take me back so easily. Not saying I haven't, I was just smarter about my shit than her.

"What... that nigga must got tired of your ass and sent your ho ass back to me? Tell that nigga I don't want you so might as well go crawl back to him." I made my way to the kitchen to pour me another glass of D'USSÉ. Apparently, I was going to need it dealing with her dizzy ass.

Ava came over placing her small hand on my large bicep. "I wasn't with a nigga. I had to heal up from that gunshot you gave me. The time away from you I had so much to think about and yes, I did fuck up when I let him into your sacred place. But I swear to you that I will never let anything like that ever happen again if you just give me another chance," she pleaded. Gazing into her dark brown eyes, I couldn't tell if she was sincere about her so-called apology or not.

Once upon a time, I used to could tell but not so much anymore. Tears soaked her red cheeks and snot attempted to drip from her nose. The whole scene before me seemed believable but it also could be fraud. Ava was good at playing games. Look how long she was playing me before I even found out she was fucking another nigga. I felt stupid as fuck behind that shit. No matter how much she begged and pleaded, there was no forgiving her ass for that shit.

"Get on your knees," I ordered her. Licking her lips getting all eager, she did exactly what I told her to. I tossed my drink back then unzipped my pants unleashing my monster. My shit was so long and thick that most bitches ran when I dropped my pants but not Ava. Her nasty ass always did that muthafucka just right. I had the urge to bust a nut and she was there so why not use her to my advantage? "Open up that mouth."

Ava opened her mouth as wide as it would go, and I shoved my dick right down her damn throat. Usually, she would suck it a little bit to warm up but that time I didn't even give her a chance to. The only thing on my mind was how my bitch betrayed me in one of the worst ways imaginable and all I wanted to do was punish her ass for it. I held her by the back of her head as I roughly fucked her mouth. She kept gagging and it was only turning me on even more. Soon, she caught on to my rhythm and was sucking me with ease.

"You little stupid bitch, how the fuck you just going give my shit away like that then expect me to just forgive you? I should've fucking bodied your dumb ass."

Ava pulled back from my dick staring me up into my dark eyes with tears in hers. "I'm sorr-" I hushed her by ramming my dick back down her throat. There wasn't shit she could say that would make me feel better about the situation. Her freaky ass kept slurping my shit until I released all my seeds down her throat.

Once she was done, she got up from her knees with a smirk on her face. "So, we good now, daddy?" she anxiously asked, bouncing on her tippy toes. Just because she gave me a little top didn't mean everything was going to be kosher. All she did was help me relieve a little built up pressure. That ho couldn't do anything else for me; she already proved she wasn't wifey material.

Without saying another word, I violently gripped her by her weave and drug her ass to the front door kicking and screaming. I opened the door and threw her ass outside onto the porch like the trash she was. "Don't bring your ass back here and if you do, I'ma let Cocaine have her way with you," I warned and shut the door in her face.

Unity

"FUCK!" I yelled powerfully punching the punching bag. Ever since I ran out on that guy the other night my focus had been gone. The night before I had a kickboxing match. I didn't know where my head was at but that was the first time, I lost a competition. The shit had me pissed the fuck off and now I was taking my frustrations out on this punching bag like it had done something to me. How could I let someone I didn't even know cause me to lose my motivation? That was the main reason why I didn't have a man in the first place. I kicked the bag so intensely that it slid away from me.

"What's your problem?" a voice asked me from behind. I didn't even have to turn around to know who it was that was lurking—the distraction himself.

"Why do you care?" I queried, pulling the bag back where it was and continued to punch the shit out of it. It kept trying to slide, so he stepped behind it, holding it still.

"What bitch or nigga do I need to fuck up for making your face look like that?" he seriously asked with furrowed brows. He was pertaining to the black eye and busted lip I had. Him reminding me of my failure just made me go harder. "So, you're just going to ignore me like I'm not standing here?" I stopped hitting the bag sighing heavily. I already felt like I was losing it because of him so, therefore, I needed to get as far away from him as possible. As I was walking away, he clutched me by the hand stopping me. "I do want to know what happened to your face." He gripped my chin, tilting my face so he could get a good look at it.

"I just don't understand you. You wanna pretend like you give a damn about me, but you don't. You don't even know shit about me, and I don't know shit about you, yet you're fucking up my mind and shit causing me to lose focus on what's important. That alone is letting me know I need to stay away from you," I said, snatching my face from him.

"I don't have to know shit about you to know that you're going to be mine one day. You can play all the games you want but a nigga going to break your ass. Just watch, you're going to be Mrs. Karrington real soon."

Did I just really hear that nigga correctly?

"No thank you. Think I'll pass on that." He wasn't about to set me up for disaster. I was good on my own; the same place I had been all this time. Ever since I had been through my very first real heartbreak, I left the relationships alone completely. I still couldn't believe that it had been almost four years since I had some dick and to keep my heart protected, I'll go another four.

"What are you so afraid of? You scared to fall in love or something?" he quizzed, staring me profoundly into the eyes.

"I'm not afraid of falling, I'm terrified of being a fool for it. Love will make you do and accept things you usually wouldn't. My best friend had to learn that the hard way." I wasn't trying to go through the things that Nix's ass was going through over dick. Speaking of which, I hadn't spoken to her since the night she left me at the club, and I had to show up and break my foot off in her ass.

"That's 'cause you haven't been loved by a real nigga." The shit rolled off his tongue like it was the God to honest truth.

"Whatever." The ringing of my phone broke our extreme stare down. I rushed over to my duffel bag, pulled it out and placed it up to my ear not even looking at the screen. "Hello?"

"Unity, baby, this your grandmother. Can you come to Calvary Hospital? I need a way home."

"Yes, of course, I'm on my way." I quickly ended the call and gathered my things.

"Something's wrong?" he asked, treading behind me as I rushed out the door. I attempted to flag down a taxi, but none were stopping.

"I have to get to the hospital." I stuck my hand out as a taxi was approaching, but it kept going. "Shit," I mumbled, scrolling through my phone to find the Uber app. It probably was going to take forever for one to get there.

"Which one? I can drive you there," he replied, pulling his keys out his pocket.

"No, it's cool. I'm sure you have other things you have to do."

"Stop bullshitting with me and get your ass in the car." He gripped me by the forearm pulling me toward a cocaine-white Maserati that was parked right in front of the entrance to the gym. He opened the passenger's side door, and I sighed before climbing inside. If I wasn't so worried about my grandma, then I would've never gotten in there.

∞ ∞ ∞

"GRANDMA!" I frantically yelled as I rushed through the emergency entrance of the hospital doors. Not spotting her anywhere in the waiting area, I went over to the nurses' station. "I'm looking for a Justine Galore," I told the nurse, impatiently chewing on my thumbnail as she typed away on her computer.

"She's in room four," she said, handing me an emergency room pass.

"Go ahead, I'll wait right here for you," he assured me, and I took off for the double doors.

"Grandma!" I called out as I entered the room. She was sitting on the bed with her infamous smile on her face as if nothing was wrong with her. "What happened?" I questioned, inspecting her to see if she had hurt herself or something.

"My sugar just was a little low that's all baby. We can head home now." She got down off the bed. I palmed myself in the middle of my forehead. It was all my fault because if I hadn't been so distracted lately, then I would've remembered I hadn't brought her medication by like I was supposed to. Just as I had said, he was a distraction already.

"I'm so sorry, it's all my fault," I apologized feeling bad as fuck.

"It's okay baby; I understand you have your own life to live." She smiled at me again.

"I promise you I won't ever forget about you again no matter what I have going on." I led her out of the room to the waiting area. He was still standing there just as I had left him, worry written all over his face. I don't know why I thought he was going to leave me there.

"She's okay?" he asked when we approached. The look she gave him was priceless.

"Grandma, this is my friend, uh..." I realized that yet again, I still hadn't gotten his name.

"Miles," he said, extending his hand. I snickered a little bit because he didn't really look like a Miles. After giving me the side eye, he left out the hospital and opened his passenger's side door. I helped my grandma climb inside then he shut it and opened the back door for me.

When we got to my grandma's apartment, he helped me get her situated. On our way there, we stopped and picked up her medicine from the Walgreen's up the street. "You need anything else, grandma?" I asked her.

"Why you have to be so country?" He chortled.

"I can't help how I sound." I frowned at him.

"No, I'm good." She was comfortably tucked away in her bed. Miles left out of the room giving us some time alone. "I like him. Where did you find him at?"

"More like he found me." I mumbled. I didn't care what she liked, he needed to go, and I was going to try my best to push his ass away. "I'll call to check on you later. Love you." I kissed her on the forehead and left out of her room.

Once I got into the living room, Miles was standing by the door talking on the phone. When his eyes landed on me, he quickly ended the call. "You don't gotta hang up with yo' bitch on my account," I made known.

"I was talking business."

"You don't gotta explain nothing to me." I sauntered to the door.

"You know my name now, so are you going to tell me yours?" he asked once we made it outside to his car. Ignoring him, I reached for the door, pulling it open, but he pushed it closed.

"Unity," I sighed, knowing that he wasn't going to give up on his question.

"Was that so hard?" His lips curved up into a smile and he pulled the door back open so I could climb in.

Nix

After Kase had put me in my place at my mother's restaurant, we had been talking nonstop. I was trying my best not to go around him and shit because he already fucked up my head with the dick. But that didn't stop him from trying to come to me. Even though my pussy was craving him, I steady kept turning him down coming up with all kinds of excuses not to see him. So far, he didn't really seem to mind since he was a pretty busy man himself, but soon I was going to run out of lies and was going to have to face him.

"Earth to Nix," Unity snapped her fingers in my face, trying to get my attention.

"Huh?" I asked, bringing my attention back to the movie we were watching on Netflix.

"What the hell are you over there daydreaming about?" she questioned, bringing her spoon up to her mouth that was loaded with butter pecan ice cream. We were supposed to be just chilling and watching movies for the night, but my mind was on Kase where it seemed to have been for the past few days since I got his number.

"About how much I fucking hate you," I admitted.

"What I do?" she asked with an arched brow.

"If it wasn't for you telling me I needed some new dick in my life, then I would've never fucked Kase." That nigga got my head gone more than Axel did and I only got the dick one time. The way I was feeling at the moment, I wouldn't mind being in a relationship with him. From what I could tell, he was the perfect package. Rough around the edges yet gentle just how I liked my men.

"Ho, you act like I put a gun to yo' head and forced you to fucking fuck the nigga." She scrunched up her face.

"Damn near; he just pulled the trigger." Out of nowhere, my phone began ringing. I reached down, picking it up off the coffee table, seeing it was Kase calling me. "Heyyyyy, Kase," I sang.

"I was just sitting here looking at this picture that you sent me earlier. A nigga faded as fuck and you looking like a whole meal. You need to pull up 'cause I got the munchies," his deep voice boomed through my line causing my pussy to purr.

"I'm on my way," I quickly ended the call and jumped up from the sectional. The way that nigga was talking to me, I knew he was about to bust that pussy down like never before.

"Uh-uh bih where the hell you going?" Unity asked, coming behind me as I made a beeline for my bedroom.

"I gots to go. Daddy called and a bitch about to come running."

"So, you just gon' leave me again for some dick?" she quizzed, folding her arms underneath her breasts. From the scowl on her face, I knew she was feeling some type of way. I stopped, tossing clothes everywhere and gripped her by her shoulders, staring her directly into the eyes.

"Bitch, you damn right. You think I'm about to pass up on that perfectly good dick for, you must be out your rabid ass mind." All that shit I was talking earlier and here I was about to go running straight to the nigga just because he called boosting my got damn head up. Kase had me so sprung off the dick.

"That dick ain't that good," she fussed, and I let her shoulders go.

"Does a prostitute sell pussy?" She rolled her eyes at me, "Aight then ho so shut the fuck up. Maybe if you opened your legs for a nigga every once in a while, then you'll see exactly where I'm coming from." After finally finding something to wear, I went into the bathroom to take a shower. I had taken one earlier, but I still wanted the pussy to be fresh when he dived into it. By the time I was done with my shower, Unity was sitting on the couch pouting like a little ass kid. "Love you too, chick. Lock up when you leave," I blew her a kiss and left out the door.

∞ ∞ ∞

"Aww fuck!" I cried out as I gushed onto Kase's dick. He had just given me yet another soul-sucking orgasm, and I was drained. Rolling off his dick onto my back, I laid staring at the ceiling, trying to catch my breath. Running over there was definitely well worth it. Turning on my side, I propped my head up with my hand and traced the diamond tattoo underneath his collarbone with the tip of my index finger. I was feeling a certain type of way and wasn't sure if it was good or bad.

As I stared at the side of his handsome face, I realized what I had with Axel was far from love. He had me so dickmatized I thought what we had was love. One thing for sure, what I could feel coming on with Kase, probably was the real deal and it was kind of terrifying me. I been cheated on, lied to, left for someone else, dropped without any explanation whatsoever, and here I was trying to love like I had never been hurt before.

My phone rung, but before I could grab it, Kase reached over and took it from the nightstand. There was a grimace plastered across his face when he looked at the screen. "Who the fuck is this?" he asked, answering my phone. With the expression on his face, I was too scared to object so I just laid there quietly, trying to see if I could hear who was on the other end. "Nigga, you calling my girl phone so don't be tryna question me and shit. Whatever business you had with her is dead so don't call her phone no fucking more."

He paused for a moment and his eyes locked with mine. I already knew it had to be no one other than Axel who he was talking to. It kind of bothered me because Axel was a straight hood nigga and I wasn't trying to have them two beefing, and shit and Axe try to do something to Kase. "Boy, I promise you that you don't want these problems. You don't know who the fuck you playing with. I'll pull up on your ass 'cause I'm that nigga." He popped up straight in bed, "What the fuck you just called me?" Not long after, he ended the call and bent my phone backward like the Hulk until the screen went dark.

"WHAT THE FUCK KASE!" I didn't know what everybody's problem was with destroying my got damn phone like they paid for them or the fucking bill.

Reaching into his nightstand, he pulled out an iPhone X and tossed it toward me. "Fuck Axe, bruh."

"Wait, how the hell do you know Axel?" I questioned.

"That fuck nigga is my baby mama's brother. I'on fuck with him period. What I wanna know is what is he doing calling your phone and shit? I told your ass to end the shit you had with whatever nigga you were fucking with." Going in the same drawer that he got the phone out of, he pulled out a Nine and cocked it. My eyes bucked because I really thought that the crazy muthafucka was about to end my ass for my ex calling my phone. He snatched the covers back and placed the gun at my pussy while gazing me straight into the eyes. "Who pussy is this?" he seriously queried.

"If you don't get that gun away from my shit!" Kase rubbed up and down my slit with the barrel of the gun. I bit down on the corner of my lower lip, knowing that my pussy was probably dripping.

"Tell me who shit that is first. I'm not playing with you."

"Okay, okay, it's yours, Kase. All yours!" He gently sat the gun back down on the nightstand then laid back on the bed on his back.

"Get your ass on this dick and show me the shit mine," he commanded, placing his hands behind his head.

"Gladly."

Axel

That rude ass muthafucka just hung up in my face like a ho. I tried calling the phone back, but it was going straight to voicemail. What I couldn't believe was the fact that Nix was fucking around with that fuck nigga. Now I had two reasons to come at his head: one for fucking over my little sister's heart and two for sleeping with my girl.

"I'm 'bout to go take Baylee over Kase's house," Harper announced coming from the back. Not wanting to set my sister up for any more heartbreak, I had to come up with an excuse and quick.

"Take her over there another time," I told her, relaxing back on the couch, pushing my dreads back out of my face.

"Why? She has been asking for her daddy, so I'm going to take her over there to him," she replied, heading straight for the door. Just as she pulled it opened, I pushed it back closed.

"I said take her over there another time!" I bellowed. Even though she said she was taking Baylee over there because she missed her daddy, I knew she was really going over there because she missed him her damn self. I was protective of my sister and her feelings, and I wasn't about to let her get hurt knowing I could've prevented the shit.

"Why you have to holler and shit?" Reaching down, she picked up a crying Baylee, trying to hush her.

"My fault; I'm just frustrated right now. Where the hell Ava's ass at?" I asked her, going back over to the sofa.

"She's in the room sleep," she answered finally getting Baylee quiet. All Ava's ass has been doing was sleeping and shit lately. When I first started fucking around with her ass, I didn't know I was going to end up with the bitch permanently. The only reason I had been sleeping with the ho was to piss Reapa's ass off. If she didn't start pulling her own weight around here, then she was going to be out on her ass. There were no free rides around this muthafucka.

Getting up from the couch, I went into the bedroom, slapping Ava hard on the ass. "Get the fuck up," I ordered.

"Gone on somewhere, Axe!" she whined, then turned over. Guess she thought I was playing with her, so I smacked her again.

"Get the fuck up!"

"Ugh!" she huffed and sat up in the bed. "Can I not sleep around here?" If she asked me, she slept too got damn much.

"You been in this bitch sleep all got damn day, it's time that you get your ass up." I plopped down on the bed beside her. I could feel her burning a hole in the side of my face with her piercing eyes. "I got something I need you to do for me."

"Do what?" She blew air from her lips.

"I need for you to get back in good with Reapa's ass."

She shook her head, "That's not going to work. Reapa doesn't want shit to do with me." What I couldn't understand was how she even knew that. Last time I checked, she hadn't seen him since he shot her ass. He still had love for her so I was sure he would let her back in soon or later if she went back and apologized to him.

"How you know that though?" I questioned her.

"I already tired."

"Well, obviously you didn't try hard enough so get your ass up, wash your ass, comb that shit on your head, and go get that nigga back." I got up from the bed, reaching into my pocket, pulling out a knot of cash tossing it to her. "Don't bring your ass back here until you got that nigga back." I was going to use her ass to my fucking advantage.

Unity

*I*t had been a week since I last seen Miles. After he dropped me off at home, it was like he disappeared off the face of the earth. I should've known he wasn't about nothing to begin with. All he was trying to do was probably fuck me, and that was it. Something I wasn't about to let him do.

"It's boring as fuck," Nix stated. What shocked me was the fact she even had time for me. Ever since she dipped on me and ran off with Kase, she been locked up in the house with him fucking him nonstop knowing her. Guess he had to get back to his regularly scheduled life if her ass was sitting here with me.

"Don't you got a dick to suck or something?" I rolled my eyes. She kissed her teeth and picked at her nails.

"He at work. Trust if he wasn't then I would." I believed her ass too.

"Let's go see what Ma got going on. Maybe we can talk her into cooking lunch for us or something." I got up out the bed and threw on some sweatpants. Nix and I had been lying around all morning not doing anything ever since she came over there and I was getting bored as fuck as well.

"Your ass not about to get me cursed the fuck out," she quickly replied.

"Bring yo' scary ass on." I grabbed my keys off the dresser and headed for the front door. After taking the couple flights of stairs down to the exit, we stepped outside, and I sucked the polluted air into my nostrils. Sitting at the curbside was Miles's Rolls Royce. I knew it belonged to him because Tyler stood beside it.

"Whose car is this?" Nix quizzed. All I could do was smile; I had just been thinking about him, and he popped up out the blue.

"Ms. Unity, Mr. Miles sent me to pick you up and take you a few places for the day," Tyler stated, opening the back door for me.

"Wait a minute, this shit for you!" Nix squealed, gripping my hand dragging me toward the car. "What paid nigga you fucking ho and leaving me out the loop?" She climbed into the car first. This was some next level shit. No other guy has ever done anything like this or close to it for me before, and I didn't know how to react. Just because he was willing to do all that, didn't mean I was prepared to let him in.

∞ ∞ ∞

I stood there staring at my reflection in the mirror. As it glared back at me, I was seeing a totally different person. The whole day Miles sent me different places to get pampered. He definitely changed the direction that my day was heading with that surprise.

"That babe looking like a full course meal. Told you that was the dress," Nix said, coming in my room smacking on some grapes she stole out my fridge. A big smile crept across my face. The long-sleeved, deep V, white, lace dress I wore hugged my small curves just right. I was skeptical about getting it at first because most of it was see-through with a split in the front. The silver, glitter Christian Louboutin's glistened on my feet. The shit seemed surreal; they were my very first pair, and I always wanted some. Thanks to Miles, I was rocking them.

"Then you topped it off with Shona," she said, referring to one of my favorite wigs. It was a long, burgundy wing that stopped in the middle of my back with loose curls. I named her Shona after my mother because when I was growing up, and she was clean, she would always wear these gorgeous ass burgundy wigs all the time. I believe that's where I got my love for wigs from in the first place.

"I hope he likes it; I'm kind of nervous. I've never talked to anyone on his level before," I whined, finally stepping away from the mirror.

"He'll be a damn fool if he doesn't. Now go on and get you a good dick down," she encouraged with a warm smile. It was just like Nix to make a joke in a serious situation.

When we got outside, Miles was standing beside his Rolls Royce with a single red rose in his hand. My pussy instantly dripped just from seeing him in that dark blue expensive ass suit with his black button-up shirt that had the top buttons undone. He had a simple gold necklace around his neck that balanced out the diamond earring and Rolex that could be seen glistening all the way over here.

"*She see money all around me. I look like I'm the man,*" Nix rapped Goldlink's "Crew" song as she shoved me closer to Miles. "Hope y'all have fun. Call me and let me know how it goes." She flagged down the first taxi she saw and hopped inside.

"Sorry about her," I apologized, blushing as I took a step away from him.

"It's cool... For you," he handed me the rose, and I stuck it up to my nose to smell it.

"Thank you," I softly replied.

"You ready?" He opened the door, and I climbed inside.

Thirty minutes later, we pulled up to a tall glass building. I was confused as to what we were doing there, but I didn't ask any questions. Miles got out the car first then helped me out. When we stepped into the elevator, he pressed the roof button. When the doors opened, I was staring at a black helicopter that had *RK* on the side of it in gold lettering. Lucky for him, I wasn't afraid of heights or his night would've been ruined. Once I got comfortable around him, I was going to ask him exactly what he did because there was no way he could afford the things he had just from owning a gym.

"Where are you taking me?" I stopped to ask. For all I knew, he could've been trying to kidnap my ass.

"You trust me?"

"So far, you haven't given me a reason not to," I confessed—except for that night that man fell off that building, but I still wasn't too sure if he was the one that had done it, so I couldn't really hold that against him. He reached his hand out and I took it with no hesitation.

Reapa

*O*nce our date was over with, we ended up coming back to my house because I wasn't ready for the night to end just yet. Just as soon as I opened the door, Cocaine came running. What surprised me was the fact that Unity wasn't afraid of her.

"Oh my God, you got a tiger!" she shrieked, leaning down petting Cocaine and she let her pet her too. "I've always wanted one of these. Nix called me crazy for wanting a wild animal as a pet, but I just think that they're so cute." I shut the door and went into my cocaine white living room. What could I say? It was my favorite color, so almost everything was that color.

"You want something to drink?" I asked, strolling over to the mini bar that was in there to pour me a glass of D'USSÉ.

"No, I'm good," she announced, taking a seat on my sectional. I swallowed hard when I glanced over and saw her beautiful dark thighs peaking from under the slit in her dress. My dick was trying to wake up, and I had to coach him back down. Unity rolled her head around as if her neck was tensed.

"Would've sent you to a spa if I had known you needed a massage." I sat my cup down on the coffee table before sitting down and rubbing her shoulders.

"No, you've... mhm, done enough for me. That feels soooo awesome." That moan that seeped from her lips caused my dick to jump. I was glad she was facing the other way where she couldn't see the shit.

"I don't mind doing it. Being with a king you going to be treated like the queen you are," I told her meaning every word. She took a deep breath then turned to me.

"Look, I don't have time for the bullshit. If you're not tryna love me how I'm supposed to be loved, support my goals and ambitions, build with me, or show me different, then you need to keep it moving." I completely understood where she was coming from. A lot of women said good men were extinct. Men said that good women no longer exist, but a lot of people don't know good when they see it. I was staring at perfection, and I'd be damned if I was going to just let her slip right through the cracks.

Pulling my gun from my waist, I got down on bent knee grabbing her left hand. I placed the gun on her finger like it was a ring. "I promise you on my soul I can do all that and more, long as you just ride with a nigga, you can have the universe. This isn't a marriage proposal or no shit, but just me promising you that I'm going to be the best man I can be for you." She gazed deeply into my eyes, making me feel things I never felt before, not even with Ava.

"And I promise to be your calm in your stormiest of days. But please do not try to underestimate me. My heart is big, and I love hard, but I don't give a fuck even harder," she warned with a straight face. I got up off my knee, gripping her face and our lips collided.

Pushing all of her hair to the side, I planted a kiss on her collarbone. Another one of those sexy moans escaped her lips. Scooping her up into my arms, I carried her upstairs to my bedroom that was fit for a king. I was about to show her what this pipe game do and hit that shit until the sky turned blue. By the time I was done with her, her pussy was going to be sore for days. Sitting her back down on her feet, I pushed her dressed down off her shoulders and watched it cascade to the floor. The sight before me was so beautiful that I just had to step back and take her all in. The only thing she wore was her heels.

"Why you staring at me like that?" Her face flushed.

"You just sexy as fuck to me." I licked my lips. Unity slowly strutted over to me, and placed both of her hands on my chest, pushing my jacket down, letting it drop to the floor. Her hands zigzagged down to my belt and unbuckling it. She unleashed the monster and got down on her knees taking my head into her mouth.

Roughly gripping her by the back of her head, I bit down hard on my lower lip as I fucked her mouth. Her gaze matched mine as she twirled her tongue around the tip. To me, the sexiest shit ever was when you were getting top and the chick locked eyes with you. Her whole mouth was filled with nothing but my dick. The way she deep throated me had a nigga ready to scream out like a little bitch. "Fuck, bae," I groaned.

"You like that babe?" she asked, coughing up a mouth full of saliva and spit it on my dick before licking it all back up. My breath caught in my throat; I couldn't even respond to her. Deep-throating me a few more times, I finally emptied my seeds down her throat.

Grabbing her underneath her arms, I picked her up and carried her over to the bed, tossing her down on it. If she wasn't my girl before, she damn sure was now the way she just sucked the soul out of me. Little mama deserved an award or trophy or something. Got damn.

"Hope you know your ass about to be in trouble," I warned, stripping out the rest of my clothes. "Put that pussy up in the air." At first, I was going to make love to her but the way she had me feeling, I needed to bust that pussy down one good time. Her pussy was drenched with anticipation of wanting to feel me fill her walls up. Without hesitation, I stood behind her, placing my dick at her opening.

Other than Ava, she was going to be the second woman I ever plunged in raw. That's how come I knew that shit was going to be real. Safe sex was the best sex, but tonight I felt like sinning and was going swimming in her pool without my swim cap. Gripping her by her hips, I eased my way inside. That pussy squeezed the hell out of me like a Magnum. She let out a whimper once I made it all the way in, making me bite down on the corner of my lower lip.

"You a fucking virgin? Got damn," I asked, giving her slow deep strokes. Her small hands balled up into tiny fists clutching the sheets underneath her. Leaning down, I planted kisses on her back. Sliding my hand up her soft skin to her neck, I slammed her down on my dick. She was soaking wet as she hit the base of my shaft.

"Fuck, Miles!" she screamed out in pleasure.

"You thought this shit was going to be that easy? Miles gone... this Reapa." And I was about to murder the pussy. Gripping her tightly around her throat, I sped up my thrusts. "Put that arch back in that back," I ordered. Unity was trying to run from the dick, but I wasn't about to have that shit. Letting her neck go, I pressed down on her back.

"Oh God, Reapa!" she screeched.

"Yeah, gone bust that shit for me." Not long after, I felt them juices gushing.

An hour in, I was still tearing up that shit. I lost count of how many times she had cum, but I was working on my second nut. Her breasts bounced up and down as she rode the hell out of my shit. Sweat beads dripped from her forehead and that wig she was wearing started peeling. I snatched that shit right off and tossed it to the side. I didn't give a fuck she had them Queen Latifah jail braids in her head, I was still going to fuck the pussy up.

"Fuuucckk, I'm cumming!" she screamed, slamming her hand against my headboard. After she came, I released my seeds inside her, and she climbed off me, falling on the bed along side me. Man, a nigga turned shorty ass out within an hour, that was a new record. Reaching over into the nightstand, I pulled out a pre-rolled blunt and lit it.

"You know your ass stuck with me, right?" I seriously asked, inhaling the blunt. She waved me off and turned over scooting her ass closer to me. I don't know why she thought I was playing with her ass, but she was stuck with me forever. In for one hell of a ride, so I hope she ready.

Harper

uck that shit Axel was talking, I was going to take my baby to see her daddy. Baylee had been crying for Kase going on three days now, and I was not going to keep her away from him no matter what we had going on. Yeah, I did want to see him as well, but she was really what was more important in the situation. Maybe once we got in there, we could do a little talking on our issues. I prayed that he came to his senses soon because I wasn't prepared to lose him just yet. I felt like he was the one made for me and I for him.

Adjusting Baylee on my hip, I knocked on the door waiting for him to come to it. When I saw the door being pulled open, a smile crept up on my face. It quickly faded once I saw that bitch from the club standing there in only a t-shirt. If only my daughter weren't in my arms; I probably would've lunged for the ho.

"Can I help you?" she had the nerves to ask like this was her house or some shit.

"No, you can't. Where the hell Kase's ass at?" I questioned, peeking around her looking into the house to see if I could spot him.

"What you looking for him for?" she folded her arms underneath her breasts.

"Not that it's any of your concern, but his daughter wants to see him. Can you move?" I went to step into the house, but she stuck her arm out stopping me.

"I can take her to him," she said, reaching for Baylee but I turned where she couldn't get her. That bitch must had lost her everlasting mind if she thought I was going to give her my fucking child.

"No, what you can do is go get Kase's muthafuckin' ass," I warned. I didn't know what type of games him and her were playing, but I was not the one especially when it came to my daughter. She shrugged and walked off.

"That nigga just going to do you the same fucking way he did me." I mumbled. At least I thought I mumbled it under my breath, but I guess I said it louder than I intended because she swiftly turned around on her heels and charged back my way.

"What the fuck did you just say?" she angrily queried. She didn't scare me, so I repeated myself loud and clear.

"That sorry ass muthafucka just going to do you the same way he fucking did me. That's what the fuck I said."

"Listen here little ho, you had him before me. I don't give a fuck how long you had him... what your motive was, but you will never compare to me, and that's a given fact. So no, he won't just do me how he did you, babe. He going to do me better." Right before I could even check her little ass, Kase appeared behind her out of thin air. "Handle that shit," she said and stormed off.

"What you doing here?" He sighed, stepping back from the door so I could finally come inside.

"I brought Baylee by here to see you, but now that I see you're busy I guess we should just go." I was trying my hardest to fight back the tears trying to escape my eyes. The hurt that I was feeling inside was indescribable. Kase really hurt me to my core with this one.

"I can keep her for the day," he implied. There was no way in hell I was going to even allow him to keep her while he had that ho parading around his house half naked and shit.

"No, you good on that. You're not getting my child with that bitch in the house." His eyebrows furrowed. The way he was eyeing me, I couldn't fight back the tears any longer. They were now coming full force.

"Maaannn, don't start that shit, Harper. Either you want me to get her or not. I'on got time for this shit," he scoffed, falling back into the wall behind him, folding his arms across his chest.

"Why her though? I have been holding you down since high school, and now you want to kick me to the curb for some gold-digging bitch?" I just had to know what she had that I didn't.

"Watch your mouth," he cautioned.

"But why, Blake?" I sobbed. It was hard trying to come to grips that the love of my life didn't want me anymore. The least he could do was give me an explanation.

"The shit complicated," was all he said.

"How is it complicated? Look, I don't want anyone else; I don't need anyone else but you. I'm hurting, and you're usually the one that I come to in times like these. You're my best friend, Blake other than Ava—"

"None of that has to change. I can still be that; it just isn't no more you and me."

"Blake," I wept. That bitch had to have been putting shit in his head because he had never switched up on me like that before. Even though he was treating me like shit, somehow deep inside I still craved to be loved by this man. "You told me you would never leave me. Said that we were in this for the long haul."

"Things change... people change, Harper," he camly replied.

"Will you just stop embarrassing yourself and take that L. Clearly you're not wanted here," the girl said, walking back up on us.

My heart was shattered, and suddenly I realized what Kevin Gates said, 'Imagine losing somebody you love and they not even dead' felt. Glancing over at Kase, he didn't say a word, so I knew I wasn't wanted there. I was done begging him to be a part of our little family. If he wanted to be with the ho, then I was just going to let him. Simple as that.

"Fine," I said and left out the door.

Kase

It had been two weeks since the incident with Harper. I didn't feel bad about the situation because she was the one that had fucked things up with all her mind games and shit. She was trying to make it seem like she was innocent when that was far from the case. I'll be damn if she was going to keep me away from my child all because a nigga didn't want her ass anymore. If I had to, I'd take her ass to court. I was supporting her ass; she doesn't have an income so of course, I'd win. What was crazy to me was the fact that she had been quiet for two entire weeks. That just wasn't like Harper and it kind of bothered me. It had me feeling like she was up to some shit.

"Here go that money," I announced dropping the duffel bag down at Reapa's feet. He was sitting on the couch in the warehouse running cash through the money counter. A lit blunt dangled from his lips, so I pulled it out sticking it between mine before flopping down on the sofa next to him.

"What the fuck you waiting for? Get to counting, this shit not going to count itself." He kicked the duffel bag over by my feet. After dumping the ashes from the blunt, I reached down unzipping the bag and pulled out a couple of stacks, taking the rubber band from around them. Just as I started counting, my phone vibrated in my pocket, so I pulled it out to see who it was. *I know you busy but let me come get thirty slow deep strokes right quick.* I chuckled at the shit Nix texted me. What was funny was the fact that I think she was serious as fuck.

Me: *Your ass just going to have to wait on them strokes.*

"Ain't you supposed to be counting while you're over there texting like Donald Trump with Twitter fingers?" Reapa side eyed me.

"Get you some fucking business." I chortled. My phone vibrated again, but that time it was a picture of Nix's fingers deep off in her dripping wet pussy.

Me: *Daddy's on the way. Hit me with that location.*

"Sorry, but you going to have to count this on your own. I got something slippery and wet to fall into," I said, standing up from the couch.

"I'll remember that when you're looking for your fucking cut, fuck boy," he scoffed, placing another stack in the money counter.

"Know I'll body a nigga about mine. Play with it," I warned, patting my waist where my Nine was.

"You're not the only one packing. You know I keeps the chrome on me," he said, pulling his Glock from his waist, lying it on the table where the money counter was.

"Man, I don't have time; I'm about to go get my girl."

∞ ∞ ∞

"Got damn!" Nix's body trembled on the masseuse's table as she threw her ass back on me one last time while she squirted all over my dick. I wasn't long after her, and the shit only took probably a good twenty strokes since she was teasing the hell out of me the whole way over to the gym.

"Don't ever try to fucking test me again," I boasted, stuffing my dick back down in my jeans and zipped them up. I'd just go and wash it off in my office bathroom once I was done in here.

"You going to get me fucking fired." She laughed, pulling her scrubs back up. The way that pussy was dripping, she was going to have to change clothes.

"Nah, you good. Me and my partner own this muthafucka. The only way you'll get fired is if you fuck up." I flashed her a smirk.

"Wait a minute, you own this place?" she asked, sounding surprised.

"Yeah, you hungry? A nigga done worked up an appetite after that work out you just gave me," I told her, leaving out the room, pulling her behind me by the hand.

"I can eat; let me take a quick shower. No way I'm going anywhere with your nut running down my inner thighs."

"Take all the time you need. I'll be in my office," I told her, then kissed her on the lips, letting her hand go.

As I headed for my office, I couldn't help but think about how good things were going between Nix and me. I knew everything wasn't going to stay kosher, but it felt good for the time being. After washing my dick off in the sink, I sat down behind my desk. Harper crossed my mind, so I called her phone just to make sure she was all right. The crazy muthafucka sent me straight to voicemail. Guess she was still in her feelings about what happened the last time I saw her. It was cool though, I knew where she stayed, and if I had to, I was going to go over there and get Baylee from her ass. There was nothing she could do about it either. The knock on my office door brought me back from my thoughts.

Moments later, Nix's head popped in. "Took me forever to find your office. You ready?" She was standing in the doorway in some simple Seven jeans and a white tank top. She made something so plain look sexy as fuck.

"Yeah, let's go."

About ten minutes after pulling off from the gym, I saw flashing lights in my review. "Got damn," I grumbled, pulling the car over. I hadn't done anything, so I didn't understand what they were pulling me over for unless it was driving while black. Keeping my cool, I reached over to the glove compartment pulling out the registration so that I could have everything ready for them once they made it up to the window.

"License and registration," the cop said, peeking into the car looking over at Nix.

"Um, excuse me, but what did you pull him over for?" she questioned, leaning over me to look up in his face.

"Just calm down, bae," I told her. I didn't feel like arguing with that man because of her mouth.

"Sit tight," was all he said before walking away from the car. Five minutes later, he came back, and his partner came over to Nix's side. "Can you step out of the car?" he asked with his hand resting on his piece.

"Step out of the car for what!" Nix yelled. I gave her a look that said she needed to shut the fuck up, but she wasn't worried about me. She was too busy ready to go in on the cop.

"This car was reported stolen about a week ago. Step out of the car, sir," he repeated.

"What the fuck you mean stolen! This is his car you ass hole!" Nix shouted.

"You too, ma'am." He eyed Nix.

I calmly got out the car so I could see what the hell was going on. "There has to be a mistake officer, this car isn't stolen. This is my car, but it's in my baby mama's, Harper name," I tried to explain, but he roughly gripped me by the arms, slamming my body down onto the hood of the car.

"Don't be manhandling him like that! What the fuck is wrong with you!" Nix came around the car getting all into the man's face, so the other cop grabbed her.

"Bae, chill out. I'll get this shit situated." I tried to calm her down, but she wasn't trying to hear that shit.

"Get your fucking hands off of me!" she shouted, trying to squirm away from the cop but he slung her to the ground. That shit pissed me the fuck off.

"Don't be treating her like she a fucking nigga, you stupid bitch. I swear to God y'all both going to pay for that shit," I warned. All I saw was fucking red. Nix was still talking shit on the ground while the officer's knee was in her back. "Nix, just calm down babe, we going to be straight!" I yelled as the cop dragged me over to the squad car, placing me in the back of it. A few seconds later, another car pulled up, and they placed Nix in it.

As I sat there watching them search my car without a fucking warrant, thoughts of me murdering Harper were racing through my mind. Who else could've reported the fucking car stolen? It made me wonder what else her stupid ass had done. When I had first came up, I fucked around and let her put her name on a whole lot of my shit just so she and Baylee would be straight if I was to ever get caught the FEDS couldn't take all my shit. Like she said, I told her that I would never leave her. I thought the shit I had with her was real but quickly found out it was an illusion.

Nix kept hitting the window with her shoe until it busted out. She was just that fucking mad. I tried telling her to calm her little ass down, but she just wasn't listening and making things worse on both of us. Just as soon as they got me to the station, I was going to make a call to Reapa and get him to come and get us out.

Reapa

*W*hen I got to the gym to put some money in the safe, I saw everyone standing outside when their asses were supposed to be inside working. Grabbing my Louis Vuitton bag, tossing it over my shoulder, I got out the car. As I got closer to the crowd, I saw Harper standing at the entrance with a cop and another man that was chaining the door shut. "The fuck?" I mumbled, pushing through the crowd to get to her. "Harper, what the hell are you doing?" I asked, stopping directly in front of her. She had a wicked smirk on her face.

"You guys are closed for business until further notice."

"How the fuck you going to close some shit that isn't even yours?" I pushed her to the side and yanked on the chains, but they wouldn't budge. "Take this shit off my got damn doors!" I barked.

"I'm sorry to tell you, but I do own *RK*." Harper shoved the deed into my face with a huge smile on hers.

I balled the shit up and threw it at her. I didn't give a damn that her name was on there or even how; *RK Fitness* was mine. Kase and I put our blood, sweat, and tears into this fucking place. It was one of the first places we opened with our dirty money. After counting to ten in my head and it not working, I yoked her ass up, slamming her hard against the building. The cop that was with her tried his best to pry my hand from around her throat.

"Harper, I'm just going to ask you one more fucking time to take that shit off my doors before I put a hollow tip in your ass," I advised. My vibrating phone in my pocket took my attention away from Harper's bulging eyes for a slight moment as I slipped my free hand into my pocket, pulling it out. "What! I'm fucking busy!" I bellowed.

"Aye, I need for you to come down to the jail and bail me and my shorty out. Harper did some fucked up shit and got us locked up," Kase quickly replied.

"Tell me about it. You just spared the bitch's life for the time being, but I'm on my way." I squeezed her throat tighter, then dropped her to the ground. "That shit better be off my fucking doors by the time I get back, or you got a hollow tip with your fucking name on it. Play with me if you want to."

∞ ∞ ∞

I stood outside posted up against my car waiting for Kase and his girl to walk out the doors. I had posted their bail thirty minutes ago, and they had yet to exit. The way I was feeling, if they didn't come out of there soon, I was going to go in there and get their ass myself. Kase had some fucking explaining to do when he got out of there too. Obviously, his stupid ass was the one that put the bitch's name on the deed without consulting me first. That shit was a dumb ass move. If he wanted to use someone else's name, he could've at least used his parents'.

Kase walked out the door with a mug on his face, but he was alone. Guess his shorty was still in there trying to handle her business which gave me time to handle mine. "Thanks for coming to get us," he said, then was met with my closed fist. I had been waiting forever to knock his ass the fuck out.

"You put that bitch's name on the gym you stupid fuck!" I loudly bellowed.

"Yeah, I was only trying to protect us that's all. Didn't think much of it when I had done it," he explained, wiping the blood from the corner of his mouth.

"You know how I feel about that ho. You pissed the dumb bitch off and now she done chained our shit up." I swung on his ass again, and we began tussling right there in front of the police station.

"Hey, hey, break it up!" a woman said and tried to pull us apart, but she couldn't. "Kase! Stop it!" she yelled. When she called his name, that was when I knew it had to be his girl. I shoved him hard off me.

"You just fucking stupid! What the fuck else you put the bitch name on?" I panted out of breath.

"That was it that we shared. I put her name on a few other things of mine like the house and shit," he admitted, and both me and his girl glared at him like he had two heads.

"You do realize that if she got the gym, she probably got your house too. Hope you know you homeless and no fuck niggas allowed across my threshold. At least you weren't stupid enough to put her name on your offshore accounts." From the dumbfounded expression on his face, I couldn't help but ask. "You didn't, did you?"

"Hell nah," he replied. Swear if he did, I was going to put Harper's hollow tip in his ass.

"Uh, I have to get home. My mama blowing my phone up," the girl chimed in.

"Oh, my fault. Reapa this my girl, Nix."

"Yeah, I know who he is," she replied. I just nodded my head at her and hopped into my car. Kase was on my body list, and I needed to hurry up and get his ass as far away from me as possible before I ended up killing his ass. He knew I would, that's why he got his stupid ass in the back seat and let Nix get in the passenger's seat. She told me her address, and I headed in that direction. All I could think about was putting Harper out of her misery. She knew better than to fucking play with me, but she did it anyway. Stupid bitch.

Nix

"Where the hell have you been?" my mother asked as soon as I walked through the door. From the displeased look on her face, I knew she was pissed off about something. I didn't know what her problem was or how come she was questioning me like I was a child. This was the first time she had done something like this. Maybe she was on her period or something.

"I was with Unity," I quickly lied.

"Why the fuck do you think that it's cool to lie to me? Have you forgotten that Unity is gone out of town for a competition? You don't have to answer me because I already know where you were." She walked closer to me putting a little fear in my heart. There weren't a lot of things I was terrified of, but Olivia Quartz was one of them especially when she was mad. "Have you lost your fucking mind?" she asked through clenched teeth, mushing me in the head.

"Ma, just let me explain," I pleaded.

"Explain? I told you that boy was nothing but trouble when you were at his house that day. I already know how you get about men. You act like you don't have the sense that God gave you. How the hell you go from one nut to another beats the hell out of me," she scolded, tossing her hands in the air. I knew she was disappointed from her facial expression. Even though she was mad, I was not about to let her downplay Kase like that because he didn't do anything wrong.

"It wasn't his fault we ended up in jail. He didn't do anything wrong." I cried.

"You're young Phoenix. Beautiful and smart but you're stupid as fuck when it comes to men. Why don't you do something better for yourself? You were with Axel so long, why don't you try to focus on yourself for a change and just take some time alone," she implied.

"But Ma, I love him." I couldn't believe I just said that. That was the first time I even thought about possibly loving Kase. My eyes shimmered with tears.

"I don't want you seeing him anymore, and that's that," she firmly stated. I was not about to let go of this fight that easily.

"Ma, please don't do this." The tears were flowing freely down my cheeks. She walked away from me, but I gripped her by her forearm stopping her. "I'm not a child. If I want to keep seeing Kase, then I will."

"Not under my roof. If you don't like my rules, then there's the door."

"Fine," I sobbed, wiping the tears from my eyes and stormed off to my bedroom. When I got in there, I grabbed my suitcases and began stuffing them with clothes.

"What are you doing, Phoenix?" She sighed.

"I'm going to Unity's somewhere I know I won't have to leave my man. How could you deny me my chance at true love? Do you want me to end up like you... all alone?" My mother's eyes grew wet with tears. I wasn't trying to hurt her, just wanted her to see where I was coming from.

"All I want is what's best for you. Being in and out of jail behind a worthless man isn't going to do anything but ruin your life, Phoenix. I'm your mother, I'm supposed to care."

I slammed the suitcase shut zipping it up. "That's right, you're my MOTHER not my best friend so stay out of my business." I grabbed both of my suitcases and brushed past her out of the room and out the front door.

∞ ∞ ∞

I used the spare key Unity gave me to let myself in. Once I was inside, I was going to text her and let her know I would be crashing at her place for a while until I got a place of my own. When I got inside, she was sitting on the couch flipping through the channels.

"What the hell you're doing here?" I asked her dropping my suitcases at the door.

"I live here. I should be asking you what you're doing here?" she replied, eyeing my belongings.

I blew air from my lips then went over sitting down on the couch beside her. "Got into a fight with Ma. Some kinda way she found out I got arrested and she went ballistic. She wants me to stop seeing Kase. I told her that I loved him and couldn't do it."

"Do you want me to try and talk to her?"

"No, she needs to learn how to stay out of my business." I laid my head down in Unity's lap. She stroked my hair for a second then stopped, pushing my head off.

"Hold up, you got arrested! AGAIN, NIX!"

"It wasn't even my fault this time. That's why I told you I don't fuck with niggas with baby mama. If I get my hands on that ho, I'ma drill her fucking face in the ground." I was getting heated all over again for the shit I been through. The day was going so perfectly until we ended up getting pulled over because she was salty and couldn't let her baby daddy go.

"So, what you going to do now?"

"I'ma try to find me somewhere to stay. I hope that it's cool that I stay here till I do?" There really wasn't anywhere else I could go other than Grandma Justine's house. Shoot, I was an only child and my father been died or at least that's what my mother told me.

"Well, since I'm home, I'll take grandma her medicine tomorrow, and you can just use that day to try and focus on finding you somewhere to stay. I mean I love you to death, Nix but I don't know if I'll be able to live with you that long." She laughed but I knew she was serious as a heart attack.

"Bih, I won't be able to stay here that long anyway. My bedroom bigger than your whole got damn apartment," I joked with a smirk.

She got up from the couch, "You mean your old bedroom." Unity stuck her tongue out at me. "At least I got somewhere to stay heffa, but you know you're more than welcome to stay here for as long as you need to."

Unity

"You sure? Check again." I was trying to pick up my grandma's medication, but the pharmacist kept telling me that someone had already picked it up. I knew for sure that I had told Nix I was going to get it, but maybe she had forgotten already.

"Yes ma'am, someone already has it."

"Ok, thank you," I told her, walking away from the counter. Pulling my phone out, I dialed Nix's number. "Did you pick up grandma's medicine?" I asked her once she answered the phone.

"No, you told me not to worry about it, so I didn't go."

"Humph, they said someone else picked it up. I'm about to head over to her apartment now and see what's going on. I'll call you back." I disconnected the call as I was leaving out the drug store. The shit just wasn't adding up. If Nix didn't pick the medicine up, there was no one else left that could've. I know damn well grandma didn't come down there and get it herself. Even though the drug store was only up the street, she wasn't going to make that walk, that's why I volunteered to bring it for her.

"Grandma!" I called out when I walked into the door. The smell of food hit my nostrils as soon I as I got inside. "Ma, what you in here cooking? It smells good making my stomach growl." Following the scent, I froze in place when I got to the kitchen. Standing in front of the stove was Reapa. "What are you doing here?" He came over pecking me on the lips.

"You were gone for two weeks, and I figured that I should come and check on your grandmother." I swear this man was going to make me fall in love with him for the things that he had been doing. The entire time I was gone, he would FaceTime me just to check in and tell me how much he missed me. I missed him like crazy since I had to leave out of town to Cali the day after we had sex. That nigga had fucked my mind up. I been fiending for his dick so bad that I pleased myself almost every night. It wasn't getting it, I needed the real thing—that long thick pipe.

"That's so sweet. Thank you, but you really didn't have to," I made known, going over, lifting the lid off the pot that was on the stove.

"You're my girl so yeah I did."

"Girl?" I queried with a raised brow.

He gripped me by my pussy, causing her to throb. "Yeah, I told you that you stuck with a nigga or did you think I was playing?" I bit down on my lower lip praying he would just slip one of his fingers inside my pussy. She longed for his touch. "Calm down; I'll take care of that later." He winked, then picked up the plate off the counter and took it to my grandma's room. I went behind him so I could speak.

"Hey, Ma!" I sang, going over, kissing her on the forehead. "I missed you, how are you feeling?"

"I'm good baby. How was your boxing?"

"You know I'm the champ. Your baby had to bring that belt home." A smile passed my lips. I was surprised that I did because I had come so close to losing. Had I lost, I wouldn't have been in the best mood when I made it back. Everybody would have been getting my backlash.

"That's good."

I kissed her on the forehead once more. "I'll be in the living room if you need me." Grabbing Reapa by the hand, I led him out of her bedroom so that she could enjoy her meal in peace. Just as soon as I closed my grandma's door, Reapa gripped me by the hips, pulling my frame straight into his.

"I missed you while you were gone," he made known, gawking down into my eyes.

"Oh, yeah? Why don't you show me just how much you missed me," I purred, biting down on my lower lip. I didn't know what the hell I was thinking, telling him to do something like that while my grandma was in the other room, but I finally realized what Nix meant about all the dick jokes. My pussy was fiending in the worst way imaginable.

"Your grandmother would think I was trying kill your ass if I slide up in that pussy right about now." He lifted me up into his arms, and I wrapped my legs around his waist. "But if you want the dick, I'll give you the shit."

Carrying me into the bathroom, he shut the door and turned on the sink and shower so that the water could drown my moaning and screaming out. He sat me down on my feet. I dropped to my knees, wanting to savor his dick. It had been so long since it filled up my mouth and I was yearning to feel it again, hitting my tonsils.

There used to be a time when I said I would never suck another dick again because I had a bad experience doing so, but Reapa's dick made a bitch want to beg to suck the muthafucka. The way that it was sculpted, it was like God took his time creating it. The curve in it was just impeccable, and those thick veins made it look as if it was on steroids. Licking my lips, I went to shove him inside, but he stopped me.

"I want to feel that pussy." Reapa shoved both of his hands into my natural kinky dark brown hair and pulled me up off the floor. His lips fell atop of mine as he lifted my foot up on top of the toilet seat and tugged on my thong underneath my sundress until it ripped off. The tip of his dick slid up and down my slit teasing me. "You want this dick?"

"Yes, pleeeaaassseee stop teasing me." I attempted to slide my pussy back on his dick, but he just pulled it away, teasing me even more. Finally, his dick rammed inside my soaking wet center. I bit the corner of my lower lip as my face contorted into ugly ass expressions. That shit was so powerful, and he fucked around giving it to a fool. Reapa had the type of dick that would make a bitch go crazy, slash his tires, curse out my grandma, hell, even one of Nix's moves... go to jail.

My walls were holding on to him for dear life as he beat it up from behind. "Good God!" I whimpered. I must was too loud because not long after I had said it, Reapa's hand covered my mouth. I threw my ass back on him, matching his rhythm thrust for thrust.

"Don't ever leave me for that long again." He pounded harder inside me, and my moans muffled by his hand. I guess it was safe to say that I was officially dickmatized. A few more pounds into my pussy and we both released at the same time.

He pulled out then grabbed a rag so that he could clean his dick off. I sat there on the toilet just stuck in a daze, watching him. My mind was so fucked up behind this man, and we hadn't even been talking that long. The way he had me feeling, I felt like I could actually love him. I didn't want to say it because I just might jinx it, especially with me not knowing how he felt about me. Once he was clean, he came over and cleaned me off.

"Now I gotta walk around in a sundress with no panties on," I cried, staring down at my ripped-up thongs on the floor.

"No, you don't I'll take you by the house so that you can change." He picked my panties up off the floor, stuffing them in his pocket.

"Where we going?" I queried, pulling my dress down.

"I want to spend the day with you. Go say bye to your grandmother, and I'll be waiting for you in the car."

I swore that man seemed surreal. Hopefully, things would keep going the way they were, but the way life was set up, I just knew something was going to fall out the sky on my ass and fuck up my fantasy. Nothing in life was this perfect.

"When I said make me some great grandbabies, I didn't mean in my house." My grandma laughed. My face turned beet red. I hadn't realized I was that loud until she said something about it. There was no way I was about to stay in there talking to her about my sex life.

"I don't know what you're talking about. I gotta go, Ma. Call me if you need anything." I hurried over to kiss her on the forehead like I always did, but she stopped me.

"Uh uh, I don't know where them lips been."

"Ma!" I rushed out of there as fast as I could.

Harper

"I told you that shit would work," Axel gloated with ease.

"Yeah, but now Reapa wants to fucking kill me!" I cried. Listening to Axel was probably the worst mistake of my life. He was the one that talked me into shutting down the gym to piss them off like that. What I hadn't realized was that I would have to deal with Reapa's crazy ass. Axel could only protect me to a certain extent. When Reapa was pissed off, there was no calming him down. Trust me, I've known him for years and saw him at his worst.

"Don't worry 'bout him. I'll take care of that fuck nigga. Did you get the house too?" he asked, turning to face me.

"No, Reapa scared the shit out of me, so I just came straight here to get out of his way." He wanted them chains off the door by the time that he got back, but I didn't take them off. When he found out, he was going to be searching high and low to find my ass.

"Go do that and like I said, I'll take care of Reapa." After he said that, the front door opened. Ava walked in with a grimace on her face. It had been two weeks since I had seen her and didn't know where the fuck she had been. "Did you do what I told you to?" Axel questioned, eyeing her.

"No, I told you he wants nothing to do with me, Axe," she whined. He got up off the couch and went over, gripping her tightly by the throat.

"Where the fuck you been at for two weeks then, huh?" he asked through gritted teeth.

"I-I been trying to figure out a way to get him back," she stammered. I kind of felt bad for her the way he was doing her, but she should have known that it was coming soon or later. That just was the type of nigga Axe was. I've never had to worry about him putting his hands on me but them other bitches, I've seen him choke, stomp... all type of shit before.

"And it took you two weeks to do that and come back empty handed?" He slammed her body hard against the front door.

"Swear that's all I was doing." She swore, but I didn't believe not one word coming out of her mouth. Knowing Ava, she had gone and cashed out on a nigga, and once the fucking money went dry, he kicked her ass to the curb.

"Harper, go handle that right quick while I take care of her." Without any hesitation, I got up from the couch, rushed to the bedroom to grab Baylee and zoomed out the front door. I didn't want to stick around to see whatever the hell he was about to do to her ass and definitely didn't want my child to be around it. Before I went over to Kase's house, I was going to drop Baylee off at my friend Brittany's.

∞ ∞ ∞

When I made it to Kase's house, he wasn't there, so it gave me a chance to do what I needed to do. Since I found out that I was the owner of the muthafucka, I got me a key made. While he was out in the streets doing only God knows what, I was going to put all his things out on the lawn excluding the furniture. It took me a good two hours to pack up all of his belongings and get them outside. I know that I had said I was going to just let her have him, but after having some time to think on it and Axe in my ear, I concluded that that's not what I really wanted. Any chick that was willing to give up on her man and everything they built was a fucking fool. And I was far from that.

Kase whipped into the driveway like a madman just as I was tossing his last bag out into the yard. He hopped out his car with a mean mug on his face. If things were to go left with him, all I had to do was call the cops since I knew my name was on the deed. "What the hell are doing!" he bellowed.

"Getting your shit out of my house. What does it look like I'm doing?" I flashed him a smirk.

"This isn't your shit; this my shit." He stopped short right in front of me. His nose flared, and his eyes were dark. I could tell he was mad as fuck, but he was only feeling fifteen percent of the anger I felt for him.

"Not according to the deed. I'm going to take everything you have from you if you keep fucking with that bitch. I tried to be nice 'bout it but it was fuck my feelings, right? So, fuck yours! If you don't want everything you've ever built taken from you, then I suggest you get rid of that bitch."

"You can't force someone to want to be with you, Harper. I did that shit to ensure that you and Baylee were straight if something was to ever happen to me and now, you're making me regret doing it."

"It's too late now, what's done is done. I'll give you a couple days to think on it. Till then, you can stay in your funky ass house. I'll be back to see what your decision is." I went to walk away but stopped mid-stride turning back to him. "I'm not playing; I will take everything you have 'cause I'll be damned if she will get her hands on anything I helped you build. You can be with that bitch but broke on the streets." If he knew what was best for him, then he would make the right choice. Maybe Axe was on to something when he had come up with that plan after all. Kase just stood there with a dumbfounded expression on his face. "A couple of days!" I said over my shoulder before climbing into my car and pulling off.

Kase

*T*hat shit Harper pulled had me thinking like a muthafucka. It was crazy how she was trying to force me to choose then want to blackmail me with my own shit. She knew I wouldn't do too much to her for the sake of Baylee, but she was pressing her luck. My mind was fucked up because I couldn't lose everything I worked so hard for. But then again, the feelings I had for Nix were strong as fuck, and I wasn't prepared to lose her either. All in all, I was in a messed-up situation. My vibrating phone pulled me from my thoughts.

"Yeah, Ma?" I sighed, not feeling up to the shenanigans that my mother was sure to be with at the moment.

"I haven't seen you since our anniversary party. You think you're too much to come and visit your mother now?" she quizzed me, and I rubbed my hand up and down the nape of my neck.

"It's nothing like that. I just been really busy. You know you're my world, I'd never neglect you, Ma." That was the truth. My mother was my everything, but she should've understood by now that I was a busy man and had a life so I couldn't just come by there to spend time with her that much even though I wanted to.

"Uh huh. I'm cooking dinner, and your grandmother is in town tonight so have your behind here at seven sharp. Oh, and bring Harper, I haven't seen her in a while either," she suggested.

"Ma, me and Harper isn't together anymore." She had to know soon or later. I knew she was going to be shocked since she liked her so much.

"What! Why!"

"It's complicated. I talk to Phoenix now," I told her and prayed she didn't ask me to bring her because I didn't know how she was going to react to Nix. My mother was funny as fuck when it came to the women I dated, that's how come I was surprised when she fell in love with Harper so quickly.

"Well, bring Phoenix by so I can meet her even though I think that it's a little early for you to be dating someone else. What do you know about this girl anyway? You sure she's not one of those heffas out here wanting you for your money?" she seriously asked. Never once did I think that of Nix. Plus, her mother had some money of her own, so that was the least of my worries. She never came off as the gold-digging type to me.

"No, Ma, and I'll see what I can do." I quickly ended the call before she tried to pry into my business any further. I wasn't sure what Nix had planned for the day, but I was hoping she would be able to swing going with me. If she didn't, then I would never hear the end of it from my mother.

Me: *You busy tonight like around sevenish?*

While I waited for her response, I finished bringing my things into the house. That crazy ass girl had my shit packed all up in trash bags and shit. Not having the time to go through every bag just to find me something to put on, I decided to just go to the mall and find me and Nix something to wear. *No, why you asked?* She finally texted back.

Me: *We got plans. Where you at?*

Not even two minutes later, my phone vibrated again. *Unity's apartment in the Bronx. I'll text you the address.* After locking up the house, I hopped back into my silver Lambo and headed for the mall.

∞ ∞ ∞

Once I picked out our outfits, I stopped back by the house, took a shower, and got dressed. I was mentally preparing myself for dinner at my parents' house. Having to deal with my mother was bad enough, but my grandmother, Karissa was just as bad. Hopefully, Nix would be able to survive both of them. My father was usually the chill one out the two, so there shouldn't be a problem there with him.

I knocked on the door and stood there waiting for someone to come to it. Moments later, the same dark-skinned girl from my parents' anniversary party was standing in the doorway. "You must be Unity." I stuck my hand out for her to shake and she politely took it with a smile. I thought it was strange how she had freckles, but the shits were dope as fuck on her.

"And you must be the nigga that got my best friend dick crazy. Joshua, I suppose?"

"Oh, hell nah, who the fuck is a Joshua? Nix!" I barked. I knew damn well she wasn't playing any fucking games with me.

"I'm just kidding, Kase. Calm down I don't want you to kill my best friend over a harmless joke." She snickered. Nix came out of a door with a sexy scowl on her face. Lucky for me that I did stop and grab her something to wear when I bought myself something. Don't get me wrong, she looked good in those jeans and crop top, but that wasn't the right attire to be wearing to meet my mother for the first time.

"What you yelling my name like that for?" she inquired, placing her hand on her hip.

"You look good as fuck no lie but you going to have to change that shit where we're going."

"Well, if you would've told me before you brought your ass over here, where we were going then I would've dressed for the occasion."

"No worries, here," I said, stepping into the door, handing her the Neiman Marcus bag I had in my hand.

"Where I'm going in this?" she asked, taking a peek into the bag. She hadn't even seen the whole dress, so I didn't know why she was tripping.

"Just go get dressed. We already pressed for time," I announced, glancing down at my Rolex that was glistening on my wrist.

Blowing air from her lips, she disappeared into the back, so I took a seat on the burnt orange couch. "Sure, just make yourself at home." Unity rolled her eyes, shutting the front door, then headed to the back as well. I checked my watch for the tenth time. Nix had been in the back for an hour. I didn't think it would take her that long just to change her clothes.

Just as I stood to go back there and drag her ass out, she came out looking spectacular. That gold bondage dress was hugging her small curves, and for the first time, she had straightened her curly hair. It was way longer than I thought it was stopping almost at the top of her ass. She was matching my fly to the fullest. I had on black Armani slacks and a matching button-up shirt. My parents were going to expect us to be at our best coming over for dinner with my grandmother. Yeah, they truly did the most with everything that they did.

"Got damn girl, the way you over there looking, I'm thinking about just saying fuck dinner." Placing both of her hands in her hair, she slowly strutted over to where I stood, never breaking eye contact.

"Let me find out you just realized what the fuck you had." I bit down on my lower lip. My dick stood straight at attention.

"Nah, a nigga been knew what the fuck he had," I confidently stated.

"Come on let's go 'cause my shit brick and I'll been done raped your little ass right here." I snatched her by the wrist, dragging her out the front door.

It didn't take long for us to get to my parents' house. I got out opening the door for Nix and grabbed her hand. "Where are we?" she asked. The whole way over there she kept questioning me, trying to figure out where I was taking her but I wouldn't tell her.

"Just chill, you're good." I brought my free hand up, knocking on the door. Moments later, my mother came to it.

"You're late," she scoffed.

"I know Ma; it was my fault," I told her, pulling her in for a hug. "Ma, this is my girl Phoenix, Phoenix my mother, Karen," I introduced them. If looks could kill, I'd sure be dead right now.

"Hi," Nix shyly said.

"Well, come on in don't just stand there."

When we got inside, my grandmother was sitting on the couch, drinking a glass of white wine. I kissed her on the cheek then introduced her to Nix as well. "Is that my boy I hear?" my father walked into the room with a wide Kool-Aid smile on his face. He pulled me in for a fatherly embrace.

"Pops, this my girl Nix. Nix my father, Blake Senior."

"Your real name is Blake, Kase?" she laughed so hard. I wanted to slap the shit out of her ass for joking on my damn name. That was the reason I rarely told people my name now. When I was younger, I stayed in and out of court, so Reapa just started calling me Kase and ever since it just stuck. I'd take it over my government any day.

"Nice to meet you, Nix." My father shook her hand. After that, my mother pulled her down onto the couch with her and my grandmother. My father took me to the side so that we could talk privately. "What's going on with you and Harper?" I shrugged. Harper had me two point five seconds away from putting a bullet in her ass.

"I messed up big time. Harper and I had been having problems for the longest and then one day Nix walked into my life, everything just changed. Yeah, there was a point in time where I saw myself with Harper, getting married and all that other good stuff, but when I met Nix, I realized I was only doing all that 'cause Harper and I had a daughter together and felt like it was the right thing to do. Now Harper got a nigga in a bind 'cause her name was on most of my shit and she threatening to take everything away from me unless I leave Phoenix." I glanced over at Nix and just watched her as she interacted with my mother. It was as if my mother liked her more than she did Harper which was a good thing.

"I never thought she would do something like that." He sighed, reaching down, picking up a cigar. While he wasn't paying attention, my eyes locked with Nix's. I stuck my fingers up in a V, flicking my tongue between them. The way she crossed her legs, I knew I probably opened the floodgates.

"Son, I think you already know what you need to do." I was afraid he might say something like that. It was one of the hardest decisions I could ever make, but he was right.

"Dinner is ready," their maid came out and announced. I didn't know her name since they stayed changing help like they changed their underwear.

"We'll talk later but for now let's go eat." I nodded my head and gripped Nix's ass, squeezing it as she walked by.

"Kase!" she squealed, blushing. I just couldn't help myself; the shit was there for the touching.

The whole time at the dinner table, I was zoned out, thinking about what my father told me. I couldn't take my eyes off of Nix; she seemed to be enjoying herself. The more and more I stared at her, the harder my dick got. Placing my hand on her thigh, I slid it underneath her dress to her warm center. Her head snapped around to me so quick I tried my best to hold a straight face. Pushing her thongs to the side, I slipped my index finger inside of her. That pussy was gushy than a muthafucka.

"Nix, didn't you say that was your mother that had did our anniversary party?" my mother asked. I slipped another finger into her pussy.

"Ugh, mhm," she replied, trying her best to hold her poker face. I stared around the table to make sure no one was paying us any attention before I sped up my pace. Nix dropped her fork onto the plate and held onto the sides of her chair.

"I really enjoyed her food and would love to use her for another party," my mother continued.

"Mhm." Nix more so moaned causing my dick to jump.

"Blake, I like her, so you better not fuck that shit up," my mother warned, pointing her steak knife in my direction before taking her attention back to her plate.

Nix's body shivered, and I knew she was close to climaxing. Her eyes rolled to the back of her head. More moans escaped her plump lips, but no one really paid attention to them since they were so low. "Awwww fuck!" she screamed out and squirted all over my fingers. A smirk crept up on my face.

"You okay?" my father asked Nix.

"YOU PLAY ALL DAY!" she shouted, mushing me in the side of the head and got up from the table, storming off.

"What's wrong with her?" my mother asked.

"Nothing, I just made a mistake and stepped on her foot. Let me go check on her." I found her, pacing back and forth in the living room with a smug expression on her face.

"Why you had to do that!" she snapped. I placed my two fingers into my mouth, sucking her juices off them. Pushing her down over the edge of the couch, I unzipped my pants and pulled my dick out. The shit was so swollen that I thought it was going to burst. "Wha-what you doing? Your parents are literally a few feet away."

"Don't be loud then." I pushed her damped thongs to the side and eased myself on in her wet walls.

"Fuck," she moaned. I long stroked her so she could feel every bit of that monster. Biting down on my lower lip, I tossed my head back while she bounced that ass on my dick. Got damn, I swore Nix had the best pussy I ever had, that's why I couldn't stay out the shit. "Damn, I'm about to cum," she whimpered. Not long after she was cumming and I released my seeds inside her. I slipped my dick out and stuffed it back into my pants.

"The bathroom down the hall, second door on the left," I told her as she pulled her dress down. I went back into the dining room, and everyone was still eating.

"Is she okay?" my mother questioned.

"Yeah, she good."

"Son, hand me one of the rolls," my father said. I picked up one of them with the same hand I fingered Nix with and passed him a roll with a smirk on my face.

Axel

*A*fter breaking my foot off in Ava's ass, I truly thought she finally got my point. That was the first time I ever laid a finger on her. It wasn't like I was going around beating bitches for no reason. I only did it when I saw fit to teach them a lesson or pretty much get my point across. With her, it was both. She thought I was stupid as fuck. There was no way she had been gone for two got damn weeks, trying to figure out how to get Reapa back. Since she wanted to play games with me, I was going to use her for the next part of my plan. We were going to rob him blind, and if she didn't agree with my proposal, then I was going to get rid of her ass.

Ava sat on the bed with a mean mug on her bruised-up face. Despite the slight markings, she still looked somewhat beautiful. I just wished she would have done what I asked her to then she wouldn't have had to worry about me putting my hands on her. I actually did like her up until then.

"I'on know why you sitting there looking stupid and shit. This your own fucking fault. You're the only one to blame," I scolded her.

"But did you really have to put your hands on me the way that you did, Axe! Look at my fucking face!" she screamed, pointing at her eye. She was lucky as fuck that was the only thing I had done to her. Things could've been far worse.

"You'll be alright." I shrugged, going over to the dresser, picking up my Nine and tucking it in my waistline. "You ready to go or no?"

"Please don't make me do this," she begged, but I wasn't hearing it.

"You won't have to if you would've just done what the fuck I told you to." Gripping her roughly by the wrist, I snatched her up from the bed and took her to the bathroom. "Put a little makeup on that eye. That shit look fucked up." Ava cut her eyes at me. "What the hell you waiting for? Hurry the fuck up; you act like we got all fucking day or something."

Sucking her teeth, she picked her makeup up off the sink and attempted to fix her battered eye. All I could think about was getting my hands on all Reapa's shit. The life he was living was meant for me. I knew that I could have the same things as them if I had equal hustle mentality as them, but I didn't. I wanted to take the easy way instead of working hard for my shit which was all right with me. "Alright, that's enough bring your ass on." Grabbing her by her forearm, I pulled her outside to the car and forced her inside.

∞ ∞ ∞

"You sure this it?" I questioned, staring at the project building sitting across the street.

"Yes," she dryly responded not even looking at me.

"Swear if you lying, I'ma black that other fucking eye. Your ass isn't going to be able to see for days. Get the fuck out the car."

I followed her up the stairs to one of the apartments that Reapa and Kase used as a trap. It wasn't anything extravagant but whatever was inside was going to cause enough noise. The muthafuckas weren't going to know what hit them. All they were going to know was that their shit was missing. Ava only knew of a couple of their small traps so I wouldn't be able to get away with much. Reapa was a smart ass nigga and barely trusted anyone, not even his own bitch.

"This it," she said, pointing at the door. I pulled the skull cap down over my head, not wanting anyone to see my face. I may have been stupid, but I wasn't that fucking stupid; I didn't need them banging on my fucking door.

"Knock on it," I demanded, stepping to the side of the door against the wall. Hopefully, there wasn't too many of them niggas in there since I was going in blind. I was trying to get out of there with my life still intact.

"Who is it?" one of the guys asked through the door. Obviously, they had taped up the peephole, not wanting anyone to be able to look inside. That's what most of them paranoid niggas did.

She briefly glanced over at me, "Ava," she finally answered. Mumbling could be heard coming through the door before it pulled open.

"What the hell you doing here?" he inquired.

"Uh, I was looking for Reapa. Is he in there?" She hesitated. The dumb bitch was going to get us both caught.

"Nah—" That was all I needed. Without saying a word, I stepped behind Ava, shoving her into the house with my gun drawn.

"Get the fuck back and don't try shit," I warned, aiming my piece directly at his head.

"Yo, what the fuck you got going on, Ava?" he quizzed, throwing his hands up in the air.

"I'm sorry!" she cried.

"Shut the fuck up and go see if someone else is in here," I told her, not taking my eyes off the nigga standing in front of me. Just as soon as she left out of the living room, I began questioning his ass. "Where the drugs and money at?"

"Are you fucking stupid? Reapa them don't keep no money in here 'cause of fuck boys like you!" he spat, spit flying from his lips. I guess they really were smarter than I thought. He didn't say there weren't any drugs in there though. I'd just take those and flip them hos on the street somewhere.

"I'll show you a fuck boy." I shot him in the knee, and he dropped down to the floor. "Where the drugs at?" I aimed the gun straight into his face.

"What the fuck are you doing, Axel!" Ava ran back into the living room and asked. Her eyes diverted to the guy, rolling around on the floor, holding his knee.

"Was anyone else in here?" She shook her head. I took my attention back to the guy on the floor. "Where the drugs at, nigga?"

"You might as well kill me now 'cause I'm not telling your pussy ass shit!"

"Okay." I shot him right in the head, and Ava screamed out. I had to quickly cover her mouth before she got us jammed up. "Shut the hell up and help me find them damn drugs." We ransacked that whole apartment, looking for the drugs. Right when I was about to give up the search, I passed something that looked off on the hallway wall.

Banging on the wall with the butt of my gun, I heard a thud. Stepping back, I shot through the wall then peeked into the hole. "Jackpot." They had a secret room with their drugs hidden in there. Kicking the wall in just enough where I could get inside, I went into the room and grabbed as much shit as I could. "You going to help me or just stand there looking stupid?"

"I'm not 'bout to help you steal Reapa's shit. You may have a death wish but I damn sure don't." She went to leave, but I quickly gripped her by her weave, pulling her into the room.

"If you don't help me, I'm going to kill your ass now." She could tell by the stern expression on my face that I was forreal, so she grabbed a bag and began tossing cocaine into it. "That's what I thought."

After filling up four bags, we made a dash for the door. As we were about to hit the stairs, a guy was coming up. He stopped once his eyes landed on me then went to Ava. Before I knew it, he had caught out running. I dropped the bags and ran behind him because I didn't need any fucking witnesses. Who was to say that Reapa found out Ava had something to do with his shit coming up missing then he came for her and she snitched on me? I didn't have time for that shit.

That nigga was running like a got damn track star. Lucky for him, I smoked too much, and my lungs weren't how they use to be. God was on his side because he had got away without a scratch on him. Going back inside the building, Ava was still in the same spot where I left her.

"Come on; we have to get out of here. And if you speak a word of this to anyone... well, you already know what's going to happen." I hurried up and got the hell out of dodge. There was no telling where that nigga was going, and I couldn't handle any damn back up by myself.

Unity

$\mathcal{E}$ven though the gym was shut down for whatever reason, Reapa was still making sure all his employees were still getting paid. Basically, we were on paid vacation. With it being closed, I had to find another gym to work out at for the time being, then on the side, I was meeting my clients at their homes and other gyms to work out with them. My hustle was not going to stop. Bills still needed to be paid. Call me crazy or whatever you wanted, but I refused to just sit back and let Reapa pay my shit for me. I had been independent this long and planned on staying that way.

"What you got planned for the day?" Nix barged into my bedroom eating a bowl of cereal. The least she could've done was knocked first. I could've been naked or had my man over or something. She never knew what was going on and apparently, she didn't care.

"I got a meeting this morning with Keke," I replied. Keke was my kickboxing manager. She had called me yesterday talking about that I needed to come down to her office because there was something important she needed to talk to me about. I had been anxious as fuck ever since I got that call.

"Aww man, I thought that maybe we could do something." She pouted.

"Sorry, boo; maybe later." I picked my phone up off the nightstand, checking to see if I had any messages or missed calls from Reapa. When I saw I didn't have any, I blew air from my lips. I kind of missed him but he seemed busy as fuck lately. Understanding that he was a busy man, I gave him his space whenever he chose to shut me out. Sometimes I just wished he would fully let me in, but the way things were looking, it didn't seem like that would ever happen.

"Guess I'll just lay around the house all day by myself then." Nix was so dramatic.

"I got a suggestion, how about you take your ass home and make up with your mother." She scrunched her face up at me before walking out of my room. It pissed me off how she was doing her mother. Some people just never truly understood how lucky they were to still have their mother or father in their life. Me, I had neither and would give anything to have my mother back even though she was a drug addict. Shona never once let me see that side of her. The side that I always saw was the loving mother that would do anything for her child. I just wished that whoever gave her that laced heroin never took my mother away from me. What could she have possibly done to them for them to want to kill her? That woman was loved by so many people; she just got mixed up with the wrong crowd.

Getting up from my bed, I headed into the bathroom so I could handle my hygiene and get out of there. I was supposed to have met Keke at nine, and it was going on seven-thirty. After my thirty-minute shower, I stood at my closet door, trying to figure out what I was going to wear for the day. It didn't take any time before I decided on just wearing some simple gray leggings and a dark blue hoodie. It was starting to get cool outside, so it was time to start putting up the summer clothes. What I couldn't wait for was when the snow started dropping. That was my favorite thing about the winter.

"I'll be back, Nix!" I yelled as I headed to the front door and stuck my feet into my UGGs.

"Yeah, yeah."

∞ ∞ ∞

"Hi, Jenny, I'm here to see Keke," I told the receptionist.

"Let me see if she's ready for you." She smiled and got up from her seat, heading for Keke's office door. Even though she was a black manager, Keke was doing quite well for herself. She managed a few well-known boxers, UFC fighters, and kickboxers so I was excited when I found out she wanted to work with me. One day out the blue, she found me in the gym, taking out some frustrations on the boxing bag and instantly wanted to sign me. Things were rocky in the beginning because she wanted to change so many things and I hated change. But once I saw that she was only trying to do what was best for me, I just let her have her way, and everything had been smooth sailing ever since.

"You can go right on in," Jenny announced, taking her seat.

"Thanks."

I pushed Keke's door opened and stepped inside, closing it behind me. She was sitting behind her big, dark wood mahogany desk, scrolling through her phone. Once her eyes landed on me, a huge smile appeared on her face. "There goes the champ," she gloated. She stood long enough for us to hug briefly.

"What's going on? How come you dragged me all the way down here to Manhattan?" I loved having our little chit chats, but I wanted to get straight to the point. She had tortured me long enough when I had to go through the entire night, trying to figure out what she had to tell me.

"Get straight to the point, huh?" She laughed. Keke intertwined her fingers together on her desk and stared me directly into the eyes. "Well, I called you down here because I got an important call yesterday. I got you into one of the biggest competitions of your life." That news was like music to my ears. It sounded just like the type of announcement I had been working so hard for. Finally, people were actually going to know my name.

"Sounds good."

"There's just one problem though," she blurted. I should've known there was a catch to it. "The competition is like a tour. If you accept, then you'll be gone for four months."

"Four months!" That was a long ass time to be gone. I had never been gone that long for a competition like that before.

"Yes, I know it seems long, but the money is definitely worth it, and I'm sure you need it." There was no way I would be able to leave for that long. I had my grandma to think about, my job, then there was Reapa. How could I just be selfish and leave all of that behind?

"Can I at least have some time to think about it?"

"If I were you, I'd jump straight on it. The tour starts in two weeks. But if you need some time to think, I'd suggest that you do it quickly. Let me know your decision in a couple of days. In case you decide you want to do it, we have to get you an endorser and start advertising. There's a lot of work that has to go into this."

"Okay, I'll get back with you in a couple of days."

Nix

I never thought I would end up back in a courthouse behind another man but yet here I was. When my court date came in the mail, I was nervous as fuck not knowing what was going to be my fate. If God was on my side, then I would have any other judge in the world besides Judge Martin. That woman hated the ground I walked on and me telling her that I was going to stay out of trouble didn't make the shit any better. It really was my intention, but I just keep getting put in fucked up situations. This time, it really wasn't my fault. We had done nothing wrong and ended up in jail over bullshit.

Everyone filed into the courtroom. I quickly took my seat, bouncing my leg and chewing on my thumbnail since I was nervous as fuck. "Please rise. The Court of Criminal Division is now in session, honorable Judge Martin presiding."

"Wait a minute, who the hell he just said!"

"Everyone but the jury may be seated," Judge Martin announced. "Ms. Quartz, I see that you just can't seem to stay out of trouble. What did I tell you were going to happen the next time you were in front of me?" Tears filled my eyes because I knew I was about to be a goner.

"But this time it wasn't my fault, Judge Martin," I pleaded.

"Doesn't matter whose fault it is. I don't even care what you did, but I'm sentencing you to two years," she said, slamming her gavel down.

"Wait! Please, Judge Martin!" I begged. The bailiff came over grabbing me, but I kept fighting him. I wasn't about to let those people take me without a fucking fight. "Don't fucking touch me!" The tears streamed down my cheeks. "Please! It wasn't my fault," I cried.

"WAIT!" The doors flew open, and there stood Kase. I immediately stopped fighting and let the bailiff slap the cuffs onto my wrists. Kase walked straight up to Judge Martin and spoke something to her.

"Give me a second, Cortez," she told the bailiff then got up from her seat, heading to the door with Kase right on her heels. I had no idea what they were about to talk about and really didn't give a damn. I was too busy trying to get this man to let me go.

"Gone let me go and just say I ran out on you."

"I can't do that," he responded, not even making eye contact. My heart beat a hundred miles a minute. I could see if she would've said some months, but the bitch said two years. Her hatred for me must really run deep.

"Fuck your bald-headed ass. You probably don't get any pussy. That's why you sucking up to Martin the way that you are. Little dick bitch." I was mad as fuck that he wouldn't let me go. He tightened the cuffs on my wrist. "Ouch!"

Her and Kase seemed to be in that room forever just heightening my anxiety. They finally came from the back, and the both of them were all smiles and shit. If those cuffs weren't on my wrists, I probably would've slapped the shit out of him for laughing when I was about to go to jail behind his dumb ass baby mama. That bitch was getting fucked up on sight every time I laid eyes on her ass.

"Let her go, Cortez," Judge Martin said, and he did as he was told. I rubbed my wrists, side-eyeing him. Everything in me wanted to kick his ass but it was a miracle I was getting set free, so I just chilled my ass out for the time being.

"Let's go," Kase said, grabbing my hand and pulling me out of the courtroom.

"Please tell me what the hell just happened."

"Let's just say, Judge Martin is one of the judges that we got in our back pocket."

"How come you didn't say something about that earlier?" He could've saved me a lot of trouble. He stopped walking and cocked his head to the side.

"Well, for one you didn't even tell me you had court today. I just so happen stopped by Unity's place looking for you, and she told me where you were."

"Yeah, sorry about that." When we got outside, he walked up to an Uber opening the back door for me.

"It's already paid for to go wherever you need to," he made known.

"Why can't I go with you?" I quickly queried. It had been a few days since I last seen him and I was fiending for the dick. I did owe him for saving my ass and just wanted to show him how much I appreciated him.

"Look, me and you need to talk. I was going to wait till later to do this, but I think I should right now." My heart thumped in my chest. From the sound of his voice, I knew something wasn't right. I shut the door and stepped back up on the curb, folding my arms underneath my breasts.

"I'm listening."

"This with me and you not working Phoenix. With everything I got going on at the moment, I don't too much have time for a relationship," he explained, rubbing his hand across his waves.

"Look me in my eyes and tell me that shit. You supposed to be a man, right?"

"Don't make a big thing out of nothing, Nix."

"Are you fucking serious right now!" I yelled, tossing my hands in the air. If I hadn't just walked out of that courthouse, I would've punched his ass in the fucking face. "Basically, what you're telling me is, that you just been using me for sex? What was I? A got damn rebound? You want that stupid bitch back? Huh! What is it!" I was fucking livid.

"Nix, calm down."

"No, I'm not doing shit!" I shoved him hard in the chest. Tears cascaded down my red cheeks. "You ain't fucking shit, Kase!" I shoved him again. He gripped me by both of my wrists and pushed me into the side of the car, pressing his body against mine.

"I'm not going to let you continue to fucking put your hands on me, Nix. I asked you nicely to fucking calm down." I couldn't believe this shit. This nigga had made me fall for him just to basically rip my heart out of my chest.

"Get the fuck off me!" The tears were coming full force. "I got into with my mama 'cause I refused to stop talking to you. I can't believe I was so fucking stupid to actually fall in love with you. You just like Axel; both of y'all ain't shit niggas!"

"You in love with me?" For a second, I thought I saw a tear in his eye, but he quickly blinked it back.

"Why does it fucking matter, we not working right?" I tried to push him off of me, but he wouldn't budge. "MOVE KASE!"

"Answer my question." I didn't have to answer shit.

"Nah, I fucking hate you." How the hell could he switch up on me the way he did? I'd never understand. It seemed like he just changed up overnight. "If you want to fuck with that stupid ho, I'm not going to stop your ass, now get the fuck off of me." He finally let me go and took a couple of steps back from me. "Stay the fuck away from me." I climbed into the car and gave the driver Unity's address. As we pulled away from the curbside, I broke down worse than I ever done before. I was truly crushed... scarred.

Harper

Kase's couple of days were finally up. Being the nice bitch, I was, I actually had given him an extra day to figure out what the hell he was going to do. When I got to his house, I used my key to let myself inside. I found him in his man cave smoking a blunt with Reapa. He was the last person I wanted to see since I had to yet take the chains off of his gym. I thought he would've come and hunted me down by now, but surprisingly he didn't. Once they spotted me, their talking seized.

"What the fuck you doing here?" Reapa asked, screwing up his face. He didn't have to let it be known any more than he already had, I knew he hated me. What irked me was that he didn't really have a reason to up until recently.

"I came here to talk to Kase. This is my house so I should be asking you the same thing." Reapa shot from the couch so fast. Out of nowhere, both of his hands wrapped tightly around my throat, squeezing it.

"You wearing the shit out of this *my* shit. It might work on Kase, but I'd be damned if it works on me. If I were you, I'd tread lightly. Kase might be scared to put a bullet in your ass, but I wouldn't hesitate to put a hollow tip in you. Try me." It felt like his hands were getting tighter by the second every time I struggled to breathe.

"Reapa," I begged, trying to peel his fingers from around my neck.

"Aye man, let her go before you kill her," Kase said, approaching him. Reapa finally let go, dropping me to the floor. I gasped for air; it felt like he crushed my windpipes.

"That was my plan. You need to do something with that bitch. Hit me up when she gone 'cause if I stay around her any longer, I just might kill her ass for real," he warned before leaving out of the room.

Kase reached his hand down to help me up off the floor. "You good?" he questioned. It surprised me he was treating me the way he was when I was just threatening him the other day. But that was Kase for you.

"I will be." I took a seat on the dark brown sectional, trying to regulate my breathing. If he hadn't stopped Reapa when he did, I probably would've indeed been dead. "Did you figure out what you wanted to do?" Even though I just damn near died, that wasn't going to change my mind about what I had come there for.

Kase sucked his teeth. "I broke up with Nix. Now take them fucking chains off the gym and leave all my shit alone. The first chance I get, I'm taking your name off everything."

"I'll take the chains off the gym, but I'm not taking my name off the deeds and stuff. You got me fucked up. How I know you just won't run your ass right back to her once I do that?" Mama didn't raise no fool. I wasn't even sure he had broken up with the ho but I sure as hell was going to find her ass to see.

"Man, I don't have time for the games you be playing, Harper. That's the reason you lost me in the first place. You need to fucking grow the hell up."

"I know you're mad, but I'm not taking my name off of shit. And while I'm at it, I think it's time that Baylee and I moved in here."

"Baylee can move in but your ass ain't."

"You can't tell me what to do in my own house. We'll be here first thing in the morning." I happily stood up feeling like I just accomplished some shit. With me being around all the time, he was bound to go back to his old feelings for me. Soon, everything was going to be back to normal, and we were going to be all good.

"I keep trying to tell you that you can't force someone to want you, Harper." He sighed a deep breath.

"Yeah, that's what your mouth say now but just watch."

Reapa

I don't know how the hell Kase was putting up with that bullshit from Harper. I swore it couldn't be me. She would've been had a bullet in her ass. Get her some of that act right real quick. Every time I tried to kill her, he was standing in the way playing captain save a ho. If she kept on, I was going to get her ass when he wasn't around and just tell him she disappeared and left Baylee for him to raise. How wishy-washy the bitch was, he just might believe the shit.

At the moment, I didn't have time to be trying to solve his problems; we had another issue on the rising. JT hit my line, telling me that we had a problem at one of the traps. Since Kase was busy dealing with his baby mama from hell, I went over by myself to check things out. When I got to the building, JT was sitting outside on one of the benches smoking a cigarette with a few of the other guys surrounding him.

"Wassup, Reapa," he spoke when I walked up. This wasn't any friendly visit, so I immediately got to the point.

"What you called me over here for?" I sternly asked.

"Somebody been in the trap. They killed Jug too while they were at it." This particular trap was known by a lot of people, so there was no telling who had actually been in there. Lucky for us, we never kept any money at any of traps for those reasons right there. I just hated they had to kill Jug; he was one of my best soldiers. What was fucking with me was the fact they were able to catch him slipping like that.

Usually, Jug was always on his A game so for him to get caught something wasn't adding up about the situation. "But check this though, when I was coming back to the trap, I ran into Ava and some nigga on the stairs. They both were carrying duffel bags so I wouldn't be surprised if they were the ones that had done it. I caught out running before they tried to kill me and just hid out at my partner's house for the time being. You know me, if I would've had my strap, I definitely would've taken both of their asses out."

"'Preciate it. Did you call the clean-up crew?" I stood there, stroking my goatee, not believing what this nigga just told me. Ava wasn't that fucking bold to fuck around with me like that so I couldn't understand what made her do it. She was never one to have tough skin, but that right there was a dummy move. I had been with Ava for two years so of course I knew what made her tick, her strengths, and her weaknesses. I was about to flush her ass out and make her regret the day she ever crossed paths with Reapa. That was a fucking fact.

"Yeah, I did that as soon as I got situated. I know we don't need no cops sniffing around."

"I'll get up with you later." I dapped him up then headed into the building. When I got into the apartment, I went straight to the secret door to see what all they had taken. Of course, they took something because JT said they had duffel bags. The shit that we kept in there wasn't anything major so obviously, they didn't dent our pockets, but it was just the principle that Ava had the balls to come and take something of mine. It wasn't bad enough she gave my pussy away to some random ass nigga but then she took product from me probably giving it to the same nigga. That bitch is dead no doubt about it.

As I observed the room, I saw that they stole almost everything that was in there. They wouldn't have had that much to take if Jug hadn't just re-upped. Pulling my phone out, I dialed Kase's number. "Aye, Harper still with you?" I asked him, glaring at the big ass hole in the wall.

"Nah, she left like thirty minutes ago. Why what's up?"

"Ava and some nigga hit our ass. I need to get a hold of that bitch ASAP."

"I can try to call her and see if she had seen her, but I doubt very seriously she'll tell me anything," he replied.

"Nah, you good I know exactly how I'm going to get that ho to come out. She took something from me, so I'm going to take something from her. I'll have that ass before the night is over with."

Unity

ix had me sitting in the mall at the food court checking my phone for the hundredth time. I clearly texted her when I was leaving my meeting and told her to meet me at the mall for lunch, and she said she was going to be there. She was doing all that complaining about spending time with me before I left but stood me up for our lunch date. What type of shit was that? Finally getting fed up, I got up from the table and just decided to head on home.

The mall wasn't really my scene. People thought I was weird because I didn't too much like doing what other females did. Most of them died to go shopping all the time but nope, not me. I'd rather save my money for things I really needed to do, like taking care of my grandma. Things like that were more important than buying red bottoms or expensive clothes that I would probably just wear one time and throw to the back of the closet, never letting it see daylight again.

"Excuse you!" I shouted at some woman that bumped me hard as she walked. She stopped, turning to me with a smirk on her face.

"You're excused."

"You the one that bumped me so how the fuck am I excused?" She stepped toward me sizing me up. I promise that ho didn't want these hands. All it'll take it one hit to knock her ass the fuck out. She better not take my size for granted; I wasn't the one to play with.

"Oh, I know I bumped you... I did it on purpose. You need to take your country black ass back wherever the fuck you came from." Okay, she was really pushing it now. Clearly, she didn't know me from a can of paint yet here she was trying to judge me and shit. So, fucking what that I was country. Them niggas loved my country ass so it really didn't matter. "And while you're at it, you need to stay the fuck away from Miles. That's my fucking man," she warned, propping her hand on her hip.

Was she really stepping to me all over a fucking nigga? Like there weren't plenty fish in the sea. I knew nothing of this bitch, but she knew who the hell I was. Don't tell me she was one of his side bitches because I swear to God that I wasn't about to put up with that shit from him. A lot of those delusional ass women might do it, but Unity wasn't the one. The difference between me and the other women was that they might allow him to do whatever the hell he pleased but with me, he was going to act right or get left.

"You must be one of his side bitches or some?" I asked, rolling my neck and placing my hand on my hip.

"No, I'm the one and only bitch." She snickered, but I didn't see anything funny.

"Ho, how the fuck? I be the one at Reapa's house damn near every day and I sure as hell ain't see you there so you can gone somewhere with that bullshit. Side bitch... maybe, but anything else I doubt very seriously."

"You don't know the first thing about Miles but want to be with the muthafucka so bad." She burst out in a fit of laughter. I wasn't too sure about what she meant about that.

"What are you trying to say?" My interest was definitely piqued.

"Miles could be the sweetest man ever, but he also has split personalities. Reapa is the total opposite. Have you ever sat there and wondered why they call him Reapa in the first place? 'Cause he's a cold-blooded killer. You see this?" she asked, pulling her dress up showing me a scar on her knee. "It's only a matter of time before he snaps on your ass as well. It's best that he stays with someone that actually knew him. Not no gold-digging bitch that's just after him for his money."

"I don't believe shit you're saying. And even if it's true, we might have had the same man, but we certainly didn't have him the same way so remember that. Now if you'll excuse me, I have somewhere to be." I shoved past her, trying my best to get the hell out of there. All the things she said had me thinking. What if he really did do that to her knee? Could he snap on me as well?

My mind went back to that night that man jumped off the roof. Everything in me told me that he had something to do with it. It was a bloodcurdling feeling to think that the man you love could possibly do something to cause harm to you. I had to get to the bottom of this because things just didn't seem right so instead of heading home, I was going over to Reapa's. It was time that I got the truth once and for all.

Reapa

"You sure that you want to do this?" Kase asked as if I was going to change my mind.

"You damn right. It's the only way I'll be able to get her to come out. I don't have time to be playing games with her and shit." I should've just killed her ass that night at the club then I wouldn't have to worry about going through this shit.

"Alright, I'm just following your lead," he replied, and we both climbed out of my Maserati and headed up to the front door. I knocked on it and waited for someone to come to it. I knew that someone was there because the black SUV was sitting in the driveway. Moments later, the door pulled opened.

"What you doing here, Reapa? Ava isn't here," Christine quickly said and tried to shut the door in my face, but I caught it with my palm.

"I'm not here for her, I came to see you." I pushed my way inside with Kase right on my heels. She looked down seeing the gun in my other hand. Her eyes immediately grew wet with tears.

"Look-looking for me for what?" she questioned. From the stutter of her voice, I could tell she was terrified, and she had the right to be. She owed this visit to her sister.

"Ava took something from me. Get that bitch on the phone," I ordered, and with the quickness, she ran to retrieve her phone sitting on the coffee table. Not long after, Ava was on the line, and I snatched the phone from her grasp, placing it up to my ear.

"Wassup babe," I smoothly spoke.

"Who is this?" her stupid ass asked as if she didn't know my voice.

"Come on babe, just think about it. I'm sure that it'll come to you."

After a moment of silence, it indeed did. "Reapa?"

"Yeah, where you at? I heard that you got something of mine and you already know how I roll baby girl. You take something of mine, and I take something of yours. It's only fair."

"Wait Reapa!" she screamed.

"Nah, you should've thought about that before you took my shit. All that crying shit not going to do you any good now." Ava already knew how I operated, so I didn't know why she thought that her crying was going to save her.

"Please, Reapa, I'm begging you. I'll do anything," she cried. I tossed the phone over to Kase and headed to the back of the house and pushed the bedroom door opened. Lying in bed fast asleep was Ava's five-year-old son. She had him before we got together and left him for her sister to raise. Ava felt like she wasn't fit to be a mother just yet, but she loved her son more than life itself.

Even though she wasn't physically raising him, she would still come and spend time with him every chance she got so that he would know who his mother was. What I couldn't understand was how come she never came and got Axe when we made things official. I would've let him stay with us and helped her raise him if that was the problem. Now, it really didn't matter. Picking him up from the bed, I carried him back into the living.

"Reapa, you really don't have to do this. He's just a child," Christine begged. Ava was still on the phone boohoo crying. She knew she fucked up big time.

"Miles," she sobbed, calling me by my government. Placing the cold steel at Axe's head, I locked eyes with Christine.

"Your sister stay fucking up and not wanting to deal with the consequences. This time there's no way around it." Turning the gun on Christine, I shot her right in the middle of her forehead. Ava howled on the phone. If anyone else were in the room at that moment, they probably would have gotten chill bumps from that scream. "Ava, you got till nightfall to have your ass at my house, and if you're not there, I will put a bullet in Axe's head." Kase ended the call and brought his attention to me.

"Swear I thought you were going to shoot the kid." He came over, snatching him away from my arms. I may have done a lot of fucked up shit, but I would never harm a child. He was just going to be used as leverage to get his stupid ass mama to do what the fuck I wanted her to do. Since I had him, I knew she would come running with no hesitation. I shot the clean-up crew a text then got the hell out of there.

Unity

W hen I made it to Reapa's house, I used the key he gave me to let myself inside. Usually, I would've knocked, but once I didn't see his Maserati in the driveway, I figure he wasn't home. It was cool; I was going to sit there until he made his appearance. My head was still fucked up, so I was hoping it wasn't going to take him that long to get there. Heading up to his bedroom, I pushed the double doors open, and the scent of his cologne hit my nostrils. Inhaling deeply, I wandered on into the room. The things that old girl had said earlier, I so badly was hoping that they were false. If they were true, I didn't know what I was going to do.

He had already stolen my heart so if the facts were accurate, my heart probably was going to be crushed. Just as I tossed myself onto the bed, I heard the front door open, so I got up and ran to the stairs. Right as I was about to open my mouth, I saw him, and Kase walk in with a child. It had me wondering if it was Kase's son or what. Far as I knew, Reapa didn't have any children.

"You sure she's going to come?" Kase asked, heading into one of the rooms downstairs. Once I heard *she* leave his mouth, I couldn't help but wonder who he was talking about. I knew it was wrong for me to be ease dropping the way I was, but I wanted to know what the hell was going on and what exactly I had gotten myself into.

"Trust me, I know for a fact her ass coming," Reapa gloated with a smirk on his face. Swear to God if that nigga was talking to another bitch, I was whooping both of their asses.

Kase walked out the room no longer holding the child. "I still can't believe you did Christine like that." Who the fuck was a Christine? That nigga was having too many bitches for me to keep up with. They came closer into view so I had to back up behind the wall so they couldn't see me. I was glad he left a spot for me in the garage for me to park in or else he would've known I was there and came searching for me.

"I know you said that she was coming and all but exactly what are you going to do if she doesn't?" Kase inquired.

"I haven't thought about that just yet." They both took a seat on the sectional, and I popped my head out further so I could hear their conversation better.

"So, what's up with you and shorty though?" Kase blurted as he rolled a blunt.

"Who?... Unity?"

"Nah, what other chick are you dating for him to call shorty?" I mumbled, rolling my eyes.

"Damn, yo, that's crazy 'cause that girl Nix I was talking to had a homegirl named Unity. Wonder if it's the same chick." Reapa pulled out his phone and showed it to him.

"This her?" I was still hung up on the fact he just said *was*, like when did he and Nix break up? Maybe that's why she stood me up earlier. I had to check on my girl as soon as possible.

"Hell yeah," Kase replied with a chuckle.

"Small world. But me and her we cool for now. Surprisingly, I think shorty snatched a nigga's heart and shit while I wasn't looking," he admitted, placing the blunt up to his lips.

"Awww," I said out loud and had to quickly cover my mouth.

"What the hell was that?" Kase asked, standing to his feet. Seconds later, there was a knock on the glass window to the backyard. Standing outside was the same chick that bumped into me earlier. Reapa and Kase headed over to the door, sliding it back and stepped outside onto the patio.

While both of their backs were turned, I snuck down the stairs, easing a little closer so I could see what was going on. "Where's my son?" she cried.

"Don't worry about all that, just know he's safe," Reapa answered.

"Okay, you got me here, now what?" Reapa took a few steps toward her, and with every step he took, she took one backward. If she kept on going, she was going to fall into the pool.

"I just want to know who that nigga was that you was with when you took my shit." Reapa reached behind his back, pulling a gun out. He cocked it and just held it in front of him, waiting for her to respond.

"It was Axel!" she shouted. My mouth fell ajar. There was only one Axel that I knew and that was Nix's.

"As in Harper's brother, Axel?" Kase quizzed her, and she nodded.

"But he forced me to do it! Look at my fucking eye, he did that shit," she wept. All I could see was the side of Reapa's face, and from the part I could see, he showed no emotion as if he didn't give two fucks.

"You got a mind of your own. Can't nobody force you to do shit, Ava," Reapa stated calmly. "Like I said, you take something of mine, and I take something of yours." His hand rose, and for a brief second, she and I locked eyes. His gun went off sending a bullet straight into her forehead. Her body went crashing into the water and tears came to the brim of my eyes as I gasped.

I must have been too loud because both Reapa and Kase turned toward me at the same time. The look in Reapa's eyes was so terrifying that I almost shitted bricks. As he slowly walked in my direction, I tried to back away but bumped right into the sectional. Just my fucking luck that I was now caught like a mouse with my back against the wall, and they were two hungry cats ready to eat me alive.

"Let me guess; you just saw all that," Reapa said, nearing me. I looked down at the gun in his hand. All I could think about was, that my life was over. If he just killed that girl, what would stop him from murdering me, if I just witnessed the shit? I may not have hung out in the streets, but I still knew that one code: no witnesses. "Why are you running from me?" he had the nerves to ask.

"Y-y-you just killed someone, Miles," I stammered.

"I may have left out a few minor details about myself." He placed the gun down on the end table beside him, but that still didn't mean he wouldn't hesitate to kill me. "You don't have to be afraid of me, bae. I would never do anything to hurt you," he reasoned. But there was no way I could actually believe what he was saying; not after he just killed that girl the way he did. Like, how could someone just take another's life so easily like that? I saw no remorse in his eyes, and I was pretty sure he wouldn't have any remorse if he pulled the trigger on me. Reapa once loved her, right? So, he should've felt something after murdering her the way he did.

"Please don't come any further," I cried, as I placed my hand on his chest to stop him. The look in his eyes was so disappointing. Just imagine how I was looking though. All the shit that girl said to me seemed to be true. The man that I had given my heart to, was a cold-blooded killer. How was I supposed to take that?

"I'll just let you handle that. I'm going to take little man and get going," Kase announced. As he was walking by, I couldn't help but to keep my eyes on him and stand incredibly still. One false move could cost me my life.

"Look, I never meant for you to find out about that side of me this way. I know you might be thinking I'm a fraud and all that other shit. I only withheld information from you 'cause I didn't know how you were going to react to it. Ava deserved to die. What she did was foul as fuck. As long as you don't do any cross shit, then you don't have to worry about me doing anything to you." In my book, no one deserved to die no matter what the hell they did.

"Are you God! Who are you to say who deserves to die and who doesn't!" I couldn't believe he actually had the fucking audacity to sit there and play like he was a good man all of this time. "So, that man falling from that building... that was you too, right?"

"Yeah, I did it. He also had a good reason to die as well." He shrugged without a care in the world.

"What the fuck is wrong with you!" There was no way to tell exactly how many people he had killed, and honestly, I didn't really want to even know. But, one thing's for sure, I wasn't trying to be next on his hit list.

"This just me. So, fucking what if I come with extra shit. I'm still going to be me at the end of the day. You either going to love and accept me or be against me. What I can promise you is that you will never have to see anything like that again. Why do you think I tried so hard to hide that part of my life from you? You're a good girl, Unity, and I want you to stay pure and green to the street shit," he explained.

"Oh, trust me, I will 'cause I'm not sticking around to turn bad. I can't be with someone that can kill someone else so easily. The look on your face when you pulled that trigger was pure bliss. You seemed to be enjoying every bit of it, and you never once blinked an eye. Like, do you not feel some type of remorse for killing a woman that you once loved?" I quizzed him as I felt the tears still streaming down my face. He reached out and wiped them away. Surprisingly, I didn't stop him.

"I never loved Ava. Sure, I had love for her, but I never loved her." He acted as if that was supposed to make everything so much better.

"I can't believe I fell in love with a fucking killer." I mumbled, walking away from him with my arms folded underneath my breasts. The crazy thing was the fact that I was still there. Why hadn't I run out of there screaming after seeing him murder someone right before my eyes? That would've been the logical thing to do.

"Wait, what did you just say?" he asked, running up behind me. Reapa grabbed me by the forearm, spinning me around where I was facing him again.

"Nothing," I lied. I didn't want him to know that I had fallen in love with him; especially not now. It was too embarrassing to admit. I wanted to love him, and I wanted to be with him. It just was something that wasn't humanly possible.

"No, I heard you loud and clear. You don't even have to repeat yourself. What's funny is how you promised to be my calm in my stormiest of days. But, just as soon as things get tough, you want to bail on a nigga and shit. Wassup with that?" he queried with a raised brow. Yeah, I did promised him that, but that was before I found out what he did for a hobby. What woman in her right mind would want to stay with a man that could possibly kill her ass at any moment? I could come in one day, and this nigga could be in one of his moods. He could just shoot me between the eyes for nothing; no warning or anything. I think I'll just pass on that.

"I know what I said."

"Well, what's different now besides you know I'm a street nigga at heart? I swear I will never do anything to harm you. I fell in love with you, Unity," he confessed. The twinkle in his eyes told me he was telling the truth, but I still couldn't be too careful.

"I think we need some time apart for me to think on things. I got a job offer to go on tour for four months. I think it's best I take it." I turned around and headed for the kitchen so I could go out of the garage door.

"So, it's like that?" he asked, treading behind me.

"Just please give me my space, Miles. That's all I ask." Once I said that, he stopped following me. I went out the door and climbed into my car. As soon as the door shut behind me, I broke down. Falling for Reapa was probably the worst mistake of my life. It wasn't like I could just turn my feelings off for him like it was a light switch. Maybe being away from him that long would help me sort out my feelings and see if being with him is really worth the risk that I'm willing to take.

Nix

*A*fter that stunt Kase pulled, I really didn't too much want to be bothered with anyone. I was going to go back over to my mother's house, but we weren't on good terms because of that nigga. I just wished I had listened to her when she said he wasn't shit. Well, those weren't her particular words, but she should've said it like that. It's crazy how a mother's intuition is always right. It's like they can just sense the shit. I went over to my mother's house to see if we could talk. In that moment, I decided I would never put another man before my mother ever again; no matter how good his dick might be or how deep in love I may be. The shit just wasn't worth the hassle.

"I'm sorry," I wept just as soon as she opened the front door. She didn't even say anything; she just pulled me into her motherly embrace. It was so crazy how she always seemed to be correct about everything. For once, I just wished she would be wrong. "You were right. I should've just listened to you and left Kase alone. Now look at me... I'm heartbroken," I sobbed. She gently pushed me back by my shoulders, then gripped the sides of my face. She stared deeply into my eyes with the exact same subtle brown eyes I had.

"I've learned that I just have to let you make your own mistakes, Phoenix. But one thing is for sure; you didn't lose me. I'll always be your mother, and I will always love you no matter what choices you may make in life. No matter how much I try, there just is no way possible that I can stop you from getting hurt. It's just a way of life. The only thing I can tell you is to learn from your mistakes, baby." She kissed me in the middle of my forehead, pulled me into the house, and then shut the door behind me. That man sat there and lead me to believe that he loved me; when the whole time he was just using me for sex. What other explanation could he have to break things off with me out of the blue? I really thought that we had something real. For once, I assumed I was going to be happy.

My mother took me over to the sectional. I laid down with my head in her lap as she stroked and played with my hair. "Everything will be just fine, sweetheart," she assured me. "Just fine; watch."

∞ ∞ ∞

I woke up in the middle of the night; not feeling any better about what happened earlier. The day's events had drained the life out of me. I pulled myself up from the couch and tossed the cover off of my body. I stared down at my phone on the coffee table, and it was lighting up with missed calls. Not even wanting to be bothered with anyone at the time, I powered my phone off and then headed for the front door. I would've told my mother I was leaving, but she was probably asleep considering how late it was.

I wandered the dark streets with no destination in mind. There was so much on my mind, and so many things I needed to get off of my chest. As a taxi was passing by, I flagged it down and hopped in it. After telling him where I was going, I relaxed back in the seat just watching the city pass us by. When we pulled up to the big beautiful house, I paid him his money and climbed out of the car. Hatred filled my mind, heart, and soul. Leaning down by the front door, I picked up one of the red bricks that surrounded the small garden that lined the front of the house.

"YOU AIN'T SHIT, KASE!" I screamed, tossing the heavy brick straight through Kase's living room window. His alarm system started going off like crazy, but that didn't scare me away. When I went over there, I was on a mission. And, that mission was to fuck his ass up for hurting me. I wanted to cause him the same pain he caused me.

"I'M TIRED OF THIS SHIT!" I tossed another brick into the long window that was beside his dark wood front door, and then I tossed another one into the window on the opposite side. "YOU AIN'T SHIT!" I was taking out all the anger I had built up inside of me, out on his house. It was the resentment that I had toward him, Axel, myself, any other person that may have hurt me in the past and whomever I may allow to hurt me in the future. I was sick and tired of every damn thing, and I just wanted the pain to go away—just throw my whole got damn life away.

His front door flew open, and he raced outside. I lunged a brick at his head, but he ducked so it missed. Just his luck because I was aiming to take the muthafucka off. "What the fuck is wrong with you! Got damn, Phoenix!"

I stood there, gazing at him with my glossy eyes, not saying a word. I hated I loved him so much in so little time. Kase slowly eased toward me afraid, that I might knock his ass upside that big ass head of his with the brick in my hand. "Put the brick down, babe," he coached, still inching my way.

"You fucking had me thinking what we had was real. I really thought you were going to be different, but you turned out to be exactly like Axel. Why the fuck did you pursue me if you knew you were going to break my heart? Why not just leave me alone? I fucking hate you, Kase," I sobbed.

Kase furrowed his bushy brows, tucking his juicy bottom lip securely between his teeth and bit down on it. That smooth, milky, caramel handsome face stared down at me the closer that I allowed him to get. I couldn't deny the fact that he was a ladies' man. Those ink-black waves always made a bitch's panties wet. The way he licked his plump lips when he stared at me for a long time was a straight turn on, and don't get me started on that body of his. I could wash my clothes on that firm six-pack he had underneath that tight, fitting t-shirt that he had on.

Kase had finally made it over to me and took the brick from my hand, tossing it to the side. I began pounding him hard in the chest with my small hands. "I fucking hate you, Kase!" I cried. He didn't even say a word. He just stood there and let me use him as a punching bag. I despised myself for even allowing him to get that close to my heart—to only crush it in return. That was a dumb move on my behalf, but then again, I've always worn my heart on my sleeve.

"I know you hate me, bae. I know you do, and you got every right to fucking hate me. I'm sorry, but shit between us just not working right now. I wish things could be better, but they just aren't. That's just life, Nix." He pulled me into his muscular arms and wrapped them around me. I pushed him back off of me.

"Fuck you!" I stormed away from him and headed down his driveway with my arms folded underneath my breasts.

"Nix!" he called out behind me, but I kept on walking. There was nothing behind me that was good for me, so from then on, I was going to keep looking ahead and work on myself. Fuck men and everything they stood for. All they would be and ever be good for is a hard dick and a good fuck.

Kase

The day just kept on getting better and better as it went by. After I dropped Axe off at this orphanage that was around the way, I had come home to relax and take some of the stress off of me behind everything that happened. Who would've thought I would've been awakened from my sleep by Nix, lunging bricks through my got damn windows? That girl just never ceased to fucking amaze me.

I just wished I could've told her what was really going on, but some kind of way, Harper probably would've found out about it. For the time being, I needed for Nix to stay as far away from me as possible until I could get the situation under control. With Reapa's temper, I knew I was going to have to do something quickly with her before she ended up ripped limb from limb. Knowing his crazy ass, he'd probably feed her to Cocaine or some shit.

"What the fuck was all that noise?" Harper asked, coming out of the door, wiping the sleep from her eyes. I wanted to punch her ass in her face when she had shown back up earlier with all of her shit. The bitch had even taken over my got damn master bedroom and she had me sleeping in one of the guest bedrooms. If only I could convince her ass to take her name off of my shit and get the fuck out of my life, but it wouldn't be that easy. Threatening her would be a total waste of time and effort because she already knew damn well, I wouldn't do anything to her for the sake of Baylee, and she was going to use that shit to her advantage.

"Get the fuck back in the house, this shit don't have nothing to do with your ass." She scrunched up her face, scratching her wild head and walked out further into the yard where I was standing.

"This has *everything* to do with me. Like I said a million times before, this is—"

Before I knew it, I had her little ass yoked up. My hand tightly wrapped around her neck and her feet dangled in the air as she struggled to breathe with tears sitting in the corners of her eyes. "I swear to God, if you say that *my* bullshit again, I'm going to snap your fucking neck," I cautioned. How the fuck could I have been so careless to have put her name on almost every got damn thing I owned?

"I'm only fucking tolerating your ass 'cause of Baylee. You do know that right?" She slowly nodded. "You going to stop with all this bullshit that you been carrying on with and shit. I already got enough shit on my got damn plate as it is." I was going to have to get a lawyer or something to look at the deeds and see if there was any way I could get her name off of everything since she wasn't willing to do it on her own. There just had to be a way around the shit.

I sat her down gently on her feet. Her eyes peered at me with hatred. If only she knew, the feeling was mutual. Once she had the feeling back in her neck, she turned looking at the vandalized house in awe. "Which one of your bitches tore up my shit?" When she realized the word, *my* slipped her lips, she ran into the house with me right on her ass. I was getting really fed up with her and her bullshit.

"I swear to God, I'm going put my foot so far up your ass, it's going to come out your got damn mouth. Your ass isn't going to be able to say the fucking word *my* ever again," I warned as she shut the door in my face, attempting to slow down my pace. Ever since I had been with Harper, I had never laid hands on her, but she was really pushing it. "Bring your ass back here, Harper!" I bellowed, kicking the front door right off the hinges. I was just that fucking mad. My anger was enraging me, and I was turning into someone I tried to keep buried deep inside me. Harper knew it, and that's why she was trying to get as far away from me as possible.

She jetted up the stairs, and I flew behind her. Harper disappeared into Baylee's bedroom and quickly shut the door behind her. I kicked that door in, as well, without even thinking. Most people had only known the sweet side of me, but the streets knew the beast I kept within. Harper was about to come face to face with the muthafucka for the second time in her life since she'd known me. That was the reason I always tried to remain humble when it came to certain shit. Dealing with possibly losing Nix forever, all because of her, was fucking with my mental. Even though I wasn't trying to, I was falling for her crazy ass and hard.

When I walked into the room, Harper was holding a sleeping Baylee, rocking her in her arms. The closer I got to her, I could see terror written all over her face. "Wake up baby," she cooed into Baylee's ear without taking her eyes off of me. "Come on baby, wake up. Pleeeeaaaassseeee wake up," she pleaded, and Baylee began stirring in her sleep. As I finally stopped in front of Harper, Baylee's little beady eyes fluttered open and she stared right up into my face. "You wouldn't dare do anything to me with her in the room. So just go, Kase."

Harper thought she had outsmarted me, but Baylee wasn't going to be there to save her ass the next time. Taking a deep breath, I calmed myself down and let my shoulders relax. I looked toward the door that was barely hanging on to the hinges. I realized that the front door was probably looking the same way as well. There was no way we were going to be able to stay in this house with the windows and shit busted all out.

"Pack your shit," I said, heading for the door.

"You can't put me out!" she shouted behind me. I ran my hand down my face. This bitch was clueless as hell.

"How the fuck are you going to stay in a house with no windows downstairs and the got damn door kicked in, Harp?" Shaking my head, I left out of the room to go make a quick call. I had to get someone over here as soon as possible to get this shit fixed. First thing in the morning, I was going to get me a lawyer. Harper's ass had to fucking go.

Reapa

*I*t had been a couple of days since I last heard from Unity. And, if the truth be told, I was going fucking crazy. She asked me for some time, and I was trying my best to respect her wishes, but staying away from her was driving me completely insane. Then to top it all off, she sprung some bullshit on me about taking some job.

What I wanted to know was how come she hadn't brought it up to me before? It was as if that was her plan all along, and she was just waiting for me to fuck up so she could catch the first thing smoking out of New York. I was never the type of nigga that would stand in the way of someone else's dreams and shit, but the thought of Unity leaving and not coming back wasn't sitting too well with me.

All I could think about was how she said she had fallen for me. If I would've just been straight forward in the beginning about my street life, then maybe I wouldn't be in the predicament I was in. Now, I had to deal with the fact that she doesn't trust me, and she probably doesn't want to be with me anymore, all because of my selfishness. There was a thought in the back of my mind that was telling me to just tell her, and maybe she would understand. But then, I had a gut feeling she wouldn't. She didn't seem like the type of person that would go for a street nigga, and that's exactly what I was—a hood nigga in expensive clothing.

Maybe that's why I was so drawn to her; because she was different. I was so used to those plastic clone, want to be gold-digging, Barbie bitches. Unity was a breath of fresh air for me. She was showing me that not all women were the same, and maybe I could trust another female again; even after the fucked up shit Ava had done. My stupid ass just had to go and fuck shit up for myself by withholding the truth. And, if I wasn't able to get her back then I was just going to have to live with that.

I couldn't focus for shit. No matter what I was doing, she was always crossing my mind. Little simple shit was reminding me of shorty and I just knew I needed to see her before I ended up going any crazier than I already was. After popping up at her apartment and her not being there, I went over a couple of blocks to her grandmother's building to see if she was there. As I climbed out of my Lambo, she was coming out of the building. When her eyes landed on me, a scowl crept up onto her face. I knew she wasn't pleased to see me, but I was happy as fuck to see her little ass.

"What are you doing here, Miles?" She let out a sigh.

"I needed to see you," I said, posting up on the side of my car. She diverted her attention to the colorful leaves blowing on the ground.

"I don't know what for, I asked you to give me some space."

I pushed myself up off the car and went over to where she stood. I lifted her face up so that she was staring directly into my eyes. I grazed the tip of my thumb across the beautiful freckles that lined her face as my eyes poured into hers. "I know what you said, Unity, but I just wanted to let you know I was sorry for hiding that part of me from you. As you can see, I had a good enough reason to do it," I went on to explain. What was wrong with me? I never felt the need to explain anything or apologize to anyone before; yet, here I was apologizing to Unity. I guess she had a deeper hold on my heart than I was leading myself to believe.

Her eyes filled with tears. She quickly turned her face away from me, thinking I hadn't seen them, but she had to be quicker than that. "I took the job. I'm leaving in a week. Consider this as my resignation from the gym. I can't be with a liar, Miles. If you hid that from me, then you'll hide anything from me." Unity shoved her hands into her front pockets and walked off.

"It's like that?" She didn't even look back. She just kept on walking like I wasn't talking to her.

Unity

*R*eapa was never going to understand where I was coming from. He may have looked at what he had done as just keeping something from me, but I was seeing it as a complete lie about who he was. He had this whole perception of some fantasy man, and he made me fall in love with a fake. Things would've been so much better if he would have just been honest with me from the start. Honesty was the only safe ground to stand on, right? If he had lied to me about something so simple, he just might lie to me again. And, I'd rather save myself the heartache.

When I left his house the other day, I called and told Keke I was going to take the job. It was going to be hard leaving my grandma behind for four long months, but I knew she would be in safe hands. Nix promised me she was going to go over and check on her every chance she got, and make sure she had everything she needed. At first, I wasn't so dead set on the idea because of the way that Nix had been the last couple of days.

Someone needed to check on her ass as well. So, I headed over there to make sure she was okay. Things between her and Kase weren't going too great. I guess that's what both of us get for thinking that everything was going to be all rainbows and unicorns when we fucked around and fell for the wrong men.

"Nix, open up the door!" I yelled pounding on her front door with my fist. I needed to check on her anyway since I hadn't heard from her ass all day. Usually, she would've called me. So, when I didn't receive that phone call, I already knew something was up. "Nix!" Just as I was about to hit the door again, she swung it open, looking like Celie from the Color Purple.

That ho's hair was in two nappy ass braids, sticking out like Wendy from the Wendy's commercials and shit. She had on a big ass shirt that swallowed her skinny ass whole, shorts, and UGG boots on her feet as if it was snowing outside. "Oh, no baby. What are you doing?" I asked, looking her up and down. Kase had really taken a toll on my bitch. The last time I saw her like this was... uh, never. And, I thought I was the one having a bad day.

She didn't even say anything. She just walked away from the door, so I invited myself inside. Homegirl had to be going through some shit if she was walking around looking like that. "Bitch, have you seen your head?" I scrunched up my face, shutting the door behind me.

"No," she dryly replied. Nix plopped down on the lime colored sectional, picking up her phone from beside her. "I been trying to avoid mirrors. Them bitches haven't been my best friend lately."

"Well, I'm one mirror you can't avoid, and you need to do something with that shit. Then, what's up with you and them boots? You act like it's cold outside or something. I mean damn, I know it's leaves and shit on the ground, but it ain't that fucking cold out, Nix. I know your stanky ass feet sweating in them got damn shoes."

Nix sighed deeply, "What do you want, Unity?"

"Damn, if I didn't know any better, I would think you don't want to be bothered with me." I pouted as I flopped down next to her and laid my head on her shoulder. She moved quickly, causing my head to fall back behind her.

"Because I don't," she confessed. Both of us were going through some shit but I at least thought that maybe she would at least want to hang with me before I left. We were going to be apart from each other for four months. That would be the longest time we hadn't seen each other. Of course, I was going to FaceTime her every chance I got, but it wasn't going to be the same.

"You're in a bitter ass mood today, and I thought I was having a bad day." I dug down into my pocket and pulled out my MAC lip gloss. I could feel my lips getting chapped.

Nix finally put her phone down and looked at me. "Of course, I'm bitter. That nigga toyed with my fucking feelings, Unity. He led me to believe I could've had something real with him, only to toss me to the side like I was trash. He had me going around playing house with him and shit when he knew he still wanted that bitch."

"Real niggas don't play house; they build them," I told her, hoping that it was going to somewhat make her feel somewhat better. I hated seeing her like this. Cheerful Nix needed to come back. "I refuse to sit here any longer letting you feel sorry for yourself and shit. If that nigga can't see what the fuck he got in front of his face, then fuck him. It's plenty more niggas in the sea and you a bad bitch, so it won't be shit for you to get another one," I made known. I was sitting here trying to convince her of something when I needed to be doing the same thing for myself. But it was just like me, always putting other people's needs before my damn own.

I got up from the sofa and headed for her bedroom. I went over to her all-white vanity with diamonds going around the mirror and grabbed her comb, brush, flat irons, hair grease, edge control and damn near whatever the hell I could find that I thought would be able to tame that shit on her head. Then, I went back into the living room.

"What you about to do with that?" she questioned with an arched brow.

"I'm 'bout to do something to that nappy ass shit on your head. What the fuck you thought I was 'bout to do? Comb my pussy hair?"

Nix

I felt like I had been away from work long enough. My mother was tired of me moping around the house and not doing shit, so she forced me to go to work. If only she understood that I didn't want to go there because I didn't want to bump into Kase. But I was pretty sure she wasn't trying to hear it. That woman was not bullshitting with me. She woke me up early, got dressed and took me to work her damn self. Trust, I had an attitude the entire ride there.

"Breakups are a part of life, Nix. You have to go back to work sooner or later, and I'd prefer sooner. If he's in there, then just ignore him. Just because he owns the building doesn't mean you have to put up with him." She gripped me by the sides of my face and planted a kiss in the middle of my forehead. "Love you." I rolled my eyes to the ceiling and climbed out of the car.

Standing on the curbside, I stood there looking up at the building. There was a time when I loved coming to work, especially to mess around with Unity. But, she wasn't even there anymore to make my rainy days better. She may not have known it, but I was in my feelings about her taking that job offer and leaving me behind. Don't get me wrong, I was proud of my bitch though. She worked her ass off for that shit, and things were finally paying off in her favor. Now, if only things would start looking up for me. Blowing air from my lips, I headed inside.

After putting my belongings in my locker, I went to the front to get my first client for the day. I was sure I probably didn't have a list since I hadn't been there in days. So, I was just going to wing it. "I'll take all the walk-ins," I told Jessica, walking around the desk, taking a seat in the empty chair beside her. She didn't even reply which probably was the best thing for her considering the way I was feeling. That ho always wanted to get smart and shit. I'll been done dragged her ass all up and down this got damn gym.

The day felt like a drag since I didn't really have anyone to act a fool with. I kept finding myself checking my phone over and over and it was like the time was at a standstill. As I was scrolling down to call Unity, I passed by Kase's number and stopped on it, letting out a deep sigh. I didn't know why it was even still in my phone like I was hoping he would eventually come to his senses or something. Why did I let him get me to that way? I was a strong chick, but it was like he was my fucking weakness. "Fuck," I mumbled with my finger lingering above the call button. "Your mind is stronger than your fingers, Nix. Put the fucking phone down," I told myself.

"You talking to yourself?" Jessica asked, grasping my attention.

"Bitch, don't act like you don't talk to your damn self every now and then. Fuck out of here!" I snapped.

"It was so peaceful without your loud ass mouth here the last couple of days. You need to take your ass back to wherever you were at and stay there," her white ass said, filing her fingernails. She better tread lightly because with the way I was feeling, I would have taken that filer and shoved the shit up her ass. I was trying my best to tell myself to count to ten in my head, but the shit just wasn't working.

Slamming my hand down on the desk, I pushed up out the chair and glared directly down into her eyes. I was pretty sure my nostrils were flaring like a bull. "Look bitch, I will fuck your white—"

"PHOENIX!" Kase bellowed, catching my attention. Not wanting to deal with him I decided to move around him.

"This shit isn't over with ho," I warned, mushing her in the side of her head and stormed from behind the desk. I couldn't even get far because Kase gripped me by the forearm, stopping me. I quickly snatched it away from him.

"I know you're mad at me, but you don't have to take it out on everyone else."

"Fuck you and that bitch!" I huffed. I don't even know why he was trying to act all concerned and shit anyway.

"Wish I could explain things to you. Just trust me alright?"

"Trust you?" I laughed. Any trust and respect I had for that nigga came out his busted windows last night. "Go play with another bitch life 'cause I'm not the one." I chucked him the deuces and walked off. Spinning around on my heels, I said, "Oh yeah, I quit." And shot him the bird finger before busting out the front doors. Little did he know, when I lost feelings, they didn't come back. I'll act like I didn't know you in a heartbeat.

When I stepped out the taxi down the street from my building a woman was standing on the curb. Something about her felt so familiar and the closer I got to her, I wanted to push her ass off into moving traffic. Let one of those cars drag her ugly droopy faced ass on down the street. "What the fuck you doing in front of my building?"

"I came to see you." She mugged me, folding her arms across her chest.

"Bitch, I don't have shit to say to you," I made known. She wasted her time even coming over here.

"Did Kase break up with you?"

"What's it to you?" I queried, placing my hand on my hip.

"Just answer the fucking question." Being the petty bitch I was I had to say something out the way to piss her off even more.

"Your nigga still be climbing between these legs every chance he gets."

"It's cool; he knows where home is," she had the nerves to smile like the shit was cute. Ho, I'm forever going to get the last laugh.

"Well, bitch do you want to come in there and get him? Looks like he got lost to me. Google maps can't even help the muthafucka find you."

"He in there right now?" Her eyes darted to the door of my building.

"Yeah, come on. Maybe you can pull his ass out my bed since I can't seem to get him out of there." I headed into the building with her dumb ass right on my heels. "He right in there," I pointed at my closed bedroom door. As she was heading to the door, I opened up the closet door by the front and pulled out the wooden bat that my mother kept in there and went behind her.

"I don't see Kase in here," she said, turning around and just as soon as her face turned, it met the end of the bat. "WHAT THE FUCK!" she yelled, stumbling to the floor, holding her busted, leaking chin.

"Don't ever fucking step to me about a nigga again especially not that bitch ass nigga, Kase." I swung on her again and the bat crashed into her ribs, causing her to yelp out in pain. Kase hurt me in the worst way and I was about to take it out on her ass since she was the reason he had done it. Only a fool would follow a crazy person they know don't like them into a building. Like what woman in her right mind would bring another bitch into her shit and she thought shit was going to be all sweet.

"Phoenix!" my mother yelled, catching the bat as I was in mid-swing. If she hadn't come when she did, I probably was going to end up killing the girl. "I'm so sorry, baby," she apologized to Harper as she helped her up off the floor. "Do you need me to call you an ambulance or take you to the hospital?" Harper shook her head, and my mother helped her to the front door. Once I heard the door shut, I slid down the hallway wall and cried my heart out.

Axel

A month later...

*I*t had been a month since Ava and I hit Reapa them. I guess Ava didn't run her mouth like I thought she would because no one had ever come looking for me after we took their shit. "Bruh, you straight?" Butch asked, nudging me, passing the blunt he had been smoking. For a moment, I forgot we were in the middle of a party. Usually, I didn't do those house parties and shit around the hood but some kind of way ended up letting Butch talk me into going.

"Yeah, I'm good; just zoned out for a sec, that's all," I replied. The party wasn't what you would call lit. For one, about fifty people were snug tight in this confined ass space. Somebody's shit was smelling like tilapia and shit. The music was hella wack and the niggas didn't even have any liquor for real. Might as well call this shit a fucking chill back... not even a kick back.

"I had been looking all over for you," Harper said loudly, rushing over to me. Thank God her face finally healed. That muthafucka was fucked up. When I asked her who had done it, she wouldn't tell me otherwise I would've fucked their ass up. Part of me felt like Kase did it since she was back fucking with that lame ass nigga but I had no proof so I just left it alone.

"Looking for me for what?" I asked, blowing the smoke out in Butch's direction since Harper was so damn close to my face like she was about to kiss me.

"Something's not right with Ava. I need you to come with me to check on her," she said. I didn't give a damn about no Ava so I didn't even know why she thought I would jump to go see about the bitch. Ava hadn't been on my radar since she helped me steal that dope and it needed to stay that way.

"What the hell you telling me for? Ava can die and go straight to hell far as I give a fuck." I shrugged.

"Seriously Axe, something's not right. I haven't seen or heard from her in a month and that's just not like her. Can you just please come with me to check on her?" she begged, pulling on my wrist but I wasn't budging. I meant what I said—fuck Ava.

"Ava good wherever the fuck she at, whoever dick she sucking and fucking... I'm straight. You can take your ass over there yourself but I'm not coming."

"Fine!" she huffed and stormed away. Harper was killing my damn vibe, not that I really had much of one going anyway.

"When you going to let me get at Harper's fine ass?" Butch asked and I gave him the side eye.

"The day my mama finally decide she doesn't want to be a coke head anymore." That was one thing I didn't play about—them niggas trying to talk to my little sister. No nigga from the hood or that I ran with could ever step down on her. Call it hating or whatever the fuck you want to call it but fuck nah. They straight on that.

Not long after Harper left, the front door to the apartment was kicked in. The first thought that came to my mind was it had to be the cops. Who else would kick someone's door in with that much force? Everyone's attention had gone toward the door but me... I jumped my ass across the back of the couch already trying to plan my exit out the muthafucka. There was no way in hell I was taking my ass to jail. It had me wondering exactly who party this was for the cops to be busting down the door and shit.

When I glanced over where the door once was, two niggas walked inside dressed in all black with assault rifles. I reached down to my waist where I normally kept my piece and it wasn't there. Not wanting to get killed with the rest of them niggas, I dropped straight down to the floor before I could even get spotted. As I peeked around the couch, I saw Reapa and Kase stroll into the door. Both were holding Glocks in their hands looking like they were about to fuck some shit up. Reapa's face was blank and unreadable as always but from the way Kase looked, I knew he was pissed off about something.

Reapa aimed his gun at the radio that they were using to play music from and shot it instantly, shutting the music off. "I came here for one muthafucka and one muthafucka only. All of you will survive if you just cooperate accordingly." My heart thumped in my chest rapidly as I thought about what Harper had just said not too long ago about her not hearing from Ava in more than a month. It made me wonder if she had snitched on my ass and that's why she hadn't come back around. If I made it out of there alive, I was going to hunt her ass down and put her six feet under where she belonged. Normally, I wouldn't be hiding from no nigga, but they had way more firepower than I did. Hell, I didn't even have my damn strap and I went nowhere without it. "Where the fuck is Axel?" Reapa asked, staring around the room.

No one made a peep just stood there in shock. I was praying in my head Butch didn't snitch on my ass to save his own fucking life. Honestly, I was trying to figure out how he even knew I was going to be at the party in the first place. All that shit just sounded like a setup and just as soon as they left, I was digging into Butch's ass.

"I know y'all hear me fucking talking to you. If someone doesn't toss his ass out and soon, I'm going to start dropping bodies," he warned. Keeping my eyes trained on Kase, he slowly strolled over to where Butch sat on the couch. I quickly ducked back behind the sofa so he wouldn't see me and steadied my breathing.

The sound of a gun cocking could be heard before he spoke. "Where the nigga at? You said he was going to be here, but I don't see the muthafucka."

"H-h-he was just here a moment ago. Must have dipped when y'all kicked the door in. Should've just come in—" Before he could utter another word, the gun went off and blood splattered over the sofa. From where I was sitting, I could see what looked like a tiny spec of brain matter on the floor directly in front of me.

"And we're just getting started." Reapa chortled. "Till someone produces him, niggas going to die. Start searching the rooms and none of you better not move."

I knew the niggas were crazy but didn't know they were that fucking crazy to kill innocent people like that. Well, really, they weren't that fucking innocent but still. I scanned the area, trying to find the quickest way to get the fuck out of there. "Duck, duck, duck, duck, goose, you're it," Reapa said, aiming his gun at a woman's head. Tears shone in her eyes as I was pretty sure she had a flashback of her life.

Seeing a window to the left of me I prayed there was something down there to break my fall as I lunged toward it and went crashing through. Lucky for me, we weren't up that high just on the second floor and I fell on top of an Oldsmobile denting the roof of it. Kase leaned out the window with his gun and fired at me so I swiftly rolled off the hood before I could get hit. The next bullet that had come my way I wasn't so lucky; it grazed my arm. If I would've just went with Harper when she came in there begging me to go, then I wouldn't have been in that shit. But one thing's for sure, I was about to lay Ava's body to rest.

Nix

"Oooh fuck yaasss, right there," I coached Lando as my hand slammed against the dressing room's wall. I was so close to cumming I could feel it. His tongue dipped in and out of my pussy, and my eyes roll to the back of my head. He may not have had the best head I ever gotten but it was close enough. I couldn't go long without getting me a stiff dick or some tongue.

Maybe Unity was right, I did need some type of help for my addiction. It didn't take me long to bounce back to my normal self after Kase's and I split. Going through a breakup is the worst but once you get over the shit you feel unstoppable and that's exactly what I was—unstoppable. Couldn't no one steal my shine, babe. I was shining brighter than the muthafucka sun and doing me without having anyone to fucking answer to. I finally took my mother's advice and decided to just be to myself for a while instead of jumping headfirst into dead-end relationships, and I swore that was the best choice I ever made in life.

When I said that there is a certain level of 'I don't give a fuckness' that will set you free, that shit truly will. I was walking around this muthafucka on a high horse, feeling like a brand-new person. I had to keep telling myself I wasn't built for no regular nigga. I'm way too thorough, it's a down ass nigga out there who needed and would find me when the time was right. Till then, I was just going to be free like a bird. Maybe the better term for it would be that I'm embracing my inner thot. Yeah, that sounds about right.

Lando's tongue rapidly went in a circular motion on my clit, and my body trembled, quickly bringing me back from my thoughts. I couldn't hold on any longer as he ate the soul out of my pussy. There wasn't anything I could grip, my denim acrylic nails clawed the walls as one of the best orgasms I had ever gotten took control of my body.

"Got dammit! I'm cumming!" I screamed out a little louder than I intended to.

Once he was done, he looked up at me with those chestnut brown eyes of his with my pussy juices glistening all over his face. I quickly turned my head away from him. Lando and I were coming close to the two-week mark and I was becoming attached to him, something I wasn't supposed to be doing. Reaching over beside me, I picked up my black slacks and stood to my feet to pull them back up.

"Look, Lando, we need to talk," I spoke up.

He stood to his feet, gripping me by my small hips, pulling me toward him with a smile on his face. "What is there to talk about when I just gave you that fire ass head?"

I rolled my eyes heavenward. "I can't see you anymore; it was fun while it lasted."

He let my hips go, "The fuck you mean?"

"I don't owe you no explanation."

Ever since that shit happened with Kase, I wasn't trying to be in a committed relationship. I'd rather duck that shit like the plague rather than set myself up for another heartbreak. I hated to say it but I adopted commitment issues. I came up with a rule, after two weeks I would stop seeing a guy so I wouldn't get too attached.

"You bitch, you weren't nothing but a jump off anyway!" he spat. From the look in his eyes, I could tell he was lying. It was more to him than he cared to admit.

"What the hell did you think you were?" I sarcastically asked, buttoning my slacks. I brushed my long black hair up into a tight ponytail with my hands. Taking a few deep breaths, I opened the door and stepped out. Amber stood there, glaring at me with her arms folded underneath her breasts. My bright skin turned scarlet red with embarrassment.

"Shit," I mumbled underneath my breath. "Hi, Amber." I smiled, trying to throw her off even though I knew it wasn't going to work. From the looks of it, I was a little louder than I thought I was if she was standing outside the door. The crazy thing about it was, she allowed me to finish. Why didn't she stop me while I was in the act? Let me find out her freaky ass was out there getting off from the shit.

"Don't *hi Amber* me," she mimicked. Shifting my eyes away from hers, I nibbled on my lower lip. From the tone of her voice, I knew this wasn't going to be good. "You couldn't wait until you got home to do that? You were so loud, I had to scare some of the male customers away from the door. You should be ashamed of yourself, Phoenix," she scolded.

"I'm sorry. I promise it won't ever happen again."

"I know because you're fired," she said, then walked away from me.

Lando chuckled and stepped around me, shaking his head. "Fuck you! I don't need this shitty ass job anyway!" I yelled at her.

"Good so you shouldn't have a hard time finding you another one," she shot back not even looking my way.

"Fuck!" I cried, placing my hands on top of my head.

I was lying, I needed the job. After I had quit at *RK Fitness,* I was having a hard time finding another masseuse job, so I just settled for here. Yeah, my mother had money and all that, but I didn't want to be living off of her. I did plan on moving out soon or later and I refused to go work for her at O even though I knew she would without a doubt give me a job there. If I wasn't having such a shitty morning, I would've never called Lando up there in the first place.

All last night I was having a hard time sleeping because my pussy was screaming diiiiiiccccccckkkkkkk. Lando should've had his ass at home so he could've handled the shit like he was supposed to. That was part of the reason he was getting let go. When I wanted the dick, I wanted the shit and didn't want to wait for it. Now all because of some dick, I lost my fucking job. With my head hung low I went to the back room to gather my things, trying to figure out exactly how I was going to tell my mother I lost my job.

After grabbing my belongings, I left out of Saks Fifth Avenue. On my way home I was going to grab one of the biggest bottles of liquor I could find on the shelf and drown myself in it. How I was feeling at the moment, I needed some of Lando's tongue but with the way I treated him not too long ago, I knew that was out of the question. I had to hurry up and find me another boy toy and soon.

Unity

*J*ake placed my mouth guard into my mouth as I stared at the other girl that was on the other side of the ring. So far, things had been going great for me except for the minor sickness I had been feeling. I kind of thought maybe I had caught a bug or maybe it just was all the fast foods I had been eating lately. Being on the road so much, I wasn't able to eat healthy like I did back home. It wasn't like I ate that green to begin with, but I did take better care of my body. Just before I came out, I threw up what felt like my insides. I thought I was just nervous and tried to calm myself down. I couldn't understand what I was nervous about when I was doing so good. I had won every match so far.

"You good?" Jake asked me. I nodded since I couldn't really speak with the mouth guard in. "You got this shit. She may be a little bigger than you, but you can outsmart her." He was telling me something I already knew. The referee walked out in the middle of the ring along with Chantelle.

"I want a clean fight," the referee said. Chantelle's eyes locked with mine and she looked like she was about to eat my ass alive out there, but I put on my best poker face. I wasn't about to let her see me sweat. "You hear me Chantelle? I already know how you get down so keep it fucking clean." He stepped back from in between us.

"You're a pretty little dark-skinned bitch." She smirked, placing her guard in her mouth. I hated whenever muthafuckas said that shit. I swore I was going to try and knock her head clean off her got damn body whenever I got the chance. I scanned the arena with all the screaming and cheering fans. Cameras were everywhere filming the shit live.

Just pretend you're back home, I coached myself. It was something I did before any match. However, these matches were different because they were airing on live TV. I knew my grandma and Nix would be watching because they tuned in to every match I had while I was gone. All I wanted to do was make them proud of me.

Apparently, I wasn't paying attention when he told us to fight because Chantelle had swung, decking me right in the chin. "Fuck," I mumbled, stumbling back a little bit but still held my balance. She tried to swing at me again, but I dodged it. For whatever reason, it looked like I had seen Reapa out in the crowd, so I did a double take. That shit had been happening a lot lately. Even though I had been away from him for a little over a month, I just couldn't take my mind off him. I knew there was no way he would be in Los Angeles, but I got distracted by the fact anyway. I was sidetracked a little too long because Chantelle got an intense kick to my stomach causing me to double over in unbearable pain. Something wet seeped down my inner thighs as I dropped to the floor.

The referee and Jake ran out into the ring over to where I was lying still clutching my abdomen. "Unity, you're bleeding!" Jake frantically yelled. I wasn't sure where I was bleeding but the pain was so treacherous that I had my eyes squeezed shut.

"It hurts... it fucking hurts so bad," I wept, with tears seeping from the corners of my eyes. This wasn't any regular pain I've experienced before after getting hit in the stomach. No, this shit was far worse than that.

"Fuck this shit, I'm taking you to a hospital." Jake scooped me up into his arms and carried me out of the arena. Pretty soon my phone was going to be blowing up with Nix and my grandma calling me to make sure I was okay.

∞ ∞ ∞

I woke up in the hospital hooked up to a couple machines. All I could remember was being in the middle of a fight and getting hit really hard in the stomach. Reaching over I tried to snatch the cords out so I could get back to the match. It was my first big tour and I wasn't about to miss a fight for anything, not even from being in the hospital.

"Unity, what are you doing?" Keke softly asked. That's when I noticed she was in the room.

"I have to get back to the fight," I anxiously told her.

"The match is over because you had to forfeit," she explained. She walked to the bed with a somber expression on her face. "How come you didn't tell me you were pregnant? If I had known—"

"Wait, what? PREGNANT!" She had the wrong somebody because I wasn't pregnant.

"Yes... pregnant Unity. You were a month pregnant."

"W-w-were? As in not anymore?"

Keke sighed deeply before sitting down on the edge of the bed. "When Chantelle hit you in the stomach, she caused you to have a miscarriage. If I had known you were pregnant, I would've never had you out there fighting in the first place." Everything she was saying was going in one ear and out the other. I was still stuck on the fact she said I was pregnant. A life was growing inside of me for a month and I didn't even know it. How did I not know? I could feel vomit coming up so I pointed over at the trashcan. Keke hopped up from the bed and rushed over to grab it. By the time it reached my face, I puked.

Not that I wanted a child in the first place, it still had me in a fucked up headspace that I lost it. "I have to fly out to New Mexico. I was supposed to been gone but I wanted to stay behind to make sure you were okay." She placed the trashcan down on the floor beside the bed.

"So, what does this means for me?" I queried afraid of what her answer might be.

"You go home, Unity. That's the rules. Even though it wasn't your fault you had to forfeit, a forfeit is still a forfeit." She picked up her things off the recliner and headed for the door. "Call me if you need anything," she said then left. I lost a child and my dreams were crushed all in one night. I wasn't too sure how I was going to come back from this.

Harper

*A*xel didn't want to come with me to check on Ava... fine. I was just going to do it by myself. He was so distracted that he didn't even feel me pull his gun from his waistline. Yeah, there were a few times before when Ava disappeared, but she always showed back up. This time shit just didn't feel right. A month was too damn long. I had been calling her phone and getting no answer. Finally, it got disconnected that's why I was so eager to get him to come with me to check on her.

Usually, whenever she didn't come to the house she would go over to her sister, Christine's. Unbeknownst to Axe, Ava had a son. For whatever reason, she didn't want him to know so I never brought it up. I thought maybe she was at her sister's place, but a gut feeling told me something was wrong with my best friend. I wasn't going to be able to sleep good till I checked on her.

When I got there, Christine's truck was sitting in the driveway, but the house was pitch black. I immediately felt like something wasn't right. As I walked up to the door shit just felt off to me. I stood there knocking on it for a good ten minutes, trying to see if someone would answer. Something told me to turn the doorknob so I did, and it opened. Before entering, I took Axe's gun from my purse and took the safety off. The house was so dark and quiet you could hear a pin drop.

"Christine! AJ!" I called out making my way through the house. I went and checked the bedrooms but didn't find anyone. At that point, I wasn't sure what to think. Ava was missing now Christine and AJ. Something definitely wasn't right. Hearing a loud crash coming from the living room, I rushed back up there with the gun aimed not too sure who it could've been or what. If indeed something had happened to them, I wasn't about to let the same thing happen to me.

When I got in the living room, Axe was standing there looking at a picture of Ava and AJ. The way his face twisted all up, I could tell he was pissed the fuck off. I lowered my hand as he turned to face me. "You took my fucking gun and I needed my shit! I could've been fucking killed!" he barked. He snatched the gun from my grips and mushed me in the head.

"I'm sorry Axe but you wouldn't come with me and I was convinced something wasn't right with Ava. I didn't want to come over here and something happened to me as well," I tried to explain. I didn't need him taking his frustrations out on me. Even though he had never put his hands on me before, now I wasn't too sure. He seemed madder than I've ever seen him.

"Where the fuck is Ava? She got some got damn explaining to do. That bitch snitched on my ass then there's this shit." He shoved the very picture into my face he was just looking at. "Did you know about this shit?" he asked with a scowl.

"I mean yeah, big deal that she had a child so fucking what."

"So, you mean to tell me you knew that crazy bitch had my seed and you didn't say shit to me about it?" Axe had me confused. Ava never told me she had a child by him. If she would've then I would have told him. He knew I didn't hide anything from him. I examined the picture closely and for the first time, I saw Axe in AJ. I couldn't believe out of all those years I hadn't paid attention to it. It made me wonder how come she wanted to keep that from him. My brother may had his faults but he was wonderful with kids. I was pretty sure he would have helped her take care of AJ if he had known.

"Axe, I swear I didn't know!"

"Yeah, I hear you. Where is that bitch and my seed?" He shoved me to the side and headed to the back of the house.

"She isn't here, Axe. I don't know where any of them are." The first thing that came to mind was that if she snitched on him, then maybe Reapa had got ahold of her. Lord, please don't let them been done got AJ too. I knew for a fact Kase wouldn't harm a child, but I wasn't too sure when it came to Reapa. That nigga wasn't wrapped too tight.

"If Reapa came looking for me then it only means they got her ass. Swear to God if they did something to my seed—"

"Let's just think positive about the situation," I told him, walking up behind him and wrapping my arms around his torso. As soon as I left there, I was going to find Kase and ask him about it. Hopefully, he would be able to tell me where to find little Axe.

"Both of those niggas are dead," he said, peeling my arms from around him. I just wished that sometimes I had a normal sister-brother relationship with him. He wouldn't even let me show him any kind of affection in his time of need.

"But it was kind of your fault, Axe. If you hadn't talked Ava into doing that bullshit, then maybe you wouldn't be in this mess." When he turned to me, I could see his jaws tightening so I backed up. I didn't want him to swing and hit my ass.

"How the fuck do you even know about that?" He paused for a moment before saying, "Don't even worry about it. Ava has always had a big ass mouth and she wondered how come I didn't want to be with her ass in the first place. I'm going to find my damn seed." With that being said, he stormed out of the house.

"Lord, Ava what have you done?" I questioned, shaking my head and leaving out behind him.

Reapa

I was in the middle of picking up money from my traps when I got a call from Unity's grandmother Justine. The shit killed me when she told me something was wrong with Unity. Her voice was laced with nothing but concern and terror. When I tell you that everything fucking came to a halt... everything stopped. I had to send Kase to finish doing the pick-ups because I hopped my ass on the first plane out of New York after I found out her exact location.

I knew she had to have a hold on my heart, I had never done that before, and it felt kind of weird. With me not really having much of a family, I was basically always working. This was the very first time I thought about someone other than myself. I tried calling the hospital but the stupid muthafuckas wouldn't tell me a damn thing about her. They kept asking me dumb ass questions such as am I kin to her. They were about to make me come tear fucking Cedars-Sinai the fuck up playing with me.

I walked into the hospital straight up to the front desk. "What room is Unity Galore in?" I asked the nurse. She looked up at me with lust-filled eyes and a smirk appeared on her face. Seeing her cell phone sitting on the desk, I picked it up and took a picture of myself then sat it back down. "That's the closest you are going to get to this dick. Now can you tell me what room my girl in or not?" Rolling her eyes heavenward, she typed on the computer for a brief second.

"Room 223."

I wasn't too sure how Unity was going to react once she saw me walk into the room especially with the way things had gone the last time we were together. If she wanted to kick me out after I laid eyes on her then that was fine by me as long as I made sure she was alright. One thing was for sure, if one of them hos fucked my babe up, I was going to go knock their ass the fuck out. When I walked into the room, she was lying in the bed watching TV. Once her eyes landed on me, they filled with tears which concerned me. Since I had been talking to her, this was the first time I saw her break down like that. Something had destroyed her barrier and I was prepared to go on a rampage to make her feel better.

"Miles," she sobbed. Without saying a word, I went over to the bed, sat down on it, and pulled her body into me.

"What happened?" I asked once her crying began to die down.

"I lost it." She sniffled.

"Lost what?" I queried, stroking her hair. She had me confused.

"The baby. I was pregnant and didn't know it." The shit crushed me to find out she had been carrying my seed and lost it. Had I known she was pregnant, I wouldn't have let her leave so easily. I should have never let her leave in the first place. I kind of felt like it was all my fault because I should've never kept my street life away from her.

"It's going to be alright, bae. We going to get through this together," I said, squeezing her tighter. I wanted her to feel that I wasn't going anywhere. No matter how much she pushed me away, I was going to keep coming back. The shit I had with her was the real thing.

∞ ∞ ∞

After staying the night with Unity in the hospital, I brought her home. The entire way from LA she had been silent. I knew losing her child had to still be fucking with her because it was fucking with me. Everything I had planned for the rest of the week was going to be put on hold so I could stay with her and make sure she was straight. Kase could hold down the front by himself while I was away. If he couldn't then he was just going to have to make do because Unity came first whether she knew it or not.

As we sat there on the couch watching chick flicks and shit, I massaged her small dainty feet. Her eyes glistened as she sat there just staring at the TV with a blank expression and her pouty full lips poked out. "The paint peeling off your toes. Where you keep your nail polish?" Yeah, I fucking said it. If it was going to make her feel better, I was about to paint her toes. Shit, I would've combed her hair as well if she wanted me to.

"You can't be serious." She burst out laughing. That was the first time she laughed since leaving the hospital. Getting up from the sofa, I went into her bedroom and wandered around till I came across where she kept her nail polish. Since white was my favorite color, it was the first color I grabbed along with the polish remover.

Sitting down on the coffee table in front of her, I grabbed one of her feet, planting a kiss on the bottom of it. "You about to fuck my shit up."

"Shut up girl and just let me do this. I'm about to hook your shit up like you went to the shop." As I attempted to paint her toes, I gazed up into her eyes. Unity had a shy smile on her face, and I was glad I could make her feel somewhat better than she was. It's crazy how she stole a nigga's heart, the way she had. It was never my intention of falling in love, but I guess sometimes the shit just sneaks up on you. "If you ever tell anyone about this, I'll kill you."

Nix

I found myself at Lando's apartment. I don't know why I went there instead of taking my ass on home but there I was standing outside of his door. With the way I had done him the day before, he wasn't going to want to deal with me anymore, but it was worth a try. Who would turn down this pussy anyway? That nigga would be stupid as fuck to turn this shit away.

Tired of just standing there like a fool, I banged on the door not even caring about the time. It was going on midnight, so I was sure he was still up. "Lando!" I yelled still beating on the door. "Lando!" That muthafucka heard me and I was going to continue hitting his shit till he answered it. Lando finally opened the door up with a smug look on his face.

Pulling my lower lip into my mouth biting the corner of it, my eyes wandered up and down his body. He was standing in front of me with no shirt on and his firm six-pack on display. My pussy purred in my thongs, begging to be freed. I flew into his arms, kissing him deeply and hungrily like it was something I had been waiting to do all day. We didn't kiss long before he pushed me off of him.

"What the hell are you doing? And why are you beating on my door this time of night? Are you drunk?" he asked, staring me right into the eyes. I mean, I had been drinking but not that much. I only had a couple glasses of wine. My definition of a couple was like four or five. He didn't need to know all that though.

"Just 'cause I broke things off with you didn't really mean for your crazy ass to go away." The only reason I was beating his door down this time of night was because I was horny as fuck. It was too soon to find someone else to scratch my itch for me. I tried calling some of the other niggas I used to fuck with but a couple of them cursed me out, some called me almost every name in the book except for the child of God and another threatened me so that was a done deal.

"There's something seriously wrong with you."

"Any other time I just showed up on your doorstep you didn't seem to mind but now you have a problem? Is there a bitch in there?" I questioned, trying to look past him to see if I could spot something out of the ordinary.

"No, you broke it off with me, remember? So, you don't have a reason to be here." He folded his arms across his chest. This nigga was acting saltier than a saltine cracker.

I scrunched my face up, "You're still mad about that shit, huh?"

"You're damn right I'm mad. You wanted to stop talking to me for no fucking reason."

"But I did have a reason," I made it known.

"And what was that?" As his brow went up, the corner of his mouth turned up. He was waiting for me to give him a reason but there wasn't anything that would justify what I had done. I could've told him the real reason why but then he would've thought I was crazy and possibly needed to be in the looney bin somewhere so that was out of the question.

"Can we just forget the shit ever happened and move forward?" I quickly changed the subject after concluding I wasn't about to tell him shit.

"Go home, Nix." Lando shut the door in my face then I could hear the lock click.

"Lando!" I yelled, hitting the door with my fist and kicked it. "FUCK!"

Since he didn't want to be bothered with me, I was going to have to find me a fuck the old-fashioned way at the club or bar. I was sure I would be able to find someone that was willing to have a one-night stand with me.

∞ ∞ ∞

Young Thug's "Relationships" blared through the speakers of club 718. There weren't many men I had seen in there that I even wanted to come close to dealing with. The only people that I knew for a fact could scratch my itch were dead to me. I wanted to be nowhere near them at the moment so one of these niggas were just going to have to do for the time being.

"Got damn, you looking good enough to eat, babe." When I turned around, disgust was written all over my face. Standing before me was Axel. I hadn't seen his scum ass since the day my mother had thrown him out on his ass. Don't get me wrong, he was still looking good as ever. I ran my tongue across my upper lip not even caring if he saw me do it or not.

"What you want Axe?"

"Shit, I been looking for your ass, but you been hard to get up with especially after you started fucking with that nigga," he replied, stroking his goatee. Why out of all the clubs in New York did he have to be in the exact same one I was in?

"Who Kase?" I asked already knowing who he was talking about.

"Who else?" he sarcastically quizzed. I eased a little closer to him, getting a nice whiff of his cologne. That scent always made my pussy gush and tonight was no different.

"I don't fuck with that nigga no more." The only reason I told him I was done with the nigga because I needed someone to take care of my pussy for me. With him standing right here in front of me it seemed like fate so who was I to go against the universe. Weren't they trying to tell me something?

"Is that so?" he queried, snaking his hand down to cup my ass. When he squeezed it, I took a sharp breath. Before I knew it, I was being yanked away from him by a big strong hand. Kase swung on Axel, causing him to fall back into the bar. Nothing but chaos broke loose after that. People were screaming and running, trying to get out of their way. A couple of them had bumped into me almost making me stumble to the floor. All I could do was wonder where the hell Kase had come from. He wasn't dressed to be in the club yet here he was whooping Axe's ass. I can't lie, Axe had got a few good hits in but for the most part, he was losing this fight.

A gun went off in the middle of the club, causing more havoc. For a slight second, Kase stopped beating Axe's face in and looked back at me to make sure I was okay. While he wasn't paying attention, Axe snuck off and disappeared into the crowd. By the time Kase turned back around he was long gone. That was one side of him I had never seen before. Yeah, I knew he was a little off in the head but if that gun hadn't gone off, he probably would've beat Axe unconscious. Or was that his intention all along?.... To kill him?

Roughly grabbing me by the forearm, he dragged me out the club. "Ouch, Kase, that shit hurts," I whined.

"Just 'cause we on bad terms don't mean to have your ass out here acting like a thot and shit. You should've been trying to get your shit together instead of trying to crawl back to that muthafucka." He finally let my arm go as he opened the passenger's side door to his black Range Rover that was parked at the front entrance.

"I'm not going nowhere with you," I said, rubbing my arm. That shit was hurting bad and I was sure there was probably a bruise forming as well. The look in his eyes, was a look I had never seen before.

"I'm not in the fucking mood to play with you. Get your ass in the fucking truck, Phoenix!" he bellowed.

"Okay, damn. Did you really have to yell?" I climbed into the truck and he shut the door. Kase just had to bring his ugly ass along and ruin my fucking night. I wasn't even horny anymore and my buzz was long gone. All I wanted to do was go home, soak in the bathtub, and take my black ass to sleep. "Where we headed?" I questioned when I saw we weren't heading in the direction of where I stayed.

"Shut the fuck up and just ride." He cut the music up on my ass so I couldn't object. The first chance I got, I was getting the hell away from this crazy muthafucka even if I had to jump out the truck and run when it stopped. I didn't really see what the problem was with me talking to Axe in the first place. He was the one that left me to go back to his baby mama but wanted to stop me from having fun. You can't have your cake and eat it too. I couldn't wait to find me a nigga that had more to offer than dick and a fucking headache because Kase was going to be the death of me.

The truck finally came to a halt, pulling me from my thoughts. I looked around and saw we were sitting in front of one of the local project buildings. Everyone heard all the stories about Garden Grove. People could never pay me to come around these parts. I tried my best to stay away from here. Turning the music down, Kase picked up his Glock from his lap and stuffed it down the front of his pants.

"When I get out lock the doors and don't open them up for nobody," he instructed and climbed out the truck. Who the fuck did he think he was talking to me like I was a child? I still locked those doors though with the quickness.

As he strolled up the walkway to the building, a guy dressed in all black came up behind him. I could tell something just wasn't right because he was walking up with his hand in his hoodie pocket and the hood was pulled down over his eyes. I immediately began frantically searching the truck to see if he had another gun in there since he had taken his Glock with him. Kase may not have been my favorite person at the moment but I still didn't wish anything bad on him and if I could stop something from happening then I would.

Reaching under his seat, I found a Nine tucked underneath it. Just as I lifted my head up, the guy was holding Kase at gunpoint from behind. Out of all my twenty-three years, I had never once held a gun before but had seen numerous gangster movies. How hard could it be, right?

Easing the door opened, I slowly shut it and snuck up on him. "Uh huh caught that ass slipping. I been waiting to catch one of y'all asses," the guy said. I never really understood how come men do dumb shit like that when they are about to rob someone. They did all that unnecessary got damn talking. Without saying a word, I took the safety off the gun, aimed it and fired, grazing his arm. My aim was a little off but it served its purpose. Kase quickly turned around with his gun in hand and sent two bullets into the guy's chest while he wasn't paying attention.

"Thought I told you to stay in the fucking car?" he queried, standing over the guy's body, pulling the hood back so he could get a look at his face.

"No actually, you told me to lock the doors." He cut his eyes at me and I shut up.

"Can't believe that you just tried to shoot a nigga for me." I didn't know why he was acting all surprised and shit. That wasn't all I would do for him, but he would never know that though.

"Told you that you didn't know what the hell you had right in front of you." I sat on the bench in front of the building with my butt on the part you rest your back on and my feet on the seat part. I was probably showing my thongs to the world, but I didn't care. Kase pulled his phone out and sent someone a text.

"It isn't even like that; I knew what I had. Promise you I'm going to fix this shit I got myself into then I'm coming back for you," he said, slipping his phone back into his pocket. Did he really think he could put me on hold then come back when he felt like it? Shit didn't work like that.

"Nah I'm good on that." Kase came and sat down in between my legs.

"Please don't be like that Nix," he pleaded, staring up into my eyes. I'd be lying if I said I didn't love that man. I hated myself for it too. Diverting my attention away from his eyes, I saw there was a cut above his brow.

"You need to do something about that cut and stop worrying about me." Not long after a van pulled up. Kase stood to his feet so I knew it had to be somebody for him. "I'll be in the truck," I told him, hopping down off the bench and walking off. I wasn't about to go back down that road with him.

Kase

"Where the hell you been!" Harper shouted just as soon as I stepped foot in the door. Let me find out she had been sitting up waiting for me to come home. She was acting as if we were together and I really had to answer to her. Lord knew I was sick of that ho but there wasn't anything I could do to get rid of her. After having a lawyer look over the deeds and shit finding out that everything was airtight, I just gave up on the shit and decided to ride the wave till I could come across something or she finally gave up and left me the hell alone.

Apparently, that shit didn't happen because here the ho was still in my muthafucking house, eating up all my shit. She kind of loosened up a bit after that scare she had that night Nix had thrown those bricks through the window but lately it was like she was becoming more and more attached. I couldn't have that shit, so I was trying my best to stay the fuck away from the house.

"Harper go find you some fucking business; I'm really not in the mood tonight." It was already late as fuck and I was tired as hell. I had been dealing with Nix's shenanigans all night long then there was the nigga that I had to kill for thinking he could even try me and get away with the shit. If Harper knew what was best for her, she would leave me the fuck alone.

"I just want to know where the fuck you been at all night that's all."

"You want to talk about where somebody been, how about you tell me where you be going once a week when you dip off without a trace and be gone all day?" I questioned with a raised brow. She stood there looking dumbfounded as hell. She really thought I hadn't paid attention to the shit. I just never brought it up because quite frankly I didn't give a fuck. I wished one of those days she would just leave and never come back, but I knew that shit wasn't happening. "Yeah, thought so. Get the fuck out of my way." I politely moved her to the side and made a beeline upstairs to the guest bedroom that I had been sleeping in ever since she brought her ass in my house and took over the shit.

As I stood in the bathroom in the mirror looking at the cut above my brow, my mind drifted off to Nix. The shit she had done for me, no other woman has ever done before. Yeah, her aim may have been a little off, but it was the thought that counted. When I took her home, the whole drive was silent like she was lost in her thoughts. I wanted to make sure she was all right after shooting that guy, so I pulled my phone from my pants pocket and shot her a quick text.

Me: *You good? I just wanted to make sure you were straight before I lay it down for the night.*

After standing there scrolling through her pictures for a good ten minutes and not getting a reply, I said fuck it. The bedroom door burst opened and in walked Harper like she was invited in. "You about to get in the shower?" she queried, standing in the bathroom doorway. I was sure it was obvious since I was in the bathroom with my shirt off but maybe she wasn't that bright.

"What the fuck do you want Harper?" I sighed.

"I just need to talk to you. It's about Ava," she responded. I should've known that was coming eventually. Ava was her best friend and once she hadn't heard from her in over a month, I was positive it would raise some suspicion.

"What about her?" I turned, giving her my undivided attention.

"I know her, and my brother stole from you and Reapa. Did you two do something to her?" she questioned me.

"What you think?"

"I kind of figured that." Her facial expression saddened.

"You also should know that Axe is next," I firmly stated. Her brother or not, I was killing the muthafucka. He wasn't any relation to me, so I didn't give a fuck.

"Please don't, Blake. Why can't you two just get along for my sake?" Did she really just say that bullshit? Harper knew I didn't get along with Axe. Any love or respect I had for her faded after she decided she wanted to blackmail me. So, get along with him? Get the fuck out of here.

"I don't even know why you wasting your breath." My mind was already made up that nigga had to go. Even if I was to change my mind, there was nothing in this world that would stop Reapa from killing him, so buddy was done. She could stick a fork in him.

"Can you at least tell me what you did with Ava's son, AJ?" she quizzed.

"What the fuck do you want to know for?"

"It's Axel's son. Now are you going to tell me or what?" Reapa probably was going to go ballistic once he found that shit out. First thing tomorrow morning I sure as hell was going to tell him. If it wasn't so late, I would've gone over there after my shower but like I said I was tired and all I wanted to do was lie down. It was time for Harper to get the hell out of there.

"All the more reason for me not to. Wherever he's at, he might as well stay; both of his parents going to be dead," I announced, picking her up by her waist and carrying her to the bedroom door. I sat her down on her feet out in the hallway and closed the door in her face, locking it so she couldn't get back in.

Unity

$\mathcal{F}$ inding out you lost a child just did something to you mentally. I hadn't really been myself but Reapa had been a big help. He understood I just wanted to take things slow at the moment. At the same time, I knew he wasn't going to wait around forever for me. I wasn't too certain if I wanted to be with him, but I could also see myself being with him if that makes sense. There was only one person that could help me get a better understanding of the situation—my grandma. I needed to go by there and see her anyway since I hadn't seen her since I been back. I was dreading telling her about the miscarriage. Even though I've talked to her daily I still hadn't told her what really landed me in the hospital.

Seeing how I wasn't going too far, I didn't bother to put on any clothes. My gray sweatpants and white t-shirt just were going to have to do. After throwing on my white Huaraches, I grabbed my keys and headed for the front door. When I pulled the door opened, there was a bouquet of red roses sitting outside of it with a card stuck inside them. The only thing the card read was, *I'm thinking of you, Reapa.* That instantly put a smile on my face. Once I placed the flowers inside on the counter, I left out the door.

As I made my way down the sidewalk, my mind drifted off to Reapa. Maybe I had overreacted a little bit when I found out what he actually did. That girl was trying to fill my head with all types of bullshit to run me away from him but at the same time, Reapa had never given me a reason to think he would hurt me. The way he handled me was so gentle besides when we were in the bedroom. It was like I brought out the softer side of him whenever he was around me.

I let myself into my grandma's apartment. When I stepped in, she was sitting on the couch watching Family Feud. I snickered a little bit because she used to make me watch that show with her all the time when I was growing up. Come to think of it, we had some amazing times watching it together. "Hey Ma," I finally spoke.

"Hey baby." She smiled, and I went over, taking a seat on the couch beside her. "Wish you would've told me you were coming by, I would have got up and cooked you something to eat," she said.

"No, you're good Ma. I'm not really hungry right now anyway. I came over here 'cause I wanted to talk to you about something." She powered off the TV and turned to me, giving me her undivided attention.

"What's wrong?"

"How did you know something was wrong?" I asked with an arched brow. It was as if she always knew when something wasn't right with me.

"From the twinkle that's in your eye. Now tell me what's going on."

Sighing heavily, I vented to her. "It's about Miles. The reason I had gone to the hospital that night, I had a miscarriage." From the expression on her face, I could tell she wasn't feeling what I just said. Before she could even get in my ass, I quickly went on to explain. "I know what you're probably thinking... no I didn't know I was pregnant. If I had known, I wouldn't have left in the first place. I found out something about Miles that I didn't like which caused me to make the decision out of anger instead of thinking it all the way through. Part of me wants to be with him but the other part doesn't. More and more each day, I get closer to wanting to stay."

I knew he wanted me more than anything. What man would fly all the way to the other side of the United States for a woman, if he didn't give a damn about her? The way he stared at me told me he loved me. People can say they loved you but to me, actions spoke volumes.

"No one's perfect Unity. Everyone has their flaws; Miles has his just like you do. I'm sure you probably do something he might not like—"

"Ma!" I shrieked.

"It's all love baby. But like I said, you probably do things he doesn't like but that wouldn't stop him from wanting to be with you. You're not going to like everything about someone. It's not humanly possible. Baby, if you love that man then you better go get him. Learn to accept and love his flaws or someone else will." I couldn't imagine Reapa being with anyone else. Maybe she was right.

"I have to go, Ma," I told her, getting up from the couch and kissing her on the cheek.

"Tell Miles I said hey." She laughed as I rushed out the front door.

∞ ∞ ∞

I wasn't sure where Reapa was going to be, but I was praying he was home since I had taken my ass all the way out there. As I knocked on his front door, my heart raced a mile a minute. When the door came open, a beautiful woman was standing in the doorway. I mean she was like drop dead gorgeous. Had me feeling some type of way. Her body had so many curves with the picture-perfect flat stomach. The type of body I used to pray for when I was younger while watching the other girls blossom and I was left looking like a sheet of paper.

"Can I help you?" she asked.

"No," I said just above a whisper and left from the door with tears in my eyes. How could he move on so fast though? If he was talking to someone else, why send me flowers? There was a possibility he was just being nice since I lost our baby. Wiping the tears from my eyes, I rushed away from the door heading for my red Volkswagen Jetta. Suddenly, I was grabbed from behind and spun around, coming face to face with Reapa.

"What's wrong?" he questioned, gazing deeply into my eyes.

"I should have never come here; obviously you've moved on," I replied still feeling my salty, warm tears against my cheeks.

"What? Cynthia?" He chortled, pointing his thumb behind him at the woman standing at the front door.

"Uh, yeah duh," I answered. Using his thumbs, he wiped the tears from my eyes.

"She's just my neighbor. I called her over to take a look at something for me. Cynthia is a lawyer and if it makes you feel any better, she's married. I'd never do anything like that to you." That made me feel so much better.

"I feel so stupid."

"Don't. I'm sure any woman would think the same thing if they would've come over and saw a woman here," he explained.

"Miles, I'll just do that for you later because obviously, you have something you need to take care of," Cynthia chimed in before walking away.

"But wassup though?" he asked me after she had left.

"I'm sorry for the way I acted toward you once I found out what you do. I love you, Reapa and I want to be with you; your flaws and all. I have my faults but stick it out with me. I'm working on myself." The tears were still flowing because I was so emotional.

Reapa gripped me by both sides of my face never breaking our trance. "I love you just the way you are but this time there isn't any running away when times get tough. We sticking this shit out. The only way out of this shit is in a casket 'cause you aren't about to play with a niggas feelings and shit," he warned then planted a kiss on my lips. I wasn't certain how I was supposed to have taken that shit.

Harper

"There isn't shit you can do for me behind bars, Donte." I sat there surveying his creamy caramel face as it peered back at me with no expression. He was sitting right where I knew he was going to be soon or later. Donte had become outrageous with that street shit. Hell, he was worse than Reapa and Kase, even if it was possible.

I kept telling him he needed to chill but he did exactly what all niggas do when they got a little clout—let the shit go straight to that big ass head of his. When he was out, he was knocking off people left and right over little simple shit, not thinking about the family he had sitting at home. Yeah, you heard right, I said family. The stupid muthafucka even knocked off our father and told me he did when I asked him about it.

"You been riding with me this long, Harper. Just hold on for a little while longer," he pleaded.

"A little while longer? Are you fucking serious!" His jaws tighten the louder I got with him. This nigga was basically looking at two life sentences and he wanted me to just hold on a little longer. "There was only one rule of the streets," I leaned my face in closer to him so he could hear me loud and clear, "never get fucking caught!"

"You think I don't know that?" he asked with a raised brow.

"Obviously you didn't, your stupid ass got caught!" I stuck both of my hands together, placing them neatly on my lap as I bounced my right leg up and down, chewing on the corner of my lower lip. Donte was getting on my last fucking nerves and quite frankly, I was beyond tired of making that long ass ride up there to visit his ass every two weeks like clockwork.

I should've just stopped making those trips a long time ago. If Kase would've known what I had been up to he'd kill me. Hell, Axel would probably put a bullet in my ass as well. There wasn't anyone else walking this God green earth that he hated more than Reapa and Kase and that was Donte.

"You doing too much. Don't sit right here and act like you didn't already know what was up when you first started fucking with me. You already knew the risks it was dealing with a nigga like me. You were with that bitch Kase when I met you so don't play stupid, Harp," he clearly stated while staring right into my eyes.

I looked down at the beautiful little girl sitting alongside me. She was the perfect mixture of Donte and me, as if someone had mixed us both up in a bowl and poured her out. I knew the shit I been doing was wrong on so many levels, having her confused as shit calling two men daddy. Donte would put a bullet in my ass and set me on fire if he would've known what I had been doing behind his back.

When I first found out I was pregnant, he got caught and thrown in jail. I refused to let my baby grow up without having a father present in her life, so I let Kase believe he was Baylee's father. The stupid fuck hadn't even realized I had been lying to him all along.

It pained me to be lying to my daughter every single day. The trips we were making to see him, she thought we were coming to visit him while he was away at work. It crushed my soul every time she would ask *"how come daddy, Donte loves to work more than being at home with us?"* And I would always tell her the same lie every single time, that he was only trying to make a better life for us. Pretty soon those lies weren't going to be able to work and I was going to have to tell her that her stupid ass daddy killed some innocent people just because he felt like doing it.

"I can't keep dragging Baylee up here every two weeks like this Donte."

"What you trying say?" A vein popped out in his neck and his large hands balled up into fists on the table.

"This the last visit, Donte. We're not coming back," I told him.

"'Cause a nigga fucked up, you want to keep me from seeing my seed? What the fuck you going to do? Have that nigga Kase play stepdaddy?" He frowned.

"You should have thought about that shit before you killed those people." I quickly wiped the lone tear that escaped my eye. On the ride up there when I was contemplating on telling him that, I promised myself I wasn't going to cry. He needed to understand that I was only trying to make decisions on the behalf of Baylee and me. That little girl was the only thing that mattered at the moment.

His eyes set on Baylee and they welled up. It kind of made me feel bad and I began second guessing my choice. *Be strong bitch, you're just doing what you must do.* "Times up!" one of the correctional officers yelled.

"We have to go already?" Baylee asked, looking over at me with her lower lip poked out.

"Yes baby. Go give daddy a hug so that we can go," I told her. Donte hugged me then stood to his feet as Baylee climbed down off the bench and ran around the table to him. He scooped her into his arms, hugging her tightly, nestling his face into her neck. Tears flowed down my cheeks and I swiftly wiped them so he wouldn't see them. Once he sat her back down on her feet, I went over and hugged him as well.

"I'll always love you," I whispered into his ear then kissed the corner of his mouth. That was the truth, I would always love him and I'm sure he knew that. But things between us needed to come to an end especially with me trying to work things out with Kase.

The guard came over and pried him from my grips. I stood there, watching him as he disappeared behind the closed doors. Everything in me wanted to break down and scream but I just had to keep telling myself I was doing it for my daughter.

Kase

*W*hen I got up, the house was empty and quiet. Something told me that Harper had left for her weekly disappearing act. I didn't even need to get up to go and find her because she always left around the same days and time. Shit made me wonder exactly what the fuck she had been doing but she really wasn't my got damn business, so I wasn't stressing it. Since there had been so much going on lately, I had yet to talk to Reapa about my problems. We needed to hurry up and come up with a solution because I was tired of Harper's ass.

I walked into the trap and Reapa was sitting down counting some money. I already knew how he got whenever he was counting so I just sat down alongside him and picked up a stack and began thumbing through it. Once we were done counting, I started telling him what was going on with me. I was pretty sure he probably would know what I needed to do.

"Know I told you about the nigga that had tried to rob me the other night and Nix shot him, well, that shit got me to thinking. I want my shorty back, but I don't know what the fuck to do," I admitted. Reapa cut his eyes at me. I knew he was probably tired of me and my drama with Harper. Sometimes I wished I never met her ass but then I wouldn't have Baylee. That probably was the bullshit I had to put up with for the time being.

"Know what, I'm about to solve all your problems. You can thank me later." He got up from his seat, placing the money in a duffel bag then zipped it up. Pulling his gun from his waist, he checked the clip then put it back. "Let's go."

"Where we going?" I questioned him, getting up and treading behind him.

"Just shut up and follow me," he said, climbing into his Maserati and shut the door so I got into my truck, pulling off behind him. When we pulled up to my house, I was kind of confused. Knowing him, there was no telling what he was about to do so I quickly hopped out the truck. He turned the doorknob and walked straight into the house without saying a word. I was going to kick Harper's ass for leaving my got damn door unlocked and I knew Baylee was in there with her. Anyone could've walked in on them and anything could have happened. She had a brain so why the fuck didn't she use it.

"Kase where the hell was you when I got—" Before she could even finish her sentence, Reapa's big ass hand was wrapped firmly around her throat and she was hemmed up against the wall with his gun at the side of her dome.

"Look, I'm over this bullshit. Kase has let this shit go on for far too fucking long and I'm here to fucking end it." Without taking his eyes off of her, he said to me, "Go get all the deeds and paperwork that she might have her fucking name on and a pen then bring it here."

"She not going to sign it. I already tried to get her to."

"See, that's the difference between me and you, she knows you won't do anything to her ass, but I will." I zoomed upstairs to the master bedroom and grabbed all the paperwork then took it to them. "You got two options. Either your ass going ti sign these fucking papers or a bullet going through your head and Kase going to become a single parent. Your choice," he threatened then took his hand from around her neck. Harper stood there with tears in her eyes, rubbing her throat. That was the difference between us, Harper knew I wouldn't do anything to her because she was Baylee's mother but Reapa on the other hand, that nigga would pull the trigger in a heartbeat. "SIGN IT!" he bellowed, causing her to jump and squeeze her eyes shut.

She picked the pen up in her shaky hand and signed all the paperwork. Once she was done, I put my name on everything along with Reapa. If I would've known that it was going to be that easy, I would've had him do that a long time ago. "Consider this your muthafuckin eviction notice," he said, tucking his gun back in his waistline and heading toward the front door. "You welcome," he called over his shoulder. That nigga just didn't know he made me a happy fucking man. Harper was finally out of my hair for the moment till she found something else to torture me with. Now she was about to go, I could leave and get my girl back, that's if it wasn't too fucking late.

"I want you out my shit by the time that I get back," I told her, picking up the paperwork and jetting out the door. I wasn't about to leave it there with her ass.

∞ ∞ ∞

I pulled up to restaurant 0 and went inside searching for Nix. That was really the only place I knew where to find her other than Unity's place. After she had quit working for me, I didn't know where she went. "What are you doing here?" Olivia stopped me and asked. I didn't know she even knew who I was till then.

"I'm looking for Nix," I told her.

"For what? I'm positive she doesn't want to talk to you," she stated, folding her arms underneath her breasts. Now I knew where Nix got that little attitude from.

"Please just let me talk to her, it's something important."

"I can't let you do that. There's no way I'm going to stand here and continue to let you hurt my daughter."

"It's fine mama, I can handle it," said Nix as she walked up behind her. Olivia rolled her eyes heavenward and left us standing there. Nix headed for the exit, so I went behind her. "What do you want, Kase?" she asked when we made it out the door. Without saying anything, I gripped her by the sides of her face, pulling her lips to mine, kissing her deeply.

"I'm sorry for everything. I wasn't trying to hurt you when I stepped back, but I just had too much going on with my baby mama. She was trying to take everything I owned if I didn't leave you alone since her name was on damn near everything. I got the shit situated now so I'm good," I explained.

"You could've just told me what was going on. I would've understood. If that was the case, I would've gone and whooped her ass till she took her name off everything for you. You didn't have to drop me the way you did; I'm a very understanding person. I just thought you were trying to leave me to go be with that bitch and that shit hurt me to the core," she replied.

"I know, I'm sorry. Do you forgive me?" I asked, gazing intensely into her eyes.

"I forgive you but I'm not going through this shit with you again. Either you going to step the fuck up or step down. Simple as that. My heart isn't shit you can play with. You get it; you going to handle it with care."

"Promise you that you don't have nothing to worry about," I swore. From now on I was just going to be honest with her to avoid any more problems.

"Alright, now take your ass home and get that dick ready for Mama. I haven't had no sex in a hot minute and I'm about to take my frustrations out on you," she said, gripping my dick through my pants, biting the corner of her lower lip. I could feel him bricking up.

"Fuck that shit, you coming with me now." I picked her up, tossing her over my shoulder and carried her to my car. I was about to knock that pussy straight out the frame.

Axel

I had been trying to stay out of dodge ever since I got into it with Kase at the club over Nix and then them having Butch set my ass up at the party. I didn't know who I could trust at the moment. Shit, the only person I knew wouldn't switch up on my ass was baby sister; she was always riding for a nigga.

"I'm never listening to you ever again," Harper whined when she burst through the front door. I hadn't heard from her ass in days since we found out that Kase and Reapa had done something to Ava and took my muthafucking child and now she wanted to come in the house complaining and shit.

"What the fuck you talking about?" I questioned, getting up to help her bring her things inside since she was struggling while trying to hold a sleeping Baylee.

"Your stupid ass plan backfired. I got put out and everything!" she fussed. At the moment, I didn't give a damn about what she had going on. My mind was still trying to process the fact that I had a fucking seed out there somewhere.

"Did you find out where AJ was?" I asked, shutting the door behind her. That was really the only thing I was worried about.

"Kase wouldn't tell me where he was and quite frankly, I don't give a fuck!" I slapped the shit out of her before I knew it. She stood there with her mouth gaped in awe. "Damn, I'm sorry," I apologized.

"I can't believe you actually put your hands on me while I was holding my child at that." Tears poured from her eyes. This was the first time I ever put my hands on Harper. I was letting my anger get the best of me and I was getting out of control.

"You know I didn't mean to." I went to pull her into an embrace, but she backed away from me. "Harper, come on; I said I was sorry."

"You're on your own finding AJ. I'm done with your ass. First thing in the morning, I'm moving out!" she announced, storming off to her bedroom. I would have gone behind her, but I knew it was probably best I just let her cool off before I tried talking to her. If Kase wanted to play fucking games with me then I was going to play them with his ass as well. I was going to cause hell till they got up off my fucking seed.

∞ ∞ ∞

I sat there in the parking lot just patiently waiting for the open sign to switch off and everyone to leave out. What I was about to do, I didn't need any witnesses. Looking up I saw her leading the last couple to the door. She switched the open sign off and dimmed the lights. I climbed out the car and headed up to the door taking a peek through the glass window to make sure I didn't see her before I pulled the door opened and entered, locking it behind me.

Everyone that fucked me over had something coming for their asses. Slowly easing to the back of the building to the kitchen where I knew she was going to be, I pushed the door opened and there she was, standing in front of the sink washing dishes. When she heard the door swing shut behind me, she turned around and her eyes locked with mine.

"What the hell are you doing here?" she asked with a scowl.

"I'm tired of playing games with your daughter so I'd rather just hurt her ass instead," I replied with a smirk. I couldn't understand what Nix actually saw in Kase in the first place. Maybe I should've had a tighter leash on that ass then he would've never got his hands on her. I mean, I wasn't in love with her or no shit, just didn't like the idea of someone else having her and making her happy. Yeah, I was low-key hating and don't give one fuck about it either.

"What are you talking about Axel?" she questioned me. As I neared her, she tried to back up a little but was already pinned against the sink, so she didn't have anywhere to go.

"I'm pretty sure you know what I'm talking about if you just think about it." I eased my hand behind me where I kept my strap, pulling my gun out. When she saw it in my hand, her eyes bucked.

"Axel, get out of my restaurant before I call the cops!" she warned.

"With what phone?" I spotted her phone on the other counter beside the kitchen door when I walked in. By the time she even made a break for it, she'd be dead so that was the least of my worries.

"You're really doing all this just because Phoenix doesn't want you? Maybe if you were a better man, then she just might. I couldn't see how any woman would want your ass!" she spat. I lifted my hand, hitting her straight across the face with the butt of the gun and she fell to the floor. Blood dripped from her mouth.

"Fuck Nix! If I can't have her then no one can. I'm going to slowly break her ass and she will have no choice but to come back crawling to me."

"You're fucking sick!" she seethed, palming her face where I hit her at.

"Maybe so but I don't give a fuck." Lifting my gun, I shot Olivia right in the forehead killing her instantly. I headed straight to her office so I could snatch the security tapes then dipped out the back door where I knew no one would see me leaving. Nix was going to be back before it's all said and done.

Nix

I woke up in one of the best moods ever. My man and I were back together, and it felt like the best feeling of all time. Lying there on my side, I just watched him as he slept. His chest slowly rose and fell with his light snores. That was like the best sight ever and to know he was mine and only mine. Yeah, all that. I never really thought I would be back here in his bed again after all that happened. I swore he had me where I was ready to say fuck love and everything that it stood for. It was crazy because all of this could've been avoided if he would've just told me the truth in the first place.

Climbing over on top of him, I softly planted a kiss on his soft lips and his arm wrapped around my waist. "Wake up it's going on one in the afternoon." I smiled, planting kisses all over his face. I lost count of how many rounds we had gone last night but my pussy sure as hell was paying for it now.

"Just let me sleep a little while longer," he groaned, not even opening his eyes. If he wanted to stay sleep, then that was fine by me but I was not about to waste my day away lying around in bed.

I climbed out of the bed and slipped on one of Kase's t-shirts that were lying on the couch in his room. It smelt like nothing but his expensive cologne so I couldn't help but take a whiff of it as I headed downstairs to the kitchen. Since I was in the best of mood, I hooked my phone up to the Bluetooth speaker that was in the living room and Future's "Selfish" began playing.

I danced my way into the kitchen. With the way I was feeling, I was sure that nothing could ruin my mood. Had I known I would've found happiness like this, I would have left Axel alone a long time ago. That man was toxic beyond measures. They say that once you clear all negativity from your life, things start to look up for you and I honestly believe that's what was happening for me.

After pouring me a glass of orange juice, I leaned back on the counter and just took in my surroundings. I couldn't believe this was actually my life right now. "Why you down here with all that noise when I told you I was trying to sleep?" Kase asked, appearing in the kitchen with a sexy scowl on his face. The music had fully woken him up which was what I wanted in the first place. That man was so fucking

171

sexy to me standing there with no shirt on and in his black Burberry boxer briefs, showing off that massive dick print. I couldn't help but bite the corner of my lower lip. Even though my pussy was sore to the touch, she was yearning to feel him fill her walls up. I could never get enough of that dick—Kase was the dick plug hands down.

"I'm sorry." I grinned, lying straight through my teeth.

"Oh you are, are you?" He smirked, nearing me. My eyes were still locked on that dick that was growing the closer he got to me. My pussy began releasing juices; I could feel them flowing down my inner thighs. Kase gripped me underneath my arms and sat me down on the counter. I put the cup down so it wouldn't spill all over his glossy hardwood floors.

"No, I'm not sorry at all." I ran my hands from his belly button up to his chest, staring him profoundly in his brown eyes. "I love you." It wasn't till that moment I realized exactly how much I loved that man. Of course, I did to a certain extent. I had to chuckle to myself when I thought about that night, I tossed those bricks into his window.

"What's funny?" he asked.

"Nothing," I lied. Kase gripped me roughly by the hips, pulling me closer to the edge of the counter. His hands slid up my back as his lips found their way to the crook of my neck. *Lord, just let this moment last forever.* There was no other place I'd rather be than in his arms. With every kiss he gave, it sent chills up my spine. "I want you," I moaned, spreading my legs wider so he could gain access.

Kase slid his boxers down some, pulling his dick out and eased it inside me. There was no need for any foreplay because my pussy was flowing like a river. I gasped for air when I felt him enter me. Usually, things between us were fast paced but at that moment, he was giving me slow sensual strokes. If I hadn't known any better, Kase was making love to me for the first time. We were finally becoming one. My eyes rolled to the back of my head as I was nearing a climax. Gripping the counter tightly with both hands I prepared myself for the ride he was about to take me on. Right at the peak of my orgasm, my phone began ringing.

"You want to get that?" he stopped and asked, pissing me the fuck off.

"No fuck them. Whoever it is, I'm sure it's not important and even if it is, they'll leave a voicemail." When my phone wouldn't stop ringing, I got frustrated. "UGH!" I screamed as Kase pulled out of me. I jumped down off the counter and stormed over to where my phone was. Unhooking it from the Bluetooth, I swiped the screen, placing it up to my ear without even checking to see who it was. "What the fuck do you want? I was in the middle of something!" I snapped.

"I'm sorry but is this Phoenix Quartz?" the woman's voice on the other end of the line asked. She kind of threw me off because I didn't recognize the voice whatsoever, so I was wondering how she got my number in the first place and knew my name.

"Yes, and who are you?"

"This is Detective Bailey. I'm with the homicide division—"

"Yeah, yeah get to the point," I cut her off, not caring about all the pointless details she was about to get into.

"I was calling to inform you that your mother was killed. I need you—" After she said that, my phone slipped from my grasp, dropping to the floor with me not far behind it.

"Nix!" I heard Kase yell before my eyes closed.

Unity

*J*ust as soon as I heard the news about Olivia, I was heartbroken. Like I had said before, that woman was like a mother to me, so I was hurting behind the shit probably just as bad as Nix. I couldn't grasp who would want to kill her when she was loved by so many people. It was like I was losing another mother and wasn't too sure how to take it.

Poor Nix, I knew she was dying inside because other than me and grandma, her mother was the only family she had. I had to find my best friend and make sure she was okay and not about to jump off a cliff somewhere. Even though I felt like I wanted to break down, I had to be strong for her.

After trying to call her phone for the millionth time and not getting an answer, I was prepared to head over to her house to see if she was all right. Not hearing from her was worrying me and I was pretty sure it was written all over my face. "You good, bae?" Reapa asked, walking back into the bedroom.

"No, Nix's mama got killed and I'm trying to get in contact with her but she's not answering the phone. I'm really worried about her," I told him.

"I think she over there at Kase's. Let me call him for you right quick." I sat there in the middle of the bed, chewing on my thumbnail, waiting impatiently for him to get Kase on the line. "Aye, is Nix over there, Unity trying to reach her?" he asked, diverting his attention away from me. "Alright, I'll send her right over," he said, ending the call then bringing his eyes back to mine. "Yeah, she over there. Want me to take you or what?"

"No, it's okay; I can drive myself." I sat there in silence for a moment, staring into space. I could feel the bed dip a little bit, so I knew Reapa probably had climbed in beside me. Moments later, I felt his arms wrap around my body, pulling me into him. "It just hurts so bad Miles. I looked at Olivia as a mother and now I've had two mothers snatched away from me. Who's next? You? Grandma?" I cried. It was best I got all my tears out before I made it over there to Nix because there was no telling what type of state she was in.

"I promise you that nothing's going to happen to me or your grandmother. Hell, I'd look out for Nix as well if you want me to but I already know Kase got that shit handled. But I know one thing, we definitely going to find out who the fuck did this shit," he replied. Never have I ever wished death on anyone but whoever killed Olivia needed to be dealt with, so I wasn't about to even object to what he said.

"Thank you."

∞   ∞   ∞

"Where's Nix?" I asked Kase when he opened the door. Reapa had insisted that he come along with me, but I knew he probably had things to do today. I assured him I was going to be fine and he didn't need to put his day on hold for me. Plus, Nix and I needed some alone time to grieve.

"She's in the bedroom. She fainted earlier and when she woke back up, she didn't say anything. Just sat there in silence. I don't know what to do at this point," he answered.

"Let me give it a try. Where's the room?" I queried, stepping into the door and he shut it behind me. I followed him upstairs to a closed bedroom door.

"I'll be in my man cave if you need me," he announced, walking off.

Taking a deep breath while trying to restrain my tears, I knocked lightly on the door before pushing it open. Nix was lying in the bed with her back facing me. I felt so bad for my bestie. It was a hard pill to swallow when you lose a parent. A lot of people would say they know how someone felt losing a parent when they still have both of theirs. How could you possibly know how we felt? Losing a parent is nothing compared to losing someone else and that was a known fact.

"Phoenix?" I called out, shutting the door behind me and easing closer into the room. She didn't answer but I also knew she wasn't sleeping. Pulling the covers back, I climbed into the bed behind her, wrapping my arms around her body. When I heard her sniffle, I knew she was crying. "I'm not here to tell you that it's going to be okay 'cause it's not. I'm here to let you know that you're not alone. I loved Olivia like she was my own mother.

Hell, she practically raised me alongside grandma, so I feel your pain, babe." She didn't respond. Whenever Nix was sad, she'd go into a silent state. Kase was going to have a problem on his hands because you weren't going to be able to get her to talk till she was ready to. It really wasn't anything he could do but let her grieve. Everyone grieved differently.

"I can't believe my mama is gone," she sobbed, sounding hoarse.

"Me either but we will get through this together the same way we get through everything," I promised her.

For the remainder of the day, we just laid there in silence in the pitch-dark room while I held her as she cried. Kase kept coming in to check on us till he had to finally leave the house but said to call him if we needed anything. Nix and I were blessed to find two men that loved the ground we walked on. All I could say was that she was going to come out stronger in the end—her and I both.

Reapa

When I went to check on the traps, the last thing I wanted to hear was some bullshit dealing with Kase. The things that I was hearing just wasn't adding up, so I had to call him to meet up with me. I didn't want to tell him over the phone, and he ended up upsetting Nix even more than she already was. I knew he didn't want to leave her side, but he was just going to be gone for a short period then he could get back to her.

With everything that had been going on lately, I hadn't been working out, so I asked him to meet me at the gym while I got a quick work out in. Just as soon as I hit two hundred with the weights, Kase appeared over my head so I put them down and sat up. "What's so important you had to call me all the way over here? You know I didn't want to leave Nix like that, so this shit better be an emergency."

"Word on the street is that you was the one who knocked her mama off," I told him.

"Fuck!" he yelled. I knew he wasn't going to be feeling the shit once he found out, but I felt like it would've been best he heard it from me than off the streets.

"Calm down. There's no need to blow everything out of proportion. I'm sure you didn't knock shorty's mama off. Where were you last night though?" I asked him to make sure he had a legit alibi just in case he needed one. The way that word was spreading on the streets, I was positive the cops were going to be knocking at his door at any minute trying to check into the shit.

"I was with Nix so how the fuck did I kill her mama? When we left, she was fine, so I don't know what the fuck happened," he replied.

"Well, we going to have to find out. Unity hurting behind that shit as well and I told her I was going to help her find out who had killed Olivia. That's a promise I intend on keeping." I may not have known her personally, but I did love Unity and care about her feelings.

"Shit, you think I don't? What I want to know is why they want to say I was the one that had done the shit." He stood there stroking his chin as if he was trying to figure out who could be trying to set him up.

"You got beef with anybody?" I queried, trying to help him rule out a couple people. There was no telling who was spreading them lies but we were going to get to the source of them.

"Shit, I don't know," he responded.

"Well, we going to find out what the hell going on even if we have to threaten every muthafucka in the hood to find out," I promised him. "You might want to tell Nix what's going on as well, so she doesn't find it out from someone else and think the shit is true," I cautioned. I already knew how women minds worked. They quick to believe what another muthafucka tell them especially when they're already hurt to begin with.

"Alright will do."

"Now let me jump in the shower right quick. I'll be over to check on Unity in a few," I replied, getting up from the weight bench and heading toward my office. I hadn't spoken to her since she left the house earlier. I knew she probably needed some time alone to deal with Nix, so I was just trying to give her space.

∞ ∞ ∞

When I had gone over to Kase's, Unity was fast asleep in the bed so I grabbed her and brought her home with me. Kase promised to get her car home later. As I carried her into the house, she was still knocked out. I couldn't help but to stare down into her beautiful face. Honestly, I think that her freckles were her best feature to me. As I laid her down on the bed, I pulled the covers up over her. She had to have been tired as fuck if she had been sleeping all this time.

Just as I was about to leave out of the room, she woke up stretching. "How I get here?" she asked, looking around the room with a confused expression.

"I brought you here. How else did you get here?" I quizzed with a raised brow. Did she think she teleported in her sleep or some shit?

Unity was still looking kind of sad and her eyes were almost fire red. I could tell she had been doing a lot of crying for the most part but that definitely didn't take away from her beauty. I climbed over into the bed with her, lying down and pulling her onto my chest. "How you feeling?" I queried.

"I'm kind of blah. My main concern is Nix. She's not doing too well." She sighed deeply.

"Speaking of Nix, I think you should know this." When I said that, she sat up on me and glared down into my face. "Someone's going around saying Kase was the one that killed Olivia," I told her. When I almost lost Unity, I vowed I wouldn't hold anything else from her, so I told her straight up what was going on.

"Are you serious? I'm sure he wasn't the one that did it... or was he?"

"Hell nah, he was with Nix last night. I'm just trying to wrack my brain, trying to figure out who could be spreading that shit though." It was best we got a handle on the situation before things got way out of our control.

"I'm sure everything will be fine. He has an alibi and they have no proof so don't even sweat it bae," she said, lying back down on top of me. Maybe she was right, but I still was going to look into the shit.

Harper

ike I had told Axe, I was moving out. I was not about to stay here and he had put his hands on me. Even though it was the first time, he might do it again and I was not sticking around to find out. I wasn't too sure exactly where I was going to go since I didn't really have any money or anything. I should've never allowed Kase to take care of me the way he had then when we fell apart, I depended on Axe. I needed to learn how to stand on my own two feet.

Maybe Brittany would let me come and stay with her till I figured things out. We weren't best friends, but I did consider her as a friend. She had been there for me more times than I could count. One thing I wasn't about to do, was go stay with our stepmother, Jen. After I left there, I swore I would never return. That place was a complete hell hole.

Picking up my phone off the coffee table, I dialed Brittany's number and waited for her to pick up. "Hey, Britt were you busy?"

"No, just was feeding little man, what's up?"

"I was trying to see if I could come stay with you for a while just till I can get on my feet. I can't stay here with Axe's ass anymore," I told her. I was praying she said yes, and I could get the hell out of there before he made it back to the house. Knowing him, he was going to try and talk me into staying and I was so vulnerable when it came to my brother, so I needed to get ghost.

"Uh, yeah sure. I have more than enough space for you and Baylee. You know you didn't have to ask me that, just show up and knock on the door," she replied. That was a relief. "Aw Junior," she cried, then I heard some muffling noises in the background shortly after. "I'll see you when you get here. This little nigga done spit this food all over my clothes." With that being said, she disconnected the call.

Just as I tossed my phone on the bed, I saw a letter that was sitting on it. From the return address that was on there, I already knew that it was some bullshit. Blowing air from my lips, I flopped down on the bed, picking up the envelope and ripping it open. The only thing the letter said was, *I'ma kill your ass when I get out of here. −Donte*

I thought that when you sent letters from prison the people read them so how the fuck was I able to receive a threat in the mail? What I should have been worried about was how the hell he knew where to find me. It really didn't matter because I wasn't going to be here long anyway.

"What the hell are you doing?" Axe asked—referring to the suitcases that were lying around my room—catching me off guard causing me to jump. I quickly ripped up the letter along with the envelope so he couldn't read it.

"I told you I was moving out. I love you to death, Axe but we can't stay under the same roof anymore."

"I told you I was sorry. What more do you want?" he queried, nearing me.

"I know but I just can't stay here anymore."

"Where the fuck you going to go? You don't have a fucking job, money, nothing so it isn't like you got anywhere to go." It hurt me that he was trying to downplay me the way he was. He acted as if I liked being in the situation I was in. I want better for my daughter and I and getting out of this house was the first step in the right direction.

"I'm going to stay with Brittany," I confidently responded with a smile on my face.

"And exactly how long you think that shit going to last? That nigga going to get tired of you being there and she's going to eventually put you out on your ass to save her own failing relationship. Then where you going to be? Huh?" He chuckled. "Right back here where you started. And you know what? I'ma welcome you with open arms. So, go ahead."

Tears welled up in my eyes. At that moment, I hated Axe's guts. What type of brother was he to bring his own sister down? If anything, he should've been trying to uplift me. Sometimes I just wished he was normal and not so caught up in the street life. Maybe just maybe our lives would be totally different. It was his fault our stepmother was now addicted to fucking coke. She came across some of his shit he had in his room one day. She sniffed the shit and been hooked ever since.

"Fuck you, Axe. I'm never coming back here." If indeed that was to happen, I'd sleep under a bridge somewhere before coming back here. Fuck Axe.

"Yeah, alright we will see," he said and left out of my room.

I went into Baylee's room and began packing all her things while feeling my tears falling. I was trying to understand exactly how I got here. Everything was so perfect in the beginning. I wished I could just go back to that time and do things differently. Once her things were packed, I took them out to the car, placing them in the trunk. I had to make quite a few trips to the car because Axe's stubborn ass was being petty and didn't want to help me. I probably would've never accepted his help anyway. After picking Baylee up, I headed for the front door but stopped and looked at Axe.

"I'll see you in a couple days if not a couple hours." He laughed and I stormed out of there.

Nix

Over the last couple of weeks, things had been so hard for me. I finally laid my mother to rest and the shit still seemed surreal. Of course, Unity was there with me every step of the way along with Kase and I loved them for it. They were there trying to help me even when I wasn't even speaking to anyone. I had completely shut down on everyone and everything. It was just the way I grieved.

Since Kase was hitting the streets with Reapa and it was still early as fuck, I decided to take a trip out to the park. It was a beautiful day out and I could use the fresh air. I took a seat on the bench and just watched the kids run around playing. There were so many things on my mind I needed to sort out. My mother's restaurant had been shut down ever since her murder and I knew I was going to have to get it back up and running. The people that worked for her had families and shit to feed. They couldn't stay out of work on my account. Then, on the other hand, I hadn't been back to our apartment since then.

"Wassup Nix," said Renee, walking up on me and taking a seat on the bench beside me. Renee was a girl I had gone to school with. She dropped out a month before graduation because she fell pregnant and wanted to run behind a nigga that didn't want her stupid ass. The shit was dumb as fuck if you asked me. Last time I checked, she had about five kids and was only twenty-two.

I cut my eyes at her because she knew I didn't fuck with her ass like that, so I didn't know what gave her the nerves to come over and sit down beside me in the first place. "I heard about your mother, I just wanted to say I'm sorry for your loss. I'm here if you need anything," she lied.

"Bitch cut the shit." That was the first thing I said since the day I lost my mother. I wasn't about to sit there, putting up with her fakeness. Obviously, she wanted some shit if she was trying to make conversation with me. Any other time she saw me on the street, she didn't say shit to me so why now?

Sucking her teeth, she said, "You don't have to be rude."

"Renee, what the fuck do you want? Don't you got better things to do like run behind them nappy head ass kids you got?"

"Know what... you think you're just so fucking much and untouchable just 'cause you had a little bit more money than everyone else but you're not. To me, you're stupid as fuck. How the hell you be with a man that killed your own got damn mother?" She got up from the bench, but I snatched her by the wrist, stopping her.

"What the fuck did you just say?" I questioned her.

A smirk crept on her face. "Oh, you didn't know? Your nigga Kase was the one that killed your mother," she said, and I let her wrist go. I couldn't believe the shit she just said. This bitch had to be lying. There was no way my man had done me like that then turned right around and comforted me in my time of need but better believe I was about to get to the bottom of the shit.

∞ ∞ ∞

After I had left the park, I went to my apartment to get my mother's car so I could go out and find Kase. While I was there, I went into her bedroom and got her gun out the safe that she kept in her closet. If he was the one that had taken her life, I was going to take his. I may not be a dead shot, but I was going to shoot that muthafucka till it clicked. One of them bullets were bound to hit his ass.

I went to his house and he wasn't there. The only trap I knew he had was in Garden Grove, so I headed there damn near hitting the whole dash. When I pulled up, I saw him posted up against his Bugatti rapping with Reapa. Climbing out the car, I left the door wide open and stormed over to where he was stood and shot a bullet straight through his windshield. He was so caught up in the conversation that he and Reapa were having that he hadn't seen me walk up. Once they heard the gun go off, everyone turned to me.

"HOW THE FUCK COULD YOU KASE!" I shouted, sending another bullet into his hood. The car immediately began smoking.

"Babe, what are you talking about?" he asked, easing toward me. I turned the gun on him because I was confused. I thought he loved me so how could he take the most important person on this earth away from me?

"Don't come any closer or I swear to God, I'll put a bullet in your ass," I warned.

"What the fuck did you do nigga that she ready to body your ass?" Reapa questioned.

"The hell if I know. Your guess is just as good as mine," he replied.

Tears streamed down my cheeks. My heart was so broken. How come everyone wanted to hurt me? If this was love, then I didn't want nor need the shit.

"How could you kill my mama like that? What did she ever do to you?" I inquired, feeling the snot running down to my upper lip.

"Wait, you got shit twisted. I didn't killed your mama," he replied, taking a few steps toward me so I turned the gun back to his car shooting one of his tires.

"I TOLD YOU NOT TO FUCKING MOVE!" I yelled.

"Alright, alright," he said, stopping in his tracks.

"Told your stupid ass to tell her," Reapa chimed in, reaching into his pocket and pulling out his phone then walking away. I didn't know who he was calling, and I didn't give a damn. My beef was with Kase and no one else. He was going to tell me why he killed my mother.

Unity

J was awakened from my sleep by my ringing phone. Since I had a busy last couple of weeks and things had finally begun to die down, I decided to sleep in, but my phone said nah bitch you getting the fuck up today. Reaching over, grabbing it from the nightstand, I swiped the phone, sticking it up to my ear.

"Hello?" I groaned.

"Bae, I know you're tired, but I need you to get up and get out here to Garden Grove like ASAP," Reapa said.

I sat up in the bed, "Why what's wrong?" I asked, tossing the covers back and getting up.

"Nix got Kase at gunpoint. From the look in her eyes, she just might shoot him. I don't know how much longer we can hold her off, so you need to hurry up," he replied, ending the call.

Nix must have finally lost it all. She was fine besides the fact of losing her mother, so I didn't know why she wanted to kill Kase. Far as I knew, she loved the ground that nigga walked on, so something just wasn't adding up. Looking down at my attire, I knew I didn't have time to change so these shorts and t-shirt just was going to have to do. I grabbed my keys off the dresser and disappeared out the door. Hopefully, I could get there before she killed him, or someone called the cops on her. Fuck Nix!

∞ ∞ ∞

When I pulled up, Nix was still holding Kase at gunpoint with a crowd of people standing around them. I knew my girl was hurting from something because I could see the tears streaming down her cheeks. Shoving my way through the crowd, I made my way over to her. "What's going on?" I asked, walking straight up to Nix. Her eyes stayed trained on Kase as her lower lip quivered.

"He killed Ma," she answered. All this shit could have been avoided if their stupid asses would have told her about the rumors instead of having her find out on the streets.

"Nix put the gun down," I told her, and her head snapped in my direction.

"Put it down! If anything, you should be telling me to shoot his ass! You loved her like a mother, right? Do you not want vengeance for her death?" she bemusedly questioned.

I went closer to her with tears in my eyes as well. "I want nothing more than that but if you pull that trigger, I swear you going to regret it, Nix. Just think about it. How could Kase have killed Ma when he was with you that night? He didn't kill her, babe." By then I had made it all the way to her and placed my hand on hers that was holding the gun. "Give me the gun."

Her eyes went back to Kase but the tears were still pouring from them. "I'm sorry," she wept, loosening her grip on the gun and I took it putting the safety on.

"It's alright babe, I know you're hurting and shit," Kase said, throwing his arms around her, pulling her into his body. She broke down crying harder than she ever cried before.

"I'm sorry," was all she could muster.

I sighed deeply, placing the gun in the small of my waist then folded my arms underneath my breasts just standing back watching all the love that poured from Kase and Nix. "I really thought she was going to kill him," Reapa blurted, appearing at my side.

"She was."

Nix's mother was her world and now she doesn't feel complete since she's gone. If she had to, she would have put a bullet in Kase's ass without a doubt. People be underestimating that girl but she was as solid as they come and went hard for the ones she loved. If he was to fuck that relationship up, then he was a fucking fool and didn't know what the hell he had. That girl would put her life on the line for him long as he showed her, he was worthy.

"Don't be getting no fucking ideas and shit. If you were to do some shit like that, I'd put a bullet in your ass then nurse you back to health," he stated with a straight face, then walked off. Certain shit that he said always had me questioning him but I knew it was all just love.

Nix and Kase kissed and made up then she slowly walked over to where I was standing. "You good?" I asked her.

"I just feel so fucking lost. I was really about to kill Kase 'cause I let someone put some shit in my head about my man. I should go put a bullet in Renee's ass."

I reached out, wiping the tears from her face. "Renee? You talking about the one that we went to school with?"

"Yeah, that loose pussy bitch. All this shit is her fucking fault, spreading lies about Kase."

"No, it's not; she got it from someone else. Reapa told me that someone was going around saying Kase killed Olivia. He said he was going to get to the bottom of it." I shrugged.

"All this shit is fucking with my sanity."

"You and me both, sister," I replied, wrapping my arms around her and walked her to Olivia's car. "Where you about to go now?"

"Back to the house. I just want to feel close to Ma so I think I'm going to spend the day there," she answered, climbing into the car.

"I'll follow you there."

As I was heading back to my car, my mind was all over the place. My best friend almost committed murder. If I wasn't able to talk her from pulling that trigger and she would have killed him, I wasn't too sure what I was going to do. Everything just seemed so fucked up at this point.

Reapa

ith everything that was going on and Unity's birthday being in a couple of days, I decided to get us together and go down to Miami for a short vacation. Maybe it was just something that we needed. I still couldn't believe that just the day before, Nix was trying to kill my nigga, Kase. That shit was so unexpected, but I did tell him to tell her.

Since both of the girls had stayed over at Olivia's place, Kase and I took the liberty of packing for them. The trip was kind of a spur of the moment kind of thing so neither one of them was going to know about it till they were boarding the plane. I rented a limo to come pick Kase and I up and take us over to get the girls on our way to the airport.

"A nigga haven't been on a vacation in a hot minute," Kase said as we turned on the street that Olivia's building was on.

"Shit, you and me both. We usually go out of town for business. This time we can actually enjoy ourselves. Let's just hope the girls do as well." The limo came to a halt and the driver got out to open the back door for us.

Kase and I went up to the apartment. I stood back leaned against the wall as he knocked on the door, waiting for her to answer. This was the first time I hadn't slept in the bed with Unity in two weeks and I was missing her little feisty ass like crazy. I couldn't wait to have her back in my arms. Nix swung the door opened with her hair all over her head. From the way Kase eyed her, you'd think she just walked off the runway some got damn where.

"What y'all doing here?" she asked, wiping the sleep from her eyes. I knew they probably were still sleeping since it was seven in the morning. What could I say? I was an early bird.

"We came to get you and Unity," he replied, stepping into the door.

"Yeah, where she at anyway?" I asked, coming in behind him and shutting the door.

"In my bedroom," she said, pointing in the direction of the room.

When I walked into the bedroom, Unity was knocked the fuck out with her mouth wide open. As I got to the side of the bed, I unzipped my pants, pulling my dick out and rubbed it across her lips. The precum made a long stringy line from my dick head to her lips. She jumped up so fast, wiping her mouth.

"The fuck Miles!" she yelled when her eyes landed on me.

"I'm your own personal dick alarm." I chuckled, stuffing my dick back into my pants.

"What the fuck you doing here this time of morning?" she queried, grabbing her phone and looking at the time.

"You act like you don't miss me or some shit. Let me find out you had another nigga in here and I'ma kill his ass and force you to eat his intestines," I threatened.

"I'm going back to sleep and wake up again 'cause this shit just have to be a dream." She laid back down, throwing the cover over her head and I snatched it back.

"Get your ass up, we got somewhere to be and from the smell of your breath, you need to handle that shit. I'll be in the living room when you done," I said, leaving out the room.

When I got back to the living room, Kase was sitting on the couch, looking dumbfounded. "The fuck wrong with you?" I quizzed, sitting down beside him.

"Nix don't want to go. I had to practically beg her ass to," he replied.

"Even though she may not want to go, it still might be good for her. Don't forget she did just lose her mother and shit. Give her some time to warm up to the idea. She just might end up having fun."

"Hope you're right about this."

A few moments later, Unity and Nix came from the back. Both of them were looking like they didn't feel like going anywhere but I didn't give a fuck. They were going and the jet was gassed up ready to pull off. "Let's get this show on the road," I said, rubbing my hands together and hopping up from my seat. I headed for the door, pulling it open and took a step back. "After you, ladies." Unity walked out first, and Nix rolled her eyes before she stepped into the hallway.

∞ ∞ ∞

The limo pulled up to the waiting jet. Both Unity and Nix glared over at me. I smiled back at them before climbing out the car. I grabbed Unity and my duffel bag from the truck and gripped her hand, heading straight to the jet.

"Where you taking me?" she questioned as we boarded.

"I thought everyone needed a vacation so we dipping off for a couple days. I know your birthday coming up and just wanted to do something special for you that's all," I responded, putting our bags up and taking a seat by her.

A few hours later, we were pulling into the airport. Just as soon as we pulled in there were two Rolls Royce Ghosts sitting on the blacktop waiting for us. One of them was white and the other was black. When Unity stepped off the jet, she took a big whiff of the air and immediately looked relaxed. That was all I was trying to achieve. I placed our bags in the trunk of the car and we all left for our hotel room.

We were staying at the Ritz Carlton one of the most expensive hotels in Miami. Whatever I did, was going to be the best. I had to treat my Queen like royalty. Since we left so early, we all decided to just get a little rest before we started our day.

Kase

$\mathcal{A}$ s I sat at the table staring across at Nix, I felt like the luckiest man alive. She was so beautiful in a simple black dress that flowed effortlessly. Her hair was straightened just how I liked it. Don't get me wrong, I loved her kinky, curly hair but whenever it was straightened it was like it did something to me. What was killing me was the fact that her face was turned down in a frown. I really wanted her to enjoy herself but from the looks of it, this whole vacation was going to be a bust. Unity was sitting there laughing like she was just having a good old time while Nix toyed with her food, seeming annoyed.

Finally getting enough, I stood up from my seat and her eyes shifted with me. "We'll meet you guys back at the hotel," I announced, walking around the table, grabbing Nix by her forearm and pulling her up. It was time I snapped her out of her funk because the shit was killing me.

"Where we going?" she asked as I dragged her out of the restaurant.

"I don't know. Somewhere fun or something. I need to lift your spirits 'cause seeing you like this is fucking killing me," I responded.

When we got outside, my driver was sitting at the curb, he got out the car to open the back door for us, but I stuck my hand up stopping him. "I'll call you if we need you."

"You do realize I have on six-inch heels and you want to decide that you want to walk," she complained, frowning.

"Will you stop with all this complaining and shit and just let me show you a good time? Damn." I didn't mean to sound rude to her, but she was beginning to frustrate the fuck out of me. It was as if all she wanted to do was be sad and I wasn't with that shit. I'm her nigga so she should just let me make her happy and leave it at that.

We found our way into a nearby arcade. There were so many different types of games in there. I wasn't the gaming type, but I'd try anything just to bring that gorgeous smile back to her face. "You think you can beat me?" I asked her, rolling up the sleeves of my Armani button-down.

"I don't play basketball," she replied, folding her arms underneath her breasts.

"Well, you will tonight." I grabbed her, pulling her in front of me and put the ball in her hands. "Just aim and shoot."

"But I don't want to play, Kase," she whined.

"Did I fucking ask you that or did I say shoot?" I blew air from my lips, trying my best to keep my temper down with her. Yeah, she was going through some things and I had to keep reminding myself so I wouldn't lose my cool.

"Fine, but I'm telling you now I can't fucking play." She sighed, lazily tossing the ball and it fell completely short.

"It doesn't matter if you can play or not, I just want you to have fun, that's all."

After letting Nix damn near whoop my ass at every game in there, we ended up at a yogurt place down the street. A couple times I had seen a slight smirk on her face, but I wanted her to laugh so hard that she almost pee herself. I wanted the old Nix back and I knew it was probably going to take some time before she got back there. No matter how long it was going to take, I intended on sticking it out with her.

As she sat there eating her yogurt that was topped with all kinds of shit that was sure to fuck her stomach up before she was done, I couldn't help but keep gawking at her. Nix made me fall for her and I mean completely fall. The shit that I was feeling, made me question if I ever loved Harper the way I said I did.

"Why you keep staring at me like that?" she blurted out, bringing her eyes up to mine.

"I'm just trying to figure out how the fuck you made me fall in love with you."

"So, what are you trying to say? That it's a bad thing you love me or something?" she queried with a raised brow. I knew that I better fix what I said before she started going in on my ass or better yet pull another gun on me.

"That's not what I'm saying—"

"Then exactly what are you saying, Blake?" she asked, calling me by my government name something that she rarely did so I knew she was serious.

"I love the feeling that I get when I'm around you. Whether you know it or not, you changed a nigga, Nix. All I ever wanted from someone was effort, consistency, and loyalty. You give me all those things and more. What else could a nigga ask for?"

I got up from my seat and went over to where she sat. Her eyes never left mine as I got down on one knee in front of her. "I love you more than words could ever explain. I know I don't have a ring or anything but if you say yes, I swear I'll let you pick out the most expensive one you can find. But I want you to marry me. You think that you can do that?" Nothing about my proposal was traditional. I wasn't even expecting to do the shit, but it just happened. It's how a nigga was feeling and for whatever reason, she was always able to pull my emotions out of me like a little bitch.

Tears shimmered in her eyes as she stared back at me. "No shit? You not playing games with me right now are you?" she asked.

"I'm for real, so what you say?"

"Of course, I will!" she cried. Her tears finally dropped from her eyes. She leaned down and planted a big sloppy kiss on my lips as the small people that were in the yogurt shop cheered us on. Now I had to get my babe a ring so big that blinded everyone when they saw the shit. I wanted everyone to know that pussy belonged to me.

Axel

The shit I said to Harper was fucked up. After sitting there in the house by myself for a couple days I realized that shit. Of all people, she was really the only one that had been in my corner and I treated her as if she was nothing. I guess because she was the only person that I had, I wanted her to need me—depend on me so I wouldn't lose her. I had to let my sister grow and become her own person.

"Eww, what are you doing here?" Brittany asked when she opened the door.

"Sure as hell wasn't to see your ugly ass. Where my sister at?"

"Harper doesn't want to see you so you might as well get to stepping," she made it known. If I had it my way, I'd get to stepping all over that ugly ass face of hers.

"Stop playing games with me and go get my fucking sister." After rolling her eyes, she left away from the door and not long after, Harper appeared.

"What do you want, Axe? Did I leave something over your house?" she questioned, shifting Baylee on her hip.

"Uncle," Baylee cried out, reaching for me. When I went to grab her, Harper pulled her back. That shit hurt like a muthafucka; she had never done anything to me like that before. I must have really offended her by the shit I said.

"Look, I came over here to apologize to you. The shit that I said was wrong and fucked up. I should've never put my hands on you or none of that shit. Do you accept my apology?"

She sighed, "Just 'cause you come over here saying you sorry and shit doesn't mean it will magically fix what you did. You really hurt me. I thought you loved me. Like seriously, I'm your fucking sister. You're supposed to treat me better than this." Tears flowed down her cheeks. I reached out, wiping them away.

"I know I did, and if you let me, I want to make it up to you. Starting by being a better brother to you and uncle to Baylee. Y'all really all a nigga got, and I can't lose y'all," I confessed, sticking my arms out, praying she would come into them. Surprisingly, she did, and I hugged her and Baylee tightly.

"I'm still not coming back to stay with you. I've come to the conclusion that we can't stay in the same house. The shit just impossible. I'll stay here till I can get myself a place," she said when she pulled back from my embrace.

"If you want, I can get somewhere for you," I offered, walking all the way into the door and shutting it behind me.

"No, I think it's something I need to do on my own." All I could do was respect her wishes. It was kind of hard that she was finally trying to grow up on me.

"Cool, what were you two doing anyway?" She finally handed Baylee over to me and I sat down on the couch playing with her.

"I have been trying to get in touch with Kase so she can see him. That's all she been asking for lately and it's driving me crazy," she replied, pulling her phone out and dialing a number.

"Where the fuck you been at? I went to the house and you weren't there. I have been calling your fucking phone nonstop and you haven't been answering. The fuck, Kase!" Harper looked as if she was frustrated as fuck, standing there, biting on the corner of her lower lip. If she would've listened to me in the first place, then she wouldn't have been in that shit. "Miami! And how long are you supposed to be gone?" My ears perked up when I heard her say that. "Fuck you! I'm not the one looking for you, Baylee is or have you forgotten about your got damn child!" A few seconds later, she pulled the phone away from her ear and stared at the screen. "He hung up on me," she spoke.

More each day, Kase gave me reasons to put his ass in the ground but his time was slowly but surely approaching. After I killed Olivia, I started telling people he was the one that had done it. I was kind of hoping the cops would lock his bitch ass up or something. Once Nix had got word, she was definitely going to come crawling back to me and the moment she did, I was going to treat her ass like shit.

"Don't even stress yourself out about that nigga, sis," I told her. She was going to end up driving herself insane over that nigga.

"I just don't know what the fuck to do anymore." She sniffled.

"Everything will work itself out." I kissed Baylee on the forehead then sat her down on the couch. "I have to bounce but here," reaching into my pocket, I pulled out a wad of cash, handing it to her. "Just in case you need something." After kissing her in the middle of her forehead, I dipped out the door.

Knowing that Kase was in Miami was like a blessing. I had a few niggas down there that I used to run with. All I had to do was make a quick call and send them little niggas after his ass. Reapa was probably down there with him as well. Those niggas acted as if they couldn't take a shit without the other wiping their ass. If I could get them to do my dirty work for me, I'd be straight, that way if they were to kill them and Harper asked me about it, I could tell her I didn't have shit to do with it. Yeah, that was my plan. Pulling my phone from my pocket, I dialed Bryan's number.

"Wassup Axe long time no hear," he said when he answered the phone.

"A nigga just been busy that's all. Look I need for you to take care of a little problem for me. Swear it'll be beneficial."

"I'm listening."

Reapa

After Kase and Nix left us at the table by ourselves, we finished dinner and I took Unity back to the room. The way she was looking all night long, I couldn't wait to get that ass back there so I could rip that fucking dress off her. That pussy had been calling my name for the longest.

Babe was riding my dick like a porn star doing all types of splits and tricks on the dick. If I must say, I had turned her muthafucking ass the fuck out and quickly. I stared her into her beautiful face as her eyes rolled to the back of her head. I slapped her hard on the ass making it jiggle. Out of nowhere the room's door busted opened and in walked two guys dressed in all black. Those bitches just had to fuck up me getting a nut. Just as soon as I saw their hand rise, I reached over, grabbing my Glock off the nightstand then rolled over so that Unity and I wouldn't be in the line of fire. They began shooting and bullets were eating the mattress up sending feathers and shit flying everywhere.

We fell to the floor and I gave her a couple more strokes because the pussy was feeling just that fucking good that I didn't want to pull out of the shit. I aimed my chrome at the first nigga I saw, shooting him right in the head, dropping him like a log. She was so into the dick that she kept on riding me while I dropped the other nigga that was behind him. That shit kind of shocked me that she was acting as if niggas weren't in here trying to kill both of us. Any other chick would have been jumped off the dick screaming. That was kind of what I was worried about with her innocence.

I lifted up from the floor, holding her up with one hand, placing her back firmly against the wall behind the door. Footsteps could be heard coming up the hallway. All I could do was wonder how the hell they knew where I was and who the fuck were they anyway. I didn't have any beef with anyone down here in Miami. The shit had to be personal; it sure as hell wasn't a coincidence.

"I'm cumming!" Unity screamed as two more guys walked into the room. Long as she got hers it really didn't matter. After sending two bullets through the door, I heard one of the bodies hit the floor. Backing up away from the wall with her still attached to my dick like a condom, I shot the last guy in the chest. I pulled her off my dick, placing her softly down on her feet. "You good?" I asked her.

"Am I good? I just had the fucking best orgasm I've ever had in my life," she panted, looking around the room at the dead bodies that were lying on the floor.

"Clean yourself up and get your things packed we have to get the fuck out of here," I told her. With all the shooting that just took place, I knew the cops were well on their way despite us using silencers and I refused to be here when they got here.

"Aye come help me clean this shit up in my room right quick. And I do mean bring your slow ass on now," I ordered then ended the call.

Tossing the phone on the bed, I looked around the room at all the dead bodies that were in there. I had been in Miami for only a day and niggas had already begun gunning for my head. From the way things were going, it didn't look like we were going to be down there much longer.

I dragged the body that was lying in the doorway into the room so I could shut the door. I didn't need anyone walking by seeing the shit.

Unity came out the bathroom with a towel wrapped around her body, dripping wet. I went into the bathroom to clean my dick off and get dressed so that I could help Kase get rid of them fucking bodies. The shit was going to be hard as fuck, considering the fact we were in a hotel. By the time I was done getting dressed and packed, I went back into the living room area, the bodies were gone and so was Unity. Kase was relaxed back on the couch with one in the air.

"How the fuck you got rid of the bodies that got damn fast?" I asked him as I plopped down on the couch.

"Shit, I know people that's all you have to fucking know," he simply replied.

"Where's Unity though?"

"Sent her up to the room with Nix. I'm sure you didn't want her to stay in here with them niggas lying on the floor like that," he responded. Yeah, he was kind of right about that. What I couldn't understand was how this nigga was just sitting here smoking a blunt like we didn't need to get the fuck out of this hotel. I hated they had come along and ruined our vacation, now we were going to have to go back home ahead of schedule. What was really fucking with me though, was the fact I didn't know who the hell that was that tried to kill us. Some digging was going to have to be done because they weren't only playing with my life but Unity's as well.

"We have to figure out who the fuck that was that just tried to kill me."

"Way ahead of you. I already got some people looking into it," he replied. I took one last pull then handed him the blunt back.

"Shit, while you handling everything, you should have been trying to find us another hotel for the night. You know we can't stay in this muthafucka." He put the blunt out then stood up from his seat, so I got up along with him.

"Nigga, what the fuck I look like to you? Your assistant?"

"Nah, but you damn sure acting like one so you might as well play the full position." I chortled. We left out of the room and went up to get the girls so that we could get the hell out of there.

Unity

The next morning, I woke up in bed all alone. I sat there replaying the events from the night before in my head. The shit that happened never happened to me before. I kind of surprised myself with the things I had done. It was kind of exciting to be in the middle of something like that. Just feeling the rush. I didn't panic or anything because I knew Reapa wouldn't let anything happen to me and that he did. Speaking of him, I couldn't help but wonder where the hell he was. It was finally my birthday and he let me wake up in bed alone. Apparently, he wanted my foot up his ass.

"Happy Birthday," he said, walking into the room with breakfast on a tray that of course, he didn't cook since we were still in a hotel. He sat the food down on my lap. "How are you feeling this morning?" he asked before taking a seat beside me on the bed and stealing a piece of bacon off my plate.

"I feel good. I'm here with this amazing ass man who loves me—"

"Where he at?" he asked with a raised brow.

I playfully shoved him. "Right here silly. Stop fucking playing with me." A smile passed my lips. Reapa was nothing short of amazing. Some might think we were moving too fast or whatnot but fuck what they had to say. I had this undeniable connection to him, like I just knew we were meant to be. "I love you," I said, staring him into the eyes.

"Love you too." He leaned over kissing me on the lips. "I got a few things I need to take care of, but I'll be back in a few. I wanted to be here when you woke so you don't think I just dipped off on you."

"Okay, handle your business." He pecked me on the lips once more before leaving out the room. Of course, if he was leaving then Kase probably was as well so I was about to eat my breakfast and then head to Nix's room.

***

"Happy birthday, bih!" Nix screamed when she answered the door.

"Thanks," I said, entering the room.

"So, what we doing today? You know we not about to sit up here in this room while those two roam the streets. Ain't no telling how long they will be gone."

"I was thinking that maybe we could—" Before I could even finish my sentence, I got the urge to vomit so I took off toward the bathroom.

"What's wrong with you?" Nix asked as I dropped down to my knees over the toilet. After throwing up till my stomach was empty, I finally felt safe enough to pull my head back up.

"I don't know, maybe it was the breakfast I ate," I finally answered her. Maybe something was spoiled, or my stomach just wasn't agreeing with it. Yeah, that had to be it.

"You sure? Were you drinking too much last night or something?" My head went back to the toilet and I puked again. I didn't know what I was vomiting since I had clearly already thrown up everything that I had eaten this morning and last night as well. I just had a couple glasses of wine last night, so I was far from having a hangover.

When I sat back on my ass, Nix was eyeing me suspiciously. "Why you looking at me like that?"

"Bih let me find out Reapa already knocked that pussy up again."

"Nah, no way we just had sex last—" I had to cut myself short because it was kind of possible that I was pregnant. He and I had sex before Olivia got killed. It wasn't anything spectacular and just kind of happened that's probably why I had forgotten about it.

"Get your ass up; we going to get you a pregnancy test like now," Nix said, jumping up to her feet and pulling me up along with her. If I really was pregnant, I was wondering how Reapa was going to take the news. I wasn't even sure how he felt about me losing the last baby since he didn't really say too much about it. All he was focused on, was me. Maybe that was the way he grieved or something.

∞ ∞ ∞

I sat there in a ball of nerves as I stared blankly at the pregnancy test that sat in my hand. I wasn't too sure how to feel about it saying positive. The last time I was pregnant, I lost the baby and was too terrified that I might lose that one as well. Definitely, losing my child had me thinking differently. I low-key wanted to be excited about it but kept putting all those fucked up thoughts in my mind, dampening my whole mood.

"You good?" Reapa asked, catching me off guard. I hadn't heard him come in because I was so lost in my own thoughts. I quickly put my hand behind my back, trying to hide the test from him but I was a little too slow. "What is that in your hand?" he questioned, coming over, pulling it from behind me. "You pregnant?"

All I could do was stare up into his eyes not even sure what to say. Tears filled mine, considering the fact that my emotions were all over the place. "That's what the test says," I softly replied.

"Why you crying? This a good thing. Ever since I saw how you were when you lost our baby, I wanted to knock your ass up again. I knew you wanted another baby even though you hadn't exactly said it," he said, sitting down on the bed, pulling me into his arms. How the hell did he know something that I didn't even know my damn self?

"But what if I lose this one as well?" I seriously queried. That was the only thing that was on my mind. If I was to keep the baby, everything I did on a daily basis, I'd be thinking I could harm the baby in some way.

"First one you lost wasn't your fault. You didn't know you were pregnant so you can't fault yourself for that. You got pregnant again didn't you?" I nodded. "Well, have a little faith then. Everything will work out."

Kase

We finally found out who tried to kill Reapa. The thing was, trying to find the nigga and figure out exactly why because neither one of us had heard of the muthafucka. Unless he was just on some hating jack boy shit but then it wouldn't have taken that many people so there had to be more to the story. Before we did anything, we were about to send the girls back on the jet to New York. We couldn't risk anything happening to them so that was the best option. I knew Nix probably wasn't going to be fond of the idea, but she would be all right.

"Pack your things," I told Nix when I walked back into the room. She sat up in the bed, giving me the side eye.

"For what?" she questioned.

"We ending the trip early. It's too much shit going on down here and I can't have anything happen to you. We sending you and Unity back ahead of us while we stay and take care of a few things," I answered, tossing her things into her overnight bag without even making eye contact.

"But I want to stay with you," she objected just the way I figured she was.

"No, you going home. I'll be there once I take care of this shit." I turned around, tossing her some clothes on the bed so she could get dressed.

"I'm not leaving here without you. Are you fucking crazy?" I sighed deeply; I didn't have time for this shit at the moment. Why couldn't she just do what I told her ass to?

"Yes, you are, now get dressed Phoenix."

"No," she replied, sitting against the headboard with her arms folded across her chest. We had told the pilot to be ready to pull off in two hours. Playing games with Nix wasn't on the schedule. Gripping her by her ankles, I pulled her to the edge of the bed and began dressing her ass my damn self. If she didn't want to do it then I would.

If I had to, I would carry her ass on that plane and tie her up before I let her stay here with me. There was no telling what the hell was going to go down when we found that nigga Bryan. Reapa and I were only two niggas, that nigga could have a whole got damn army with him sitting somewhere. We knew nothing of him nor what he did and was surprised we could get enough information to know he was the one that called the hit.

"Why would you try to force me to go?" From the tone of her voice, it sounded like she was crying so I stopped for a moment and stared up into her face.

"What the fuck you crying for?" The shit just seemed weird to me.

"I can't help but think that if you put me on that plane and send me off that it might be the last time I see you," she sobbed.

"You don't have to worry about nothing like that. Swear to you I'll always come back to you."

"It still doesn't make me feel any better." She sat on the edge of the bed and wiped her tears.

"Just trust me alright. I got something to come home to so I'm going to do my best to do so." I softly kissed her on the lips. "Now can you get dressed so we can go? We kind of behind schedule."

∞ ∞ ∞

"If this the wrong house, I'm going to come back here and kill everybody in this muthafucka," Reapa warned with his gun still pressed at the guy's temple.

"I promise you that it's right," the guy responded, trembling.

"Alright," Reapa said, tossing him to the side like he was a rag doll. We headed out of the bar straight to our car. It didn't matter that we were walking in there blind, I was pretty confident we both were going to make it out of there. Both of us together had always been a force to be reckoned with.

"I found out that Unity's pregnant," Reapa said when he climbed back into the car.

"Congrats nigga." I smiled; I was happy as fuck for him. When he told me about her losing the last baby, I knew it kind of fucked with him, that's really why he disappeared on my ass for a whole week. I knew he needed some time to himself, so I wasn't really stressing it.

"Yeah, a nigga finally about to be a father like your ass. I just hope I don't have the same baby mama drama as you." He chuckled.

"Marry her then you wouldn't have to worry about all that shit."

A few moments later, we were pulling up to a house. There were toys thrown all over the yard and two black SUVs sat in the driveway. Knowing that there were probably children inside, we were going to have to handle this situation a lot differently. "I'll grab the kids," I told him as I got out of the car and we headed up to the front door.

A woman answered the door with a two-year-old in her arms. She looked tired like she had been running behind kids all day. Of course, she was most likely Bryan's wife or some shit. "Where's Bryan?" Reapa asked, stepping into the house like he was invited in. I smirked at her facial expression and came in behind him, not even bothering to close the door.

"Who are you?" she asked, taking a step back from us.

"Ask your husband, he the one that sent niggas to try and kill me. Only if he knew what he was getting himself into." Reapa chortled.

"How many kids are in the house?" I asked her.

"Three... why?"

"Where the other two?" I questioned, walking off to go and find them. Before I could even bend the corner well, a man appeared with a little girl and boy running behind him. I snatched both of them up before he could even react.

"Who the fuck are y'all?" he queried.

"How the fuck you going to try and kill someone but don't even know who the hell you were trying to take out?" Reapa quizzed and Bryan's eyes grew wide.

"Yeah, it's me nigga." When I saw Reapa reaching for his gun, I took the kids outside so they wouldn't witness the shit that was about to happen.

"What's going on, Bryan?" I heard his wife ask as I shut the door behind me.

About five minutes later, I heard gunshots. The kids jumped and I just told them to not be afraid and that it was nothing. Reapa opened the door and Bryan's wife was in there screaming over his dead body. "You ready to go?" he asked, heading straight for the car with me right behind him.

Harper

A month later...

*K*ase had been finding almost every excuse in the book for him not to come around me and shit like he had something to hide from me. He even had gone as far as having his mother to come and pick up Baylee and drop her off on the days he got her. Soon, I was going to find out exactly what it was he was trying to hide. It wouldn't be me if I didn't try my best to get in his business. Even though I knew he didn't really want anything else to do with me, I still wanted to be with him. No one on this earth could switch their feelings off that easily. Look how long we had been together, and he just expected me to stop loving him like it was nothing. Hell no.

Looking down at my phone, I realized it was time for me to go over Mrs. Karen's to pick up Baylee. She had been with them over the weekend which was longer than she ever been away from me before. I couldn't wait to get her back. I knew she was in good hands, but I always loved for her to be around me. My baby was practically my best friend; I'd do anything for that girl even let Kase go if I had to. Maybe one day when she was old enough to understand, I would tell her who her real father was and hopefully, she would understand the reason why I did the things I did.

As I was making my way to my car, a Mustang pull to the side of the road. I had never seen the car before so I was assuming it had to have been someone for Brittany or her baby daddy Jeff, so I went on and climbed into my car. Just as I was about to start it up, I looked in the rearview mirror and saw Donte step out. The first thought that had come to mind was that he had to have broken out of jail and ran his ass over here. I sure didn't want to see his muthafucking ass especially with that threat he sent me in the mail. If Donte said he was going to do something, then he definitely would.

My heart pounded in my chest as I climbed back out of the car, and he slowly approached it with a big ass grin on his face. I don't know why I did it when I could've easily just backed out of the driveway and left. But knowing him, he would still be here when I made it back so I might as well go on and faced him now. "What are you doing out?" I was sure he was a goner, seeing how he was looking at two life sentences and shit. The fuck were they thinking to let him go?

"Let's just say that someone fucked with the evidence that they had against me and they didn't have no other choice but to let me out of there," he replied, stroking his fingers across my cheek. "Did you really think I was going to stay in there forever? You were supposed to have rocked with a nigga and if you didn't try to abandon ship the first chance you got then you would have known that."

I swallowed hard the lump that formed in my throat. It was just my luck the son of a bitch got lucky and got out. I never thought I was going to have to see his face again outside of those brick walls. "It wasn't even like that and you know it, Donte. Did you really want me to keep bringing Baylee up there to see you in that state? Have her growing up with her father locked behind bars and shit.

She's young now but as she gets older, she's going to start asking questions and shit. How am I supposed to explain something to her like that without having her hating you for the rest of her life?" Tears flowed down my cheeks. I wished he just would have understood where I was coming from. It wasn't like I was trying to keep him away from her like out of spite, I was just trying to save her. That's all.

"Fuck you; I'll deal with your ass later. Where the hell my daughter at anyway?" I nibbled on my lower lip, debating if I actually wanted to tell him the truth about where she was. If he would have known, he probably would flip his fucking lid.

"She's at daycare," I lied.

Donte came closer to me immediately causing my body to quiver. He roughly gripped me by my hair, pulling my face close to his. "She better not be with Kase bitch ass or I'ma kill you," he warned. From the firm expression that was on his face, I knew he was telling the truth. He was never the type of person that would say things just to say them.

"She's not I swear," I cried because he had this tight ass grip on my hair that felt as if he was pulling my shit from my head. The shit was so painful that there were tears coming to my eyes.

"Go get her and hurry up and bring your ass back here. And if you don't... I will fucking find you so don't play with me, Harp," he warned then let my hair go. The tears kept flowing as I climbed into the car quickly backing out of the driveway. I so badly wished I could just take my baby and run away or something but like he just said, he'd find me. He found me at Brittany's so without a doubt he would find me anywhere. How the fuck could I possibly let myself end up pregnant by a nigga like that? Sometimes I wished Kase really was Baylee's father then I wouldn't have to deal with this mess. He was better than Donte was for sure.

As I pulled into Mrs. Karen's driveway, I tried my best to dry my eyes so she wouldn't know something was wrong. I didn't need her all in my business then running and telling Kase shit. Dealing with him was the last thing I wanted to do. For as long as I could, I needed to keep the two apart, so I guess it was kind of good he had this little arrangement set up for us.

"Hi, Mrs. Karen. I came to pick up Baylee," I said when she opened the door.

"Come on in sweetie. She's asleep but I'll go and grab her for you." I stood there at the door as I waited for her to go get Baylee like I was scared to come on inside or something. If I would have, she probably would try to have a conversation with me and I was just not feeling that at the moment. All she needed to do was bring me my daughter so I could take her to her crazy ass daddy and not have to worry about him trying to kill me for the time being. For my sake, I just hoped he couldn't stay out of trouble long enough to get his ass locked right back up. Maybe this time their dumb asses would throw away the fucking key.

"Here she goes." Karen smiled, handing Baylee over to me.

"Thank you. I'll see you in a few days," I told her, rushing toward the door.

"Are you doing okay, Harper?" she questioned. There she go trying to get all in my business and shit.

"Yes, I'm fine. I just need to get home, that's all. See you in a couple days." I rushed out the door at the speed of lightning.

Nix

Over the last month, I had been spending all of my time trying to find a head chef for my mother's restaurant. It had been opened and we were staying afloat for the time being, but I was no chef. I couldn't do half the things my mother did so I needed someone in there running the kitchen.

"I see you have ten years of experience and you went to culinary school in Italy?" I questioned, locking eyes with him.

"Yes," Alex replied with a smile. I couldn't lie, Alex was a nice-looking black man and well educated. His bald head shined underneath the light in my mother's office—well, might as well say mine now. He kind of reminded me of a caramel Morris Chestnut.

"I say you're hired," I beamed, feeling kind of relieved. Out of twenty chefs, I finally found one I was comfortable with hiring.

"Thanks," he said, extending me his hand.

"Let me show you around the place."

Being at the restaurant was kind of bittersweet. It brought back so many memories of my mother—good and bad. Reminiscences that I wouldn't trade for the fucking world. Part of me still didn't feel complete now she's gone but I knew I had to move forward with my life. She wouldn't have liked it if I just moped around and let my life pass me by.

"So that's it," I said when we ended up in the kitchen after the quick tour. "Any questions?"

"Uh, no just when can I start?"

"Now is fine with me. That's if you're ready," I quickly replied, feeling relieved.

"Thanks again for the opportunity." He shook my hand once more.

"No problem. I'll be in the office for the next hour in case you need me."

When I opened the office door, Kase was sitting in there behind the desk with a smirk on his face. Just seeing him brightened up my day. "What are you doing here?" I queried, shutting the door behind me.

"Missed you, plus I had something for you," he answered. I loved surprises and knowing Kase it was going to be a good one.

"Oh, yeah and what is it?" I smirked, slowly strutting over to where he sat. Just as soon I got around the desk, I peeped something was sitting in his sweatpants where his dick was. "Hmph, wonder what that could be?"

"I don't know stick your hand in there and find out." He grinned widely.

Pulling his pants back, I pulled out a small Tiffany's box. "What's this?"

"Open it."

When I popped the box open, sitting inside it was a big ass emerald-cut diamond engagement ring. The shit was so big with so many diamonds that it almost blinded me. "Thought you said you were going to let me pick out my own ring?"

"So, you don't like that one?" he asked with furrowed brows.

"It's beautiful but kind of a bit much, don't you think?" It wasn't like I was complaining or anything, the ring just wasn't my style. He could have bought me something simple and I would have been pleased with it.

"No, it's not. It screams you. Different, loud, and shines bright 'cause you always brighten up my day whenever I lay eyes on you." He took the ring from the box and slipped it onto my finger. "Now it's official everyone knows that you're taken."

"I think you deserve the neck." I dropped down to my knees and pulled out his dick. "I've missed you," I cooed. From the precum oozing from the head, I could tell the feeling was mutual. I breathed through my nose, massaging his balls as his dick slid down my throat. My eyes connected with his shortly before his rolled to the back of his head, letting me know I was doing my job. I hummed a little on his dick, sending a vibrating sensation through it.

"Fuck," he grumbled, interlocking his fingers in my hair, slowly guiding me up and down on his dick.

Gently easing up from his dick, I tenderly jerked it, licking and sucking on his balls. Coughing up a mouth of saliva, I spit it on it and licked it back up with the tip of my tongue before shoving him right back down my throat. "Got damn, bae," he groaned right before shooting his seeds down my throat and I made sure to swallow them all. "Take that shit off and hop on this dick," he ordered.

With me being so busy lately, I hadn't been getting any regular dick, so my shit was fiending to feel his death stroke. Not even feeling like taking my thongs off, I straddled him and slid them to the side and eased down on him. It was kind of a struggle at first because of how tight I was but after gliding his head up and down my slit, he slid right on in. "Oooo," I moaned, mouth forming an O as I slowly eased up and down on him.

Kase pulled my dress all the way up, exposing my bare breasts. His mouth latched onto one of them, sending me into a frenzy. My pace sped up, feeling him stroke me from the bottom. My head fell back in complete bliss as my climax touched the horizon. "Yaaaassss, right there Kase," I whimpered.

"Gone make that shit cum for daddy," he demanded. Shit, he didn't even have to say it because I was already about to gush every got damn where.

"Ok daddy." I went up and down on his dick a couple more times and I was cumming—body shivering and all. "Fuck I love you!" I cried as I released my juices all over him.

Kase smacked me hard on the ass and said, "I know. Now it's time I take control."

He lifted up from the seat, placing me down on the desk with my legs spread open and plunged right back into my soaking wet center without warning. I tightly held onto the desk as it rocked. Kase was giving me a dose of that death stroke I loved so much. With every stroke he gave my pussy clung to his dick.

"Why the fuck you have to be so tight?" he asked, planting his lips on top of mine. I slightly parted my mouth he slipped his tongue inside. As they intertwined with each other, I felt another orgasm coming on. "Gone let that shit out so I can cum."

I came long and hard with him right behind me. Kase pulled his dick out then went into the bathroom to clean himself up. Once he was done, he wiped me down and pulled me back from the desk into his lap. I just sat there, staring at his handsome face not able to believe the shit was actually real. "I love you so much," I blurted out.

"I love you too. You done gave a nigga a workout. I don't even think I need to go to the got damn gym now," he joked.

"Well, if you were about to leave I suggest you gone and get the hell out of here 'causs the way I'm feeling, I'll climb back on that dick," I said, biting down on my lower lip.

"Alright, I'll see you later at the house." He sucked my lower lip into his mouth and bit down on it before lifting me up so he could get up. "Hit my line if you need anything." with that being said, he was out the door.

Reapa

*A*fter finding out Axel was the stupid muthafucka that had hired Bryan to kill me, I had been hunting his ass nonstop. I tried my best not to pull Harper's ass in the shit but it seemed like I didn't really have much of a fucking choice. She was the only person that could have known exactly where his ass was at. And I already knew she was probably going to push me to the point where I was going to want to kill her ass before she spilled anything. That was the type of shit I was trying my best to avoid.

"You good, bae?" I asked Unity when I went back into the bedroom. For the past week, she had been feeling bad as fuck just throwing up all over the place. I'm surprised she wasn't vomiting then, but I didn't want to speak too soon. It was as if nothing agreed with her stomach. I kind of felt bad for my baby since it was kind of my fault she was sick in the first place.

"Yeah, I'll be okay," she responded, sitting there looking like shit. Definitely wasn't used to seeing her that way. Babe had always been on point but for now she could get a pass.

"I have to head out for a quick second. Do you need anything?" I questioned as I sat on the edge of the bed and slipped my Jordan sneakers on.

"Bring me back some pickles and um butter pecan ice cream. Oh and some sour cream and onion chips. I think I want some candy too ." As she was rattling off everything she wanted from the store, I was thinking I had made a mistake asking.

"Got damn, you want me to bring you the whole fucking store?" I joked with a light chuckle. If she did want it, I'd go out and get the muthafucka for her.

"So what you are you trying to say? That I'm fat or something?" she poked her lower lip out at me. Getting up from the bed, I went over to where she was sitting and kissed her softly on the lips.

"No, I'm not trying to call you fat. You could never be fat in my eyes. All I was saying was if you wanted the whole store then I was going to make that shit happen," I made known.

"And that's why I love you." She smiled brightly.

"Love you too. I'm about to head out. Call me if you need anything else," I told her, kissing her lips once more before heading for the bedroom door.

Since Kase didn't know where the hell Harper had been staying, I put my ear to the streets and got the information I needed from someone. It didn't take too much pressure to get people to cough up what I needed. I was about to head over there and have a little chit-chat with her ass. I prayed she didn't fuck around and have me kill her ass in front of my niece. For her sake, I hoped she cooperated with me.

∞ ∞ ∞

When I pulled up to the address, I parked a couple houses down the street just to scope the place out before I went on there to know what I was getting myself into. As I sat there on the side of the road, I watched Harper pace back and forth in the driveway like she was nervous about something. I knew that something wasn't right how she was chewing the hell out of her fingernails. Just as I threw the car in drive and was about to pull up, a Mustang turned into the driveway. When the door swung open, I couldn't believe the shit. Climbing out the car was Donte. Last I heard that nigga was locked up on some fuck shit so how the hell was he standing there in the flesh?

Nothing about that nigga was good so my thoughts about Harper being sheisty probably stood corrected. When he had gone around the car and pulled Baylee out the back seat, I wanted to go down there and body slam both of their asses. "Where the fuck have you been had me worried sick about my got damn daughter!" Harper yelled, snatching Baylee away from him.

"This my child too. What you thought? That I was going to let something happen to her?" he asked, stroking his goatee. I know damn well I didn't just hear him right. If that bitch had done what I thought she did, she needed her ass beat, ran over, stomped out, shot and more shit. Not even wanting to sit there and listen anymore, I sped off. Axel was just going to have to wait. Kase came before anything and my nigga needed to know this shit ASAP.

I rushed over to the gym since I knew he was going to be there so we could talk. I wasn't too sure how he was going to take it. He had raised that little girl. He was there through all nine months of the pregnancy and Harper pulled some shit like that on him? The shit was going to kill him without a doubt but he deserved to fucking know what the hell was going on. There was no way I was going to withhold that information from him just to spare his fucking feelings.

When I walked into the gym, Kase was standing in the mirror, lifting weights. "Aye, follow me right quick; we need to talk," I announced, walking up behind him. His eyes shifted to mine in the mirror so I knew he could tell something was wrong. After placing the weights down on the floor, he followed me to my office. I shut the door behind us so no one could hear our conversation.

"What's going on?" he asked.

"I don't know how to put this shit to make it sound sweet so I'm just going to go on and spit it out. Baylee isn't yours."

"Is this supposed to be some kind of joke?" he bemusedly questioned.

"No, I'm serious. I went over there to holler at Harper to see if I could get out of her where the fuck Axel ass at but when I got there she was outside pacing like something was wrong. That nigga Donte pulled up and he had Baylee. I overheard them talking and shit and basically that nigga said she was his daughter and she didn't deny the shit either." Tears came to Kase's eyes. I knew he was hurt so I didn't really speak too much on it. Without saying another word, he walked out of the office.

Kase

When Reapa came and told me Baylee wasn't mine, I didn't know what the fuck to think. I had raised that little girl and I'd be damned if I was going to sit there and let him tell me my child wasn't mine. I needed to hear the words from the horse's mouth. If Harper was to sit there and tell me my child wasn't mine, I wasn't too sure what I would do. Everything inside me lived, breathed, and beat for Baylee so if she turned out to not be mine then I was probably going to flip my fucking lid.

As I was leaving out of the gym, I called Harper's phone. She wasted no time picking up. "What Kase?" she rudely asked. I had to squeeze my fist to keep from going off on her ass.

"We need to talk. Meet me at my house in an hour."

"I'm sure whatever you have to say, you can just say it over the phone." That alone let me know her ass was up to something.

"In an hour Harper and I'm not bullshitting with your ass. Bring Baylee with you too." I disconnected the call and climbed into my Bugatti. Man I swear, when I got my hands on Harper I was going to kill her muthafucking ass. She had my blood boiling beyond limits. I just don't understand how some women could do shit like that. They set themselves up to get fucked up.

I rushed home so I could beat her there. By the time I got there, she was pulling into the driveway behind me. Quickly, I hopped out and grabbed Baylee from the back seat without saying a fucking word to her. "What the hell is going on that you called me over here like this?" she questioned. Ignoring her, I just gazed into Baylee's face, trying to find the resemblance between she and I. Out of all this time I been having her, I didn't think she looked much like me but just favored Harper more. Tears sat at the brim of my eyelids as I attempted for the second time to find something in her face that favored me.

"What's wrong daddy?" she asked. I sucked my tears up and took her on into the house with Harper right behind me. After placing her in my man cave and powering the TV on, turning it up to almost the max, I gripped Harper by her forearm and dragged her out of the room, shutting the door behind us.

"What the fuck is your problem? Let my arm go; the shit hurt," she cried but that pain was the least of her worries at the moment. This bitch had some explaining to do.

When we got back down to the living room, I tossed her onto the sectional and glared at her. "What I'm about to ask you, you better think twice before you answer this shit 'cause if you give me the wrong answer, then you one dead bitch," I cautioned. Terror overtook her face as she stared me back in the eyes. Harper knew I wasn't playing with her ass, not one bit.

"Kase—"

"Shut the fuck up and let me ask my question." Looking directly into her tear-filled eyes, I asked, "Is Baylee mine?"

She was a little hesitant at first but then she finally answered. "Of course she's yours. Why would you ask me some bullshit like that?" What tripped me out was how she sat there and lied to my face for the millionth time like it was nothing.

"Bitch, don't fucking lie to me. I'ma give you one more chance to tell me the got damn truth. Is Baylee mine?" I repeated.

She slowly rose up from the couch easing toward me. "Just let me explain, Kase." In that moment, I knew that the daughter I'd raised wasn't mine. The daughter I had grown to love. She had me feeling like someone snatched my heart from my chest and my soul from my body. "I cheated on you with Donte and ended up pregnant.

I know for a fact that she's his because we weren't having sex at the time. I swear I never meant for that shit to happen. None of this. I so badly wanted her to be yours then it just seemed like the right thing to do at the time since he had got locked up and wasn't getting out." Tears streamed from my eyes. As if I never thought it was possible for Harper to hurt me, she had hurt me in the worst way imaginable. It felt like the ground had been taken from underneath me.

"I never meant to hurt you," she sobbed.

"I don't give a fuck what you say. That girl upstairs is mine. I raised her! She may not have my blood flowing through her veins but she's fucking mine! Nothing you or anyone else can say will tell me otherwise!" I bellowed, gripping Harper roughly by the hair, pulling her close to me. "I just wish you never made me do this—" I snatched my gun from my waistline, placing it at the side of her dome, sending a bullet straight through it. "But it was a long time coming," I said as her lifeless body dropped down to the floor.

My head was all fucked up at this point but nothing she said was going to change the fact that I loved Baylee more than life itself. Just because she wasn't mine, I wasn't going to throw her away as if she never existed. After shooting the clean-up crew a quick text, I headed back upstairs where Baylee was. For a brief moment, I just stood in the doorway, gazing at her as she sat on the floor, watching cartoons.

"You know daddy loves you right?" I asked her as I took a seat down on the floor in front of her.

"Uh huh." She smiled up at me.

"And I would do any and everything for you." Baylee got up and came over, wiping my tears away with her small fingers. This was my muthafucking daughter, fuck Harper.

Axel

ord on the streets was that Reapa and Kase had been looking for me. Bryan's stupid ass couldn't even do one little thing. They say when you want something done then you got to do it yourself. Harper just was going to have to hate me for taking her baby daddy out because I had to get that nigga before he got me which I knew was going to be soon. I don't know why I even trusted his stupid ass to handle the job in the first place.

Since I was about to attempt some stupid shit, I needed to get Harper out of New York for the time being. I didn't need one of them trying to come after her. I wouldn't be able to live with myself if something was to happen to her or Baylee. I headed over to Brittany's house so I could talk to her. I wasn't really going to tell her why I was sending her away till after the fact so she wouldn't be in my fucking way, trying to mess up my plan.

When I pulled up, I didn't see Harper's car and just figured that maybe Brittany was gone in it or something. "You know where Harper at?" I asked Brittany when she answered the door. She scrunched her face up at me. I didn't give a damn the bitch didn't like me. All I did was ask her a simple fucking question.

"She said something about going over to Kase's. Something seemed off with her before she left. Usually, she didn't tell me where she was going but this time she made it her mission to let me know," she replied. If something wasn't right with her, then she would have told me. I was certain of that.

"Have you tried calling her?"

"No, didn't think much of it," the stupid ho had the nerves to say.

"And how long has she been gone?" I quizzed.

"Since like earlier. Why are you asking me all these got damn questions? Harper is a fucking grown ass woman so I shouldn't have to keep up with her," she sassed. Before I knew it, I slapped the shit out of her.

"Your ignorant ass just sat there and said something seemed wrong with her when she left then say she been gone since earlier and you didn't have the common sense to call and check on her to make sure that she was alright? What type of fucking friend are you?"

"GET THE FUCK OFF MY PORCH BEFORE I CALL THE COPS ON YOUR ASS!" she yelled back.

If I wasn't worried about my sister at the moment, I would've beat her stupid ass black and blue. Pulling my phone from my pocket, I headed to my car, quickly dialing Harper's number. *"Hi, you've reached Harper. You know what to do."*

"Fuck!" I barked, hopping into the car. I swear to God if that bitch ass nigga had done something to my fucking sister, he was going to live to regret the shit. I was about to tear up the whole fucking state looking for them muthafuckas, beginning with their gym. If I couldn't find them, then I was forced to make them come to me.

∞ ∞ ∞

With it being late, I knew the gym was probably going to be dead. Everyone in the fucking state knew those two owned *RK Fitness*. Hopefully one of the muthafuckas were going to be there. When I pulled up, I saw Kase's Bugatti parked at the door. I knew it was his because Harper was driving it for a couple days after she got him locked up for stealing the shit. Pulling my gun from my waistline, I headed inside.

"If you don't want to die tonight then I suggest you get the fuck out!" I barked, waving my piece around in the air. The few people that were in there began running out of there.

Once the last person left, I searched that whole building looking for Kase's ass, finding him in an office behind the desk. I should have just pulled the trigger right then but I needed for him to tell me my sister was all right. "Where the fuck is Harper?" I asked through clenched teeth.

"Now your bitch ass want to show your face after we been trying to get you to come out?" He chuckled.

"I'm going to ask you again. Where the fuck is Harper?" He relaxed back in his chair, eyeing me with a smirk on his face that pissed me off even more. I had so much hate for this nigga probably because he had the life I wished I had. Nigga even had my bitch probably only because he had way more money than I did. I wasn't about to let him have my got damn sister as well.

"Probably laying somewhere stinking by now or turned into ashes. Better yet, her body parts might be scattered throughout the state. Who knows." He chortled. Tears came to my eyes when I heard him say that. This nigga really killed my fucking sister and for what? All she ever did was love his bitch ass. "Aww, don't tell me you're tearing up?" he teased. This nigga was talking hella shit when I was the one standing there holding the gun. "Harper deserved to die and I won't apologize one bit for the shit I did."

I sent one shot toward him, hitting him right in the shoulder. "MY FUCKING SISTER DIDN'T DESERVE TO DIE! I told her to stop sweating your bitch ass, that the shit was going to end up getting her killed or heartbroken in the end but she wouldn't fucking listen. The same shit that's going to happen to Nix if she keeps fucking with you."

"Nigga you still bent over Nix? You might as well stop worrying about that one my nigga; she cuffed already. Walking around with the ring on her finger to prove the shit." He laughed.

"She won't be for long when she finds out you're the one that killed her mama." The grin he once wore quickly wiped off his face.

"So that shit was all you?"

"Damn right I killed Olivia and now I'm about to take your ass out. She not going to have no choice but to come running back." Kase's arm moved so I already knew he was probably reaching for his strap. Being quick on my feet, I shot him dead in the chest before he even got the chance to shoot me.

Nix

K ase had called and told me what happened earlier with Harper. I felt so bad for him how he sounded on the phone I could tell he was hurt. I couldn't possibly understand how he was feeling when he found that shit out. I probably would have gone on a murking spree. To make sure he was okay, I went to the gym to check on him.

When I got in there, it was completely empty which I thought was strange. For as long as I worked there, it had never been empty like that before so I knew something was up. As I got closer to Kase's office, I could hear Axel's voice. Rushing back out the door, I checked to see if Kase had locked the doors on his car. Once I saw the doors were unlocked, I leaned inside, searching for a gun, praying he kept one in there as well.

A gun went off sending me into a panic. My heart thumped in my chest, terrified he might have killed Kase. My hand finally ran across a gun that was underneath his driver's seat. "Call an ambulance," I told a woman that was standing on the sidewalk. Quickly running back inside, I could still hear Axel talking, catching the end of the conversation.

"Damn right I killed Olivia and now that I'm about to take your ass out, she not going to have no choice but to come running back," Axel bragged then the gun went off again.

I busted into the office with the gun aimed at him. I couldn't believe that nigga had stooped that low to take my mother away from me like that all because I didn't want to be with him. Tears freely flowed down my face. Axel was becoming the worst mistake of my life and it was time to end his.

"I can't believe you fucking killed my mama, you bastard!" I yelled, cutting my eyes at Kase who looked like he was barely holding on for dear life. Blood poured from the corners of his mouth. The shit hurt me, seeing him like that.

"Damn right I did, and I'd do it again," he boasted with a smirk.

"Why the fuck do you want to hurt me so bad? What have I ever done to you to deserve this?" I had never done anything to this man but loved him when we were together despite the shit he put me through. Looking back on our relationship, it wasn't really much of one at all. Basically, I was just a convenient fuck to him.

"If I couldn't have you then no one else will," he simply replied with a shrug.

"You already took my mother and I'm not about to let you take the love of my life." I shot him dead in the kneecap, dropping him where he stood. The gun he was holding in his hand, dropped to the floor. "I don't love you. I will never come back to you." I shot his ass in the shoulder and he yelped out in pain. "I regret the day I ever met you," I said, placing the barrel of the gun in the center of his forehead. When the gun went off, his brain matter went everywhere.

By the time Axel's body fell completely to the floor, sirens could be heard from outside. The EMTs ran inside along with the cops right on their tails. "He tried to kill my fiancé." They rushed over to Kase, pulling him from the chair lying him on the floor. I dropped the gun and ran to his side. "It's going to be okay, babe, just hold on," I encouraged. One of them ripped his shirt open, taking a look at his bullet wounds while the other went to get the gurney.

Tears still flowed down my cheeks as he struggled to breathe. It was like I was sitting there watching his life slip away. I placed my forehead atop of his while my tears dropped down on his face. "I-I-I—"

I hushed him with my lips because I didn't want to hear what he had to say. In my heart, I knew he was going to be all right. One of the cops pulled me back off of him as they lifted him, placing him on the gurney. "Let me go! They can't take him without me!" I cried.

"We need to question you about what had happened," the cop said but I wasn't trying to hear that shit. He would just have to question me another time because that ambulance wasn't pulling off without me in it.

"Get the fuck off me," I shoved him and ran behind them as they were pushing him away. "I'm here babe," I told him, gripping his hand. He tried to squeeze it but didn't really have much of a grip. When they placed him in the back of the ambulance, I climbed in right behind them.

Just as the ambulance was speeding off, the EMT that was in the back with me said, "We're losing him."

"Come on babe, you're strong; you're a fighter. Please hold in there. If you leave me here by myself, I swear I'll never forgive you," I wept.

She put some gel on his chest then took two paddles into her hands, rubbing them together. "Clear!" she yelled before putting them on his chest. I sat there silently praying he would be all right.

"Lord, I promise if you bring him back, I'll do whatever it takes to get my life together."

"Clear!" she yelled again but nothing happened. My heart was aching for Kase. I couldn't believe that my babe was actually gone from me.

"I refuse to give up on you. Clear!" And that time she hit his chest, he started breathing again. "You gave us a scare, thought we really lost you for a second."

"Thank you, God," I whispered.

Epilogue

Reapa

*A*fter two months, things were finally getting back on track. Shit had got hectic after Kase killed Harper and he got shot. Everyone really thought we were going to lose him. Thank God he pulled through. Shit was still the same old around the traps and shit. Since Kase had taken off for a while, I was left running things on my own. It wasn't a big deal to me.

"So y'all going to tell me who took my shit or no?" I asked three of our soldiers that were kneeled down in front of me. I had sent these little niggas on a run and just so happened, they magically got robbed before they could get the product to its destination. The shit had never happened before, so I knew there had to be some bullshit behind it.

"Man, I don't know, I told you we were robbed," Tyga cried. Lifting my foot from the floor, I kicked him in the face with my size twelve Timb. His head jerked back and one of his teeth flew out to the floor.

"You're lying. One of you, if not all know what the fuck happened to my shit." They must have forgotten I was once there in their shoes. There were several times I ran off on the plug and more shit. Their stupid asses weren't smart enough to get away with it though.

"Someone attacked us in a black Mustang when we were in route. We're telling you the honest truth," Black said. They could have been being honest, but at the same time, I felt like they were lying. I was always told to go with my gut so I was not about to let them walk away from there lying or not. Only them and God knew the truth.

I took a seat in my chair to take a break from whooping their asses and roll me a blunt. All three of them just sat there on the floor looking stupid as fuck. "Y'all know I got a baby on the way?" I asked, licking the blunt. Neither one of them answered so I shifted my eyes from the blunt to them.

"Yeah," they all said in unison.

"I hope my seed doesn't come out as stupid as you three. If someone was in here beating my ass the way I had been beating y'all, I would have been snitched on the other muthafucka," I lied, hoping that one of them would have said something but they just sat there in silence. My got damn knuckles were black and blue from whooping their asses but at least they didn't look as bad as their faces did. "So what were y'all thinking when you took my shit?" I quizzed, firing up the tip of the blunt.

After I smoked the whole blunt neither one of them had spoken up so I was getting fed up with their asses. I was not about to waste any more energy on them. I knew exactly what to do to their ass to get them to talk. Getting up from my seat, I went over to the door and pulled it open. Cocaine pranced out and they all jumped.

"Yeah, bet y'all forgot about her didn't you," I taunted. Cocaine paraded around the room like she was out in the jungle somewhere. "This is your last chance to speak up or forever hold your peace."

"Man, Reapa we're telling you the truth. We really were robbed," Tyga said.

"Alright," I simply replied and sat back down in the chair. They all looked relieved till I said, "Eat." Cocaine mauled all three of their asses while they screamed for dear life. When I no longer heard their cries, I grabbed her. "Good girl."

Unity

"How are you feeling?" Reapa asked when he walked into the bedroom and immediately began stripping out of his clothes.

"I'm good." I was so happy that I had finally gotten over all that puking I was doing when I first got pregnant. That shit was taking so much from me and always had me drained as fuck.

"You hungry?"

"What kind of question is that to ask a pregnant woman? Aren't I always hungry?" I joked.

"Yeah, you right." He chuckled. "Let me take a quick shower then I'll go down and whip you up something," he said, going into the bathroom and starting the shower.

I climbed out of the bed and headed downstairs. I needed to get up and move around since I had been lying there ever since he left before dawn. When I got outside, I saw Cocaine walking around with blood all over her. I hated it whenever he used her on people. All he was going to do was turn her savage. Before the baby was born, he was going to have to find somewhere else to keep her because I couldn't risk her attacking my child. I'd never be able to forgive him if some shit like that was to happen.

"Bae!" I called out heading toward the kitchen where I smelt food cooking.

"Yeah," he answered.

"How come Cocaine has blood all over her?" I asked him with an arched brow. He had been gone all morning and came in like he was in a good mood, offering to cook me lunch and shit, yet Cocaine was in the backyard walking around looking like she had her period come out her mouth instead of her pussy.

"Oh, I was meaning to clean her up before we got here but I got a little sidetracked. Don't worry, I'll give her a bath," he stated like it wasn't shit.

"You need to stop using her to do your dirty work before she turns on your ass and ends up biting you," I scolded.

"Then I'm just going to bite her ass back," he said with a straight face. I wouldn't even put it past his ass to do it too. "Gone in there and sit down till I'm finished cooking. I'm almost done."

I pulled the barstool away from the island and took a seat. "I want to be in here with you. I haven't seen you all morning."

"I missed you too," he said, briefly turning away from the stove and leaning over the island stealing a quick peck.

I was now three months and my baby bump was growing. My skin was radiant and glowing. I just felt all over amazing. I had the most perfect guy a girl could ask for. Lucky for me I had listened to my grandma or else I wouldn't have him. Shortly after we got back from our trip to Miami, Reapa asked me to move in with him. And to get my grandma out the hood, he moved her in as well. At first, I wasn't too fond of the idea because I knew we weren't going to be able to do much but I loved having her around. She was a big help when it came to my pregnancy.

Reapa placed a plate down in front of me then fixed me some juice before grabbing his food and taking a seat beside me. "I love you so much." That was the truth. I had fallen so deeply in love with this man that it was crazy.

"Love you too," he replied kissing my lips.

Kase

*a*fter I killed Harper, I decided I was going to keep Baylee and just raise her. Like I said before, that was my child I didn't give a fuck what nobody had to say about it. Nix had been a big help with her and I couldn't ask for a better woman. She took on to Baylee as if she was her own. Cooking, cleaning, taking her to daycare and everything. I couldn't ask for a better woman to be beside me and patiently waited for the day she walked down that aisle to become Mrs. Watts.

It was Olivia's birthday, so I had taken her to her mother's grave. She had already been feeling kind of down about the whole day so I decided to go up there with her just so she wouldn't feel alone. As she stood there just gazing at the headstone, I gripped her hand squeezing it. I could only imagine what she was going through at the moment. There was no way I could possibly say I knew what she was going through because I didn't. Both of my parents were still walking this earth. Maybe it would have been a little easier for her if her father was still here. But she had lost both.

"I'm sorry, Ma," she wept. The tears flowed effortlessly down her cheeks. Something in me knew she felt as if her mother's death was all her fault but it wasn't. No one told Axel's crazy ass to kill Olivia the way he had. No matter what she thought, there was nothing she could have done to stop him. Even if she would have given him what he wanted by being with him, he probably would have still found a reason to kill her. If I could take away all her pain and bear it for her, then I would in a heartbeat. I loved her just that much.

"I love you," she said, placing the flowers on Olivia's grave. Without saying another word, she headed back toward the car with me following closely behind her.

When we climbed inside, she just sat there in silence. "You alright?" I asked. I just wanted to make sure she was straight even though I could already feel she wasn't.

"No," she cried, shifting her eyes to mine. "I don't think I'll ever be alright again. No matter what I do, the feeling just won't go away." I wasn't too sure what she meant by that.

"It's my fault my mother is gone. I brought that crazy muthafucka into her life. He should have taken me instead of her."

"Don't think that way. How were you to know he was going to do something like that? I'm sure your mother is satisfied with the decision he made. She would want you to still be breathing and to live your life," I told her, reaching over, wiping the tears from her eyes.

"Still can't help but think it's my fault. I've been doing a lot of thinking lately, especially when you got shot. If I hadn't come when I did, you probably would have been dead." More tears poured from her eyes.

"And I'm grateful for that." I gripped her hand, bringing it up to my lips and kissed it. Nix saved my life and I would forever be indebted to her. Thanks to her, I'll be here to watch Baylee grow up, have even more kids with her, and get to marry the love of my life. There's nothing I could do to ever repay her for that.

"Kase—" The way her voice cracked when she said my name brought worry. For the first time, I could feel my heart racing in my chest.

"Whatever crazy thing you might be thinking, I need you to dead that shit. We about to go pick up Baylee from my mama's and head home." I went to reach to press the button to start the car but she stopped me.

"Kase—" she called out again. I had a feeling what she was about to say and I'll be damn if I was about to sit there and listen to that shit. No way in hell.

"Don't Kase me. Put your seatbelt on so we can go," I ordered.

"BLAKE!" she yelled, calling me by my government name so I would know she was serious.

"Don't say what the fuck I think you about to say, Phoenix," I cautioned. My eyes watered, staring her back into her beautiful face.

"Blake, I love you so much. I really do and I've even grown to love Baylee as well but I love myself even more. That night I almost lost you, I promised God I would do whatever it takes to work on myself. I'm not the woman you want to marry right now." She was now crying harder than she was when she was standing in front of her mother's grave.

"Pleeeeaaasssseeee don't do this to me, bae," I begged. I wasn't trying to lose this girl so yeah, I was pleading like a bitch. Her and Baylee were my world, and I loved them more than anything. There was no way I could just let her walk out of my life like that.

"Don't make this any harder than it has to be, Blake. I'm sure there's someone else out there for you that will make you happier than I ever could. If I can't give you a hundred percent, then I'd rather give you nothing," she explained. Honestly, this was the first time I ever been heartbroken over a woman before and the shit wasn't sweet.

"Whatever you think you need to do, we can do it together. Just don't leave me, Phoenix," I pleaded.

"Wish we could but it's just something I have to do on my own," she said, reaching over wiping my tears from my eyes.

"But I love you."

"I know you do. Come find me in a couple years. Maybe I'll be in a better state than I am now. I just need some time to myself to get my life together." She pulled her ring from her finger and tried to hand it to me but I wouldn't take it. I refused to accept this shit as my fate. Just earlier we were fine and now all of a sudden, she wanted to leave a nigga over nothing. What type of shit was that? "I'm sorry," she said, placing the ring on the dashboard and leaned over, kissing me softly on the lips. "I'll always love you." Was the last thing she said to me before she climbed out the car and shut the door behind her. Just like that, she walked out of my life.

Nix

S ome might look at Kase's and I relationship from the outside looking in and think that what I did was fucked up but it's not. I should have just done what my mother told me in the first place and took some time to myself. Maybe we all wouldn't be in the shit we were in if I would have. That decision had been weighing heavily on my mind for some time now. It wouldn't have been fair to him if I would have married him and didn't give him a hundred percent in the marriage. Soon, he would forget all about me once he met the next bitch. At least that's what I hoped.

Drying my tears, I pulled my phone out so I could call Unity to get a ride home. "Can you come get me?" I sobbed when she answered.

"What's wrong with you?" she queried.

"I'll tell you when you get here. Are you coming or not?" Without a doubt I knew she would come especially since she knew something was wrong.

"Duh, where you at?" I heard shuffling noises in her background, letting me know she was probably getting up to get ready to come and get me.

"Ma's grave. Hurry up; I'm cold," I whined. I had to choose one of the coldest fucking days to bring my ass out here. It was snow on the ground and I was standing here freezing my ass off. I don't know why I didn't just wait till Kase had taken us back to the house to do all that.

"That nigga just left you out there!" she screamed. "When I see him I'm going to kick his ass!"

"It's not even nothing like that. Just come on," I said, disconnecting the call. I went to twirl my ring but just that fast had forgotten I had taken it off and given it back to him. This breakup was going to be harder than I thought.

Unity whipped into the parking lot, throwing her car in park. I rushed out there to it, jumping in. I was too anxious to feel that heat. I had been freezing to death out there that I could barely feel my toes in my boots. "Now are you going to tell me what happened or what?" she questioned just as soon as I got into the car. She didn't even let me shut the door good.

"I broke up with Kase!" I blurted, showing her my empty ring finger.

"WHAT THE FUCK, NIX! For what?"

"It was the right thing to do. I felt like I needed to work on myself before I could marry anyone, let alone him," I honestly told her.

"Well, sometimes you just have to do what's best for you. Are you okay?" Now that question I didn't really know how to answer. It hurt me that I broke up with him because I loved him so much, but I knew it was something I needed to do.

"I will be," I assured her.

∞ ∞ ∞

It had been a couple days since I broke up with Kase. I hadn't been feeling too well, thinking it was just probably me feeling depressed. I hadn't felt like this since my mother died but this time I felt ten times worse. Of course, Unity popped up to take care of me even though I had told her not to. Someone needed to be taking care of her since she was the pregnant one. I couldn't wait till the baby came into the world; I was going to spoil the shit out of it.

"Can I get you anything else?" Unity asked, rubbing on her baby bump.

"No, you're already doing too much as it is. Sit down somewhere before Reapa want to come over here and rip my head off from you doing too much," I joked.

For the heat to be on in the apartment, I was in that bitch shivering and shit like I was standing outside in the fucking snow ass naked. I hated this time of year and couldn't wait till the shit passed. If it was up to me, we would fast forward to got damn spring.

"You sure you're feeling okay?" she questioned with an arched brow. Unity reached over touching me on the forehead and saw that I was burning up. "Got damn you hot as fuck. Have you had this fever the whole time?" she asked, getting up from the couch heading toward my mother's room that was now mine.

"I don't know." Maybe that explained how come I was so fucking cold when I was blasting the damn heat. She came back into the living room.

"Let me check your temperature." We sat there in silence for a few brief seconds. "Your shit a hundred and four, Nix!" she yelled, hopping up from the couch. "I'm taking you to the doctor."

"But I don't feel like going out there in the fucking cold. I'm straight on that. It'll pass." At least that's what I was wishing for. It wasn't enough that I was depressed but I had to be sick as well.

"You're so fucking lazy," she fussed. Right then I got the urge to vomit so I hopped up from the couch, rushing to the nearest bathroom. As I was puking, she said, "You still think it's just going to pass?"

"You think this shit funny or something?" I gave her the side eye when I was done throwing up.

"Nah, just letting you know that I was right as always. You need to go to the doctor." I didn't feel like going in there sitting with all those got damn sick people. Everyone was sick around this time of the year and quite frankly, she didn't need to be in there herself. She most definitely didn't need to get sick.

"Fine, I'll go but I'm going to my doctor and not the hospital. I hate being around sick people." I finally gave in since I was probably sicker than what I thought and didn't need to get worse.

"Do you not know how stupid you sound right about now? You act like you're not sick or something." She rolled her eyes.

"That's different than being around other sick people, ho."

"Yeah, whatever."

∞ ∞ ∞

Even though I said that I was coming to see my doctor, there were still several sick people in there as well. Every time someone coughed or sneezed, I jumped. I may have been sick but I wasn't doing all that. I didn't know what the hell they had and certainly didn't want the shit.

"Stop being so fucking dramatic, Nix." Unity sighed.

"You talking but don't even need to be in here with all these germy ass folks." The place was so packed that we had been sitting there for an hour to see my doctor. I wished they would bring their slow asses on so I could get the hell out of there with the quickness.

"Phoenix Quartz," the nurse finally called out.

"About got damn time." I mumbled.

"Nix, don't go back there doing all this unnecessary bullshit. Just let them people do whatever the fuck they have to do so we can get the hell out of here," Unity lectured.

"I should left your ass up here with those sick ass people," I scoffed, following the nurse to the back.

"What's going on with you today Phoenix?" the nurse asked when I stepped into the room.

"I don't know. Just not feeling too well. I thought it maybe been from being depressed but then I'm running a fever and threw up," I explained.

"And how come you are depressed?" she queried. Hope that ho didn't think I was on some suicidal type shit because I valued my life too got damn much to do some shit like that.

"For reasons that doesn't concern you."

"Ma'am I'm so sorry for her rude behavior. She just has been going through a lot lately," Unity chimed in like I needed her help or something. She should have just stayed her ass up in that front like I said.

"Do you have a headache or anything?" the nurse asked.

"A slight migraine but that's all," I replied.

"Have your sides been bothering you?" She was killing me with all these got damn questions and shit.

"I don't know. Can you just fix me so I can go back home?"

"I'm just trying to help you, sweetie," she said in a polite tone. "One more question, when was your last period?" Now she had me wracking my got damn brain because that shit I didn't know. I had completely lost track of the shit since I had been fucking Kase but I was sure that my shit had come on so I wasn't too worried about that.

"I don't know." I shrugged. Unity glanced over at me suspiciously.

The nurse went over grabbing a small clear cup and handed it to me. "Can you pee in this?"

"For what?" I quizzed.

"I want to run a couple tests to see if you have an UTI and if it's possible that you're pregnant since you don't know when the last time you had your cycle."

"Hell no, I'm not pregnant but you can test me for a UTI." She needed to stop trying to jinx me.

After I peed in the cup I gave it back to her and waited as she ran the tests. Shit was just running through my mind miles a minute. The longer she took, the more anxious I got. "Ah, okay Phoenix, it says that you do have an UTI but it also says you're pregnant."

Unity's eyes almost popped from her sockets. "Fuck my life."

THE END... OR IS IT?

Please be kind enough to leave a review.

Good or bad, I'd really love to hear from you.

Facebook: www.facebook.com/authortaniece

Personal Facebook: Taniece McDaniel

Join my reading group: Taniece's Reading Group

Instagram: www.instagram.com/taniece

Twitter: www.twitter.com/_taniece_

Email: Taniece91@gmail.com

Website: www.novelsbytaniece.weebly.com

Also, by Taniece

I Wanna Be Your Girl: A Love Story (Incomplete)

She Got A Hitta Catching Feelings 1-2

A Kiss Sealed With Fate: A Novella

I'm Addicted To His Love: Complete Boxset

Bad Girls Love Trap N*ggas: Complete Boxset

A Hood Boy's Love Is Forever 1-2

That Bona Fide Hood Love: Pluto and Galaxi 1-3

Cuffed By A Hood Rich N*gga 1-3

Sprung: Lovin' A Certified Gangsta 1-3

Down For My Dope Boy: Mina & Heat

Crazy In Love With A Dope Boy: Complete Boxset

A Hitta's Valentine: A Novella

When A Thug Loves You Better: A Standalone

Made in the USA
Monee, IL
04 September 2020